SCORE

MASSEY SECURITY DUET BOOK TWO

S. NELSON

The Score/ S.Nelson.—1st edition

ISBN-13: 9781074413118

I dedicate this book to those who had the courage to ask for help. And for those who haven't yet... set yourself free and reach out.

CHAPTER ONE

Cara

There was only so much fear and anxiety a person could handle before numbness wielded a protective shield over the human psyche. Unfortunately, dread continued to slice away at every thought I had, pricking every cell in my body until I was left as nothing more than a shell of the woman I often portrayed to the world.

From the moment I'd been taken, I racked my brain trying to figure out who hired my kidnappers. I couldn't help but wonder if I knew the person pulling the strings? Was it a man or a woman? If provoked, I knew just how ruthless a woman could be in order to get what she wanted. Hell, I'd been that woman a time or two in my life. But if it was indeed a man, had I met him before? Had I slept with him?

I'd made my share of enemies over the years. None I thought would go so far as to send menacing threats to my father, though. And even if they had, I never suspected they'd follow through and abduct me or my sister, Emily.

Or did the circumstance simply boil down to the fact I was just an innocent bystander in the twisted game of revenge?

Innocent. Hmph… it'd be the first time in a long time. The concept was laughable. Although, right then, I couldn't find a speck of amusement for the predicament I found myself in.

"This couldn't have gone better." Purposeful strides brought Ford closer, and even though his hands flexed into tight fists, his expression was relaxed. Cocky, even. The glimmer in his eyes spoke of secrets and revelations.

The two men who had taken me rushed forward and grabbed me, one on each side. The force of their touch wasn't lethal but strong. I tested their grip by jerking back and then side to side, trying to somehow break free. But it was no use. There was no way I'd be able to get away. Maybe if there was only one of them to contend with, I'd have some sort of hope, but not with the two of them restraining me and Ford standing in my way.

Ford's gaze drifted to my eyes and then my mouth, and while desire for him had coursed through my veins two hours prior, everything had changed. Being the object of his scrutiny, eyeing me up like I was the top trophy in some fucking game made me bristle with apprehension.

My body trembled when he reached out to run his finger along my collarbone, the corner of his mouth lifting slightly as he toyed with me.

Ford Massey had been hired to protect me from this very same thing. Me being taken. He'd chastised me repeatedly when I'd ditched him in the past, relentless in his warning of how unsafe it was for me to be anywhere without him.

But there he was in front of me. The one who had orchestrated everything, first by sending the veiled threats to my dad, causing him and my mom to worry about the welfare of their children, then by having me taken against my will.

As the pads of his fingers elicited goose bumps to break out over my skin, a thought popped into my head. Scratch that. Many thoughts poured in as my eyes glued to his.

Was Owen part of the threat, or would he be as surprised as the rest of us? If Owen *was* in on the deed, had he taken Emily? If so, where were they?

I couldn't have misread the interactions between my sister and Ford's brother. They appeared to share a sincere connection, whispering when they thought no one else was around. Laughing and appearing to enjoy the other's company. I could admit I'd been jealous of their exchanges, wishing from time to time that Ford and I could share something similar.

The only time I'd witnessed Owen upset with Emily was at the strip joint. I'd convinced her to shut her phone off when we ditched them back at the club, and while she was hesitant at first, she'd relented. I came to find out later that night that she'd turned her cell back on, which was how they were able to track and find us.

Even though I realized my efforts would be futile, I struggled to break free from the bastards holding on to me once again. I attempted to throw myself backward, hoping the jolt would cause them to loosen their grip.

But nothing happened.

My body never moved.

Instead, their fingers dug deeper into my flesh.

And because I needed to keep trying to get away, I tried another tactic. My feet weren't restrained, so I'd use them as best as I could. I raised my foot and angled my body slightly toward the man on my left, the one with the tattoo covering the side of his neck. With all my strength, I brought my foot down hard on top of his and waited to see if the impact would be enough of a distraction for him to relax his hold on me.

"Christ!" He jostled me a bit before shifting his foot away from me. "You're lucky I'm wearing these boots, woman."

Clearly, he was startled but I didn't injure him. The man on my right, his buddy with the scar that ran from his jawline to his temple, straightened his posture and locked his grasp tighter, essentially immobilizing me.

The whole time Ford's eyes, his beautiful, captivating, treacherous, and deceitful eyes, roved over me carefully. I had no idea what ran through his mind and while I was curious—about so many things—I wasn't about to ask.

I cursed myself for not taking the self-defense class Emily had begged me to a few months prior. I bet I would've learned some karate-type shit that could've helped me get away.

"You can stop trying to escape, Cara. It's pointless." I wanted to strike his shin with the tip of my shoe, but that would get me nowhere, and because I wasn't sure what Ford would do to me in retaliation, I dismissed the thought as quickly as it had entered my brain.

"Why are you doing this?" I couldn't fathom what his reasoning was behind threatening my family. What grudge did he hold against my dad? Or was it all just a ploy to get to me? Nothing made sense, and the longer I stood there without answers, the more I was susceptible to concocting outlandish stories.

"Because."

"Because isn't an answer." The response was often what my parents said to me whenever I tried using that one-word reply.

"Do you love your sister? Your parents? Your friends? Hell, do you love anyone other than yourself?" Ford's hands disappeared inside his pants pockets right before he thrust his shoulders back slightly. He glanced briefly at the other two men before finally resting his attention back on me. "Well, do you?"

"Of course, I do." I hated that my emotions had suddenly got the better of me, the glassiness of my eyes becoming too much for me to suppress. Tears coursed down my cheeks before I could stop them, my breathing hitching every few seconds as I tried to calm down.

"I don't think you do."

My body went lax in the men's hold, but they held me upright. Defeat overtook me. I didn't understand the meaning behind Ford's questions, but it was my experience that when the captor started asking random inquiries, shit was about to go down. Okay, maybe it wasn't from my personal experience, but that's the stuff that always happened in the movies.

Fear of the unknown started to unravel whatever calm I'd been able to hold on to up until that point, and trust me, it wasn't much.

"Are we good here?" The guy with the tattoo directed his question at Ford. "Because I think you're dangerously close to that line, man."

What the hell was he talking about? What line? Was Ford planning on killing me? Was that the line the guy was talking about?

For as much as I berated myself for showing any kind of weakness, my will to appear strong was shoved to the side when the tears came faster, my breathing choppier than moments ago.

"Yeah, I think he's right," the other man added, his fingers easing up a bit on my arm.

"A few more minutes for good measure," Ford responded, tilting his head to the side before he was on me, his hands replacing those of his buddies. The switch seemed orchestrated, like a dance they'd practiced many times before. Maybe they

5

had. Maybe it was their job to kidnap people, and they were so used to it that they could predict each other's movements.

"Wh… what are you go… going to do to me?" I stammered, tasting my tears as they passed over my lips.

"I'm going to give you back to Cal and Hunter and let them do whatever they want. How does that sound?"

I looked at both men and noticed the uneasiness in their stare. They glanced at one another briefly before looking back to Ford, the tattooed one shifting his weight from foot to foot while the scarred one knit his brows and bit his bottom lip.

My heart slammed so hard against my chest, I swore the thrum of the muscled organ could be heard for miles around. Heat engulfed me and spread throughout my body, and I feared I'd pass out right then and there if I continued to fail at gathering myself. Although, the feat was much easier said than done, the look of determination in Ford's eyes pushing me toward crumbling instead of standing tall.

"I thought for sure you'd be cursing me up and down and trying to claw my eyes out. There was no way I'd ever have thought you'd become a mess." Directly after Ford spoke the words, he squeezed his eyes shut for several seconds before sighing.

I gave up trying to figure out what would happen next because it was useless. I needed to save whatever energy I had left and try and either figure out how to convince him to let me go or to try and devise a plan of escape. Both options seemed impossible, however.

What he said hit home. Why wasn't I trying to attack him? Why wasn't I struggling more? Why the hell was I breaking down? Where was the woman who was as tough as nails? The one who didn't take shit from anyone, spoke her mind, and did whatever the hell she wanted?

She was gone.

That bitch abandoned me as soon as I'd seen Ford walk through that door.

"Is it not enough you've taken me, but you have to humiliate me on top of it?" My tears had slowed, but I was a long way off from composed.

"I'm not trying to humiliate you, Cara. It's just an observation."

He finally released me, and while my inner voice shouted at me to run for the door, which was still open, I stood frozen in place, reprimanding myself for not drawing on the fleck of courage I had deep down and trying to change my circumstance.

Ford ran his fingers through his dark hair, and if I didn't know any better, I would've thought he was going to step to the side and allow me to leave. He pulled in a deep breath, then released it slowly, and I couldn't help but wonder if he questioned his actions. If he regretted them.

"What are you going to do?' I asked.

"What do you want me to do?"

"Let me go," I answered truthfully.

"Not until I'm done." He looked to his coconspirators once more before advancing closer. "I have to know you get it." He may as well have been speaking in another language for the amount of sense he made.

Out of my peripheral, I saw the other two men step to the side and farther away from Ford and me. Odd behavior for men who had just been an active part in a crime.

"I don't understand." My tears had finally dried up, but I hated that my voice was softer than I tried to project.

"You were warned over and over. You should've listened to me after the first time you ditched me, or even after the second.

But no, you had to be defiant and do it again. See where that got you?" He rubbed the back of his neck, his hand lingering there before dropping his arm to his side. "You would've been safer with me next to you."

Gone were the tears.

Gone was the trepidation I'd felt, unsure of my imminent future.

Gone was all logic of circumstance.

Utter confusion took over.

Listening to Ford ramble on like a crazy person and spinning his words in an effort to disable any rational thought, set fire to my anger.

"What the hell are you talking about? YOU took me!" I shouted, grabbing clumps of my hair and allowing the slight sting of pain to center me. For as much as I wanted to physically lash out at Ford, I wasn't sure how our encounter would progress, so I kept my hands to myself.

He was talking in circles, and I couldn't keep up with the psychological torture.

He pointed toward the other two men. "They took you, but on my wishes."

"Your wishes?"

"Yes, I set this all up."

I narrowed my eyes. "I know you orchestrated my kidnapping. But why? What did my father ever do to you?"

He swung his arms behind his back and held them in place, pacing in short spans while he glanced over at me every few seconds.

"Cara, you're not getting it." He shook his head. "I'm not behind the threats to your family. I set up you being taken because you wouldn't listen to me about how unsafe it was to ditch me." He pointed back and forth between the two other people in the room. "Cal and Hunter work with me and Owen. They're part of our security firm." The blank stare on my face prompted him to continue. "You're not in real danger. This time."

A wave of emotion crashed over me after finally allowing his words to sink in. From confusion to relief to embarrassment to rage. I settled on the last one because it was the one that would give me what I most wanted. What I needed.

Release.

There wasn't much space between us, but it felt like a mile. My feet propelled me forward until I was close enough to reach out and touch him. Or punch him. Or knee him in the fucking balls. I couldn't decide.

"So, let me get this right. You set up this whole thing? You had these two," I said, hoisting my thumb over my shoulder, "wait until I walked out of Blush, then take me and throw me into the back of their van? Then you allowed them to scare the shit out of me by keeping me locked in this goddamn room with not so much as a heads-up as to what was going on?"

"That would've defea—"

"Shut up!" My breaths picked up in intensity while I glared at him and continued my tirade. "Then you walked in here and acted like you were the one responsible for sending the notes to my father? Making me think that my life could possibly end?" Unshed tears briefly clouded my vision. "You made me think Emily was in danger." That wasn't a question. Fear my sister would be harmed sliced at my soul, and remembering the terror I felt for her safety pushed my fury to another level.

I never allowed him to answer before I clenched my fist and swung my arm directly at his face. He saw it coming, though, because he ducked at the last second, his reflexes on point. Before I could try again, he grabbed both my arms, spun me around, and pulled me against his chest, wrapping me in a reverse bear hug.

"Calm down," he growled in my ear, the rasp of his tone and the warmth of his breath knocking me off-kilter.

Despite being furious that Ford went to such great lengths with his stunt, I had to admit I was relieved my life wasn't truly in danger.

CHAPTER
TWO

Ford

"**W**hy don't you guys take off?" While holding Cara tightly in my arms, I looked to Cal and Hunter. I appreciated their help but needed to be alone with her for this next part. I didn't need anyone trying to convince me to calm down or be careful not to cross any lines.

Where I failed with my sister, Julia, was that I didn't push her. I didn't scare her enough into making her see that her actions had consequences, not only for herself but for those of us who loved and cared for her.

I wasn't going to make that same mistake with Cara.

"You sure?" Cal asked, the apprehension on his face enough to make me think about his simple question one second longer than I would have.

"I got it." The two of them walked away without so much as another glance at me or Cara, and once they'd closed the door, I knew our time here would be short. So, I dove right in.

Holding her so close, I couldn't stop myself from inhaling the smell of her hair, a mixture of fruit and coconut. Before I lost myself to unsuitable images, however, I focused on the reality of the situation. The two of us. Alone in a windowless room and away from prying eyes. If I was less of a man, I'd take advantage of Cara's attraction for me and proceed with giving her what she'd wanted back at the club when she kissed me.

But I wasn't a shit. Although, if Cara could give her opinion on the matter, I was sure she'd beg to differ.

The tremor of her body disarmed me, and for as much as I wanted to reassure her that nothing bad would happen to her while I was in her life, I couldn't do that. I didn't want to give her a false sense of security because the truth was, I had no idea what kind of predicament would befall her if the person making the threats wasn't caught soon.

Needing to ensure she finally understood the severity of her actions, more to point, her ditching me, I squeezed her tighter and anchored her to me, careful not to constrict her breathing. I didn't need her passing out on me because that would defeat the purpose of my warning. Or maybe it would drive home my point.

Cara could barely move, but she could certainly still run her mouth.

"Let me go," she shouted, the tremble in her voice betraying her typical strength. Or the illusion of it, at least. My guess was that the image she projected to the world, including her family, was someone who had no qualms about doing or saying whatever she wished, consequences be damned. Her actions never warranted any sort of real punishment and she continued to live life the way she wanted.

But I had a gut feeling her life was all a ruse. A means to hide from something, although for the life of me, I couldn't say what. Or why I even possessed such a thought, but it was there, nonetheless.

I ignored her plea, and one arm held her close while I freed the other and proceeded to continue my *lesson*. Moving her hair to the side so there was no mistaking my words, I said, "Remember the fear you felt a few minutes ago? Draw on that and picture some psycho holding you like this, thinking of all the ways he could violate you." My hand skated over the edges of her breasts, then down her sides, trailing over her plump ass before settling on the inside of her thigh. Far enough away from her pussy but close enough to make my point. She tried to squirm, and I couldn't figure out if it was in excitement or trepidation, hoping for the latter. Otherwise this whole song and dance would be for nothing.

"I don't have to imagine because *you're* the psycho. Now let go of me," she reiterated right before she jerked her head back and thumped me right below my collarbone. Any higher and that shit would've hurt, especially with the force she used.

But I chose to ignore both her words and her attempt to harm me. "Or even kill you if he so desired." My hand disappeared from between her legs and wrapped around her throat, my fingers pressing into the sensitive skin underneath her jaw. If I pressed any harder, I would surely hurt her, and that wasn't my intention. Not pain, just fear. Fear of what could happen if someone else got their hands on her.

Moments passed in silence, her breathing slow and choppy while mine was relaxed and in control. My mind, however, was a fucking mess. I inwardly cringed when I pictured a faceless man having his way with Cara right before I saw her lying in a pool of her own blood, beaten and battered. Then my brain messed with me and twisted those images into ones of her lying beneath me, the look of desire painted on her face while her body writhed from my touch. So many conflicting thoughts confused me, and before I could settle on one of them, either enough to rattle me, I thought about how to transition back into the role of her bodyguard and her my client.

"Wait until I tell my father what you've done," she threatened,

13

and even though I couldn't see her face, I knew her expression had schooled, switched from shock back into the cocky and assured smirk she typically wore. "He'll fire you and kick you out of our house so fast your head will spin."

"That's where you're wrong, *sweetheart*." My breath fanned over the side of her face when I spoke. "After I tell him about the three times you took off on me, the first one being the time you snuck off to see Kurt after he explicitly told you not to, and what you partook of while there, he will be only too happy that I stepped up and tried to teach you a lesson." Even as the words left my mouth, I only half believed them. There was a great chance Walter Dessoye would only focus on the stunt I pulled, and not on his daughter's disobedience. But there was also that chance he'd be furious with Cara's behavior and condone what I'd done as a result.

"Or, he'll be pissed off and disappointed in your lack of ability to watch over me, allowing me the time to ditch you in the first place. Not very good at your job, are you, Ford?" Even though her condescending tone pissed me off, I couldn't argue with what she said. "Or how about I tell him how inappropriate you were with me. Do you think he'd like to hear about all the ways you touched me, practically grabbing my tits before shoving your hand between my legs?"

"I didn't touch you with lust, and you know it." I said this with her body still molded to mine. I'd since withdrawn my fingers from her throat and locked that hand onto my other, which was pinning her arms across her ribcage.

"Then why are you hard?"

Her words burned me, and I immediately released her. She spun around, and her eyes diverted directly to my crotch, where sure enough, I was blatantly aroused.

14

"My body's reaction has nothing to do with you," I lied.

"Oh, is that right. Then who is that for?" She pointed at the tent in my pants. "Were you thinking about one of your buddies? Or were you excited you were all able to pull off this stunt of yours?"

"Don't be ridiculous." We could go round and round all day long, back and forth, and trying to blame the other for what happened. Technically, I was the one responsible for why we were standing there in that room, but it was her actions that led me to do something so extreme. Maybe if I'd done something similar with Julia, she'd be alive today. Shaking all thoughts of my sister away for the moment, I took a step to the side and swung my arm out toward the door. "We need to go."

Without so much as an eye roll, Cara headed toward the exit. I expected her to run, but she casually walked away from me, as if it was a normal occurrence for her to be taken against her will, scared out of her mind only to come to find out she'd been set up. The straightness of her posture and the swivel of her hips had me guessing whether I'd gotten through to her.

On the ride back to the house, I couldn't help but regret the fact I'd made her cry. Although, that was the purpose of why I'd gone to extremes, wasn't it? To scare her. To make her feel all the emotions she'd travel through if someone succeeded in snatching her.

Still, the moment the first tear wet her cheek, I had to hold myself back from wrapping my arms around her and telling her I was sorry. Instead, I let the entire scene play out as it should.

I bounced between thinking I might be screwed if Walter found out what I did and hoping Cara had finally learned her lesson.

CHAPTER
THREE

Cara

"**N**aomi is waiting for me," I snipped, yanking the back-seat door open. Once inside, my fingers glided over the keys of my phone, texting my bestie that I was on my way to the restaurant we'd originally agreed on after our shopping excursion yesterday.

Ford had been talking with Owen on the front porch, but I neither had time for pleasantries, nor did I want to indulge in them. I was still seething over what happened.

I'd contacted Naomi as soon as Ford brought me home the day prior and apologized for standing her up, even though it wasn't my fault. I promised to tell her everything once I saw her. Emily had been the first person I'd told, and while she seemed just as angry with Ford for the stunt he pulled, she agreed that I should stop taking off on him. In fact, she told me I needed to find my center and move ahead. Having no mental stamina to decode her odd message, I had turned in early and shut out the rest of the world, falling into a deep sleep as soon as my head had hit the pillow.

When I woke, I contemplated telling my dad, but then thought better of it. A part of me believed maybe Ford was right when he said my dad would be okay with what had happened, telling me it was my fault Ford thought he had to go to such lengths in order to convince me to stop disappearing. And because I didn't know which way my dad would land, I chose to keep my mouth shut.

"Why are you stopping?" My frustration barreled off me, and with the mood I was in, there was no way I could attempt to be civil toward the man. Not after what he'd just put me through.

"Because we're here." He cut off the engine, then exited the vehicle. I knew better than to expect him to open my door for me. He hadn't done it before, and I doubted he'd start that shit now. Even if he felt guilty about the faux kidnapping, which I doubted he did.

As I brushed past him, I wanted to yell at him to remove his sunglasses. I hated not being able to see his eyes. When he hid them, I felt him judging me. Although, I was sure he judged me with or without them on.

Me: You here yet?

Naomi: Back booth. You have some explaining to do.

Ford was hot on my heels as I marched toward the entrance to the restaurant. I prayed that once inside, he'd give me a bit of space, seeing as how he owed me and all that. At least, I thought he did.

Once I'd located my friend, I slid into the booth opposite her and slumped forward, placing both arms out in front of me on the table. I saw Ford headed for the booth directly across from us, but I shot him a warning look. Normally, he'd brush me off and do as he wanted, but that time, he took the hint and sat two seats up from where he originally was going to, giving us more privacy.

When I looked back to Naomi, she frowned. "What was that all about?" I opened my mouth to speak, but she cut me off with the flick of her wrist. "What the hell happened to you? You said you'd meet me, then never showed up. I called you repeatedly." She shrugged. "No answer."

I loved Naomi like a sister, and I knew she felt the same for me. I hated that I'd made her worry, but it wasn't my fault. It was probably the first time in a long time where I could actually say that and it be the truth.

"Something happened."

"I assumed. But what?"

To be sure I had the privacy needed to tell her everything, I looked in Ford's direction. He was turned to the side, looking at his cell, but I had no doubt he was still paying attention to me.

"I came out of the shop and two guys grabbed me and threw me in the back of a van." There was no use in sugarcoating my answer.

Naomi covered her mouth. "Oh, Cara!" She studied me, her eyes roaming over me slowly before she leaned across the table and placed her hand over mine. "Wait. How did you escape? Ohhh... Ford found you." She nodded continuously, satisfied she'd been able to answer her own question. If only she knew the half of it.

"You're right. Ford did find me. But it wasn't hard to do, seeing as he was the one who set the whole fucking thing in motion." I removed my hand from hers and leaned back against the red leather booth, folding my arms over my chest. Naomi looked over at Ford before turning her stare back onto me. She tugged on her ear right before she squished her eyebrows together. "Oh, yeah. You heard me right. That bastard had his two buddies snatch me up and act like they were real kidnappers.

"He's behind the threats, then?" She tilted her head to the side. If the situation hadn't been so serious, I would've found Naomi's mannerisms comical.

"No." I blew out a breath. "He set the whole thing up because he wanted to show me what could happen if I keep ditching him."

Her lips parted and acknowledgment registered on her face. "So, he was teaching you a lesson."

"Yes."

She shook her head from side to side briefly before nodding. "I can see that."

"What? You're siding with him?" I couldn't believe my ears. First Emily and now Naomi? Out of all the things I expected her to say, that wasn't it. I wouldn't go so far as to say I felt betrayed, but it was close.

"I think he went to extremes, but you have to admit that since your father assigned him to watch out for you, you've taken off on him twice."

"Three times," I corrected, wincing when I realized I'd proven her point.

"Okay, three times." She leaned closer. "Maybe it was the only thing he could think of to show you how much danger you could be in. Are in. You have no idea who's sending those notes. You could be being watched right now for all we know."

"I *am* being watched, by that guy over there," I said, pointing at Ford.

Naomi looked to him, then back to me. "That man could kidnap me anytime." She laughed, wiggling her brows in an attempt to make me laugh, but I found nothing about this situation amusing. "Oh, come on. You can't tell me you don't dream about sitting on his face."

Her bluntness was what made me crack a smile. "Only you."

"You know damn well you're hot for him, you just won't admit it."

"Yes, he's cute."

"Puppies are cute. Babies are cute. That man is gorgeous."

"All right, he's... attractive." Naomi pursed her lips. "You know damn well I think he's hot, but that doesn't mean I like him. Because I don't."

"Just think about all the angry sex you two could have." I couldn't help but laugh because she'd completely gone off topic, and while I'd initially wanted to tell her the story from the beginning, I realized it was best I didn't. The last thing I wanted to do was wade through the ocean of emotions he'd evoked from me the moment he walked into that windowless room.

I wanted to change the subject to one that was safer, one that would take all the focus off me and my shadow. "How's Benji?"

She gave me a far-off look before answering, breathing out slowly as if what she was about to tell me was bad news. I prepared myself that the rest of our lunch date would be spent in consolation of a lost relationship, but when she parted her lips to speak, she told me the opposite. Sort of.

"He proposed." My eyes landed on her left hand, but her ring finger was bare.

"Am I to assume from the lack of an engagement ring that you told him no? Or did he not have a ring? Is he one of those guys?" I smiled at the memory of us when we were younger, discussing that if any guy ever proposed to us without a ring, we'd ditch them on the spot.

"No, he's not that guy." The corner of her mouth turned up, but fell flat just as quickly. "He had a ring."

"Well?"

"We've only known each other for a few months. I think it's way too early to think about marriage, don't you?"

"You're asking the wrong one. I don't believe in marriage. Too many restrictions." I sipped my iced tea and wished I'd asked the waiter to throw in a couple shots of tequila for good measure.

"You do realize you're gonna have to give up on the 'I hate love' mantra eventually, right?" Naomi took the remaining bite of her carbtastic meal and leaned back in her seat, her eyes narrowing at me until I acknowledged what she said.

"I don't hate love." I shrugged. "I just don't want any part of that shit. No offense."

"None taken."

"So... what are you gonna do about Benji?" Before she answered, I threw another question at her. "Wait, what did you end up telling him when he asked you?"

"I told him that I wasn't ready to get married. I mean, we hadn't even talked about it and he goes and proposes. That's pushy of him, right?"

I pointed toward myself. "Again, wrong one."

"You're no help." She chuckled, patting her belly from meal satisfaction.

Naomi and I had been friends for a long time, and I realized she needed my support. I needed to stop being, well, me, and woman up. Give her some advice. Problem was, as I told her, I wasn't the right person for the job. But I needed to say something meaningful before the worried look on her face morphed into one of anxiety.

"If you care about Benji, I mean, really care about him, then give his proposal some thought. I'm not telling you to say yes, but talk to him. Hash it out." I took a few more sips of my drink, the ice cubes clanking to the bottom of the glass when I rested it back on the table. "When did he ask you?"

"Right before I came here."

I was mid-swallow when my iced tea went down the wrong pipe. Or was I choking because of what Naomi had just said? That her boyfriend asked her to marry him right before she met me here? Before I could ask her to repeat herself, a large palm slapped me on back. Not once or twice but four times. It took me a moment to figure out whose hand was smacking the hell out of me.

I hadn't seen Ford approach our booth, so to say I was startled with the sudden attention would be an understatement. I wasn't going to lie and say that I forgot he was even there, because I was all too aware of his presence, but I never thought he'd end up behind me as soon as I started choking.

I flinched to the side when I saw his hand raise in the air again. "Stop hitting me," I griped, controlling my breaths to help alleviate my coughing fit.

"Are you all right?" His voice was rougher than usual.

"I'm fine. You can go sit back down now." My tone wasn't friendly, certainly not toward the man who'd fucked with my head yesterday.

He walked back to his seat without another word, and it was only when he was away from earshot did Naomi lay into me.

"Why are you so mean to him all the time?"

"Did I not just tell you earlier what he did to me?" I swore if my eyes widened any more, they'd fall out of their sockets. "What he put me through?"

"I understand you being sour about yesterday, but from the day he started, you've done nothing but complain about him. I don't know why you just don't accept the situation and find some common ground with the guy." She peered around the booth to look in his direction. "He doesn't seem that bad."

"Says the woman who can't make up her mind when it comes to her own life." Naomi gasped and I instantly regretted my comment. "Sorry. I'm just... I guess I don't.... Fuck! I don't know."

"Trust me. Been there." We shared a smile before taking care of the bill and getting up to leave. Ford was behind me before I took a step toward the exit.

CHAPTER
FOUR

Ford

The past week was filled with tension, more so than usual, only this tension was uncomfortable. I realized tension, by its very definition, was uneasy, but ever since my "lesson," Cara had been different around me. Distant. All of it sounds redundant, but trust me, something was amiss.

I wasn't a man who typically paid attention to shit like this, but I couldn't help it. Was it because I only half regretted setting her up? Or was it because I had a feeling what happened had changed her perception of the situation? Of me, perhaps?

I wasn't making any sense and I made even less of it when I tried talking to Owen. He told me I was overthinking it, something I'd only done one other time I could recall, with my sister Julia.

"I'll take the upstairs this round." Owen and I often switched the areas of the house and grounds we checked, which happened multiple times a day to ensure everything was safe and sound. Maybe it was overkill, but I'd rather be prepared in case anything happened. The last thing I wanted was to be caught off guard.

"Nothing in Common" by Frank Sinatra popped into my head for some reason, so I busied myself humming the tune while I checked each of the rooms on the second floor. My mother often called me an old soul, telling me I was born during the wrong decade. My tastes in music gravitated toward the classics, like Sinatra, Crosby, King, and Cole. I believed that I enjoyed their sound because it comforted me, eased me when I felt out of control. Hell, I blared Crosby right after Owen left my place the day he told me about this job. I was drunk but I was content listening to the sounds of his voice.

All rooms were clear except for the last one I had to check. Cara's room. I believed her to be inside as she wasn't on the lower level, and seeing how it was cloudy outside and looked like rain, she wasn't out by the pool either.

I rapped on her door and waited. After five seconds there was no answer, so I knocked again, louder the second time. Still nothing, so I turned the handle and entered.

"Cara? You in here?" Any other time I would've rushed inside without a thought to her privacy. Okay, maybe that was a stretch. I'd been somewhat considerate but nothing like right then. Something needed to change in our working relationship, and I urged myself to extend a proverbial olive branch. And although I had nothing specific to be sorry for, I could, at the very least, alter my interactions with her so they weren't as unpleasant.

Her bathroom door was closed, so I assumed she was inside. I commenced with my check of her room, and as I turned to leave, a gust of air from her half-opened window blew a pile of paper that was resting on top of her bed all over the room.

Bending down, I gathered the mess when Cara suddenly appeared behind me. I never heard the bathroom door open, but

25

there she was, in her short silk robe and a white towel on her head.

She rushed over and snatched the paper from my hands. "What are you doing?"

"The wind blew them all over the place. I was only trying to pick them up." A simple and true explanation, but one she didn't believe.

"I think you were snooping again," she accused. "Much like you did the last time." Cara referred to the time I snuck a peek at some of her work while she'd been engrossed in watching a home movie.

Sarcastic remarks formed in my head, but I released none of them. Instead, I nodded, a simple acquiesce, a refusal to argue over something I couldn't win.

"They're quite good. You should do something with them." I hadn't realized I was going to say such a thing so her shock at my compliment was a mirror of my own. I didn't lie; she was talented. Too bad she couldn't spend more of her time and energy on something that mattered. Developing her talent would take her far, but she would rather laze about and party than think about her future.

I had to stop thinking of Julia whenever I thought about the comparisons between her and Cara. Hard to do because I saw many similarities in them.

"Contrary to what everyone thinks, I will do something with my life. I just have to figure out a few things first." She spread the drawings out on her mattress, face up so I could see them. I thought she would've continued to hide them from me, but she displayed them, instead. I took it as a sign she was willing to open up a little, maybe talk to me like someone other than the overbearing pain-in-the-ass shadow who'd been assigned to her. "I'm going to make and wear an outfit for the cancer charity event I'm attending next week. Something elegant yet trendy."

With my head pointed straight ahead, fearing I'd break whatever connection existed right then, I looked at her from my peripheral vision and saw a lilt of a genuine smile spread across her lovely face. My stomach fluttered, but I slammed that shit down immediately. One smile and one moment of her looking at ease was not enough for me to react in anyway. I refocused. My mission returning to that olive branch I planned.

"I have no doubt it'll be great." My words surprised me, but anything was better than falling back to the tit for tat we'd been throwing at each other since day one.

We turned to look at one another, our eyes connecting briefly before turning away. "Thank you," she whispered, but I heard the words of gratitude loud and clear.

I left with a lighter feeling than when I walked into her room, an odd interaction, at best. As I descended the stairs, an unease wrapped around my heart, but there was no chance in hell I'd be analyzing that anytime soon.

CHAPTER
FIVE

Cara

"How is everything?" Our mom settled into her seat on the sofa before accepting a glass of lemonade from Emily.

With the gloomy weather, I had no plans to leave the house, so it was a nice surprise when she said she was going to stop over for a visit. The skeptical part of me thought maybe she was there because she'd somehow heard about what happened with Ford and the faux kidnapping, but as soon as I saw her relaxed expression, that thought flew right out the window. Besides, if she did know about it, my father would be right by her side, I had no doubt.

I plopped down on the other couch, nestling in to get comfy, my lightweight sweatshirt and yoga pants the perfect outfit for catching up and relaxing.

"Good," my sister answered, taking the seat next to her. "Someone donated twenty-thousand dollars to Dream for Paws. That's a lot of care and food for the animals housed there." Emily smiled, her joy something I didn't understand because I wasn't much of an animal person myself. Don't get me wrong, I loved Buster, our family dog we had when we were little, but I'd never owned a pet as an adult.

Now if we were talking about fashion, I could hop on the

excited train for sure. I could go on and on about clothes, shoes, and accessories all day long if you let me. My passion had only come back into the equation over the past few months, more so these last couple of weeks.

Emily had always been a big supporter of mine, but the only other people who had seen my designs were my mother and Naomi. And of course, Ford, but that was by accident. Or on purpose on his part. When he had seen them, I'd become uncharacteristically nervous. Anxious he would say something that would crush me, crush the joy I felt when I sketched each line of the picture I had in my head. I had no idea why I cared so much about what he thought. But he'd complimented them. Complimented me, and a rush of pride had swirled through me.

There were times in a person's life when their perception of the world, and of themselves, could become altered forever. For me, it happened from a passing comment from Ford, of all people.

"Cara? Sweetheart?" My mom had been calling my name, but I'd been so lost in thought, I hadn't heard her. "What's the smile for?" Her grin was infectious, causing me to widen mine. Whenever I gazed at her, I saw both Emily and me. The family resemblance was strong. If I looked half as good at her age, I should consider myself lucky. I wasn't complaining about my appearance at all, though. I realized I'd been blessed in the looks department, but there was something about the way Mom carried herself that made her seem regal. Her dark-blonde hair was styled in a long, bob-type haircut, her bangs making her look closer to our age than fifty-two.

A fifteen-year age gap existed between my parents, and while my grandmother wasn't keen on her daughter dating a man who'd just turned forty, when she was only twenty-five herself when they met—our age to be exact—she soon allowed it to happen after seeing how in love they were. They'd been smitten from the start.

"I was thinking about the outfit I wanted to make for a charity event I'm attending next weekend."

"Ooh, is this the one with the plunging neckline? The one that stops right above your hoo-ha?" Emily laughed but my mother raised her brows.

"What dress is that?" she asked.

"She's teasing." I threw my sister a warning glare, cautioning her to shut her mouth with the narrowing of my eyes. "It's a pantsuit slash jumper-type design. All black except the sides, from under here," I said, pointing to just under my arm, "all the way to the ankle is a nude color. It looks like my skin, but it'll either be a mesh material or lace. I haven't decided yet."

"Sounds beautiful, honey. I can't wait to see you in it."

"I could send you a picture of me wearing it." I leaned back and tucked a pillow under my arm to get more comfortable.

"You don't have to do that. I'll be there."

"You'll be where?"

"At the event."

My head flinched back slightly. "What event?"

"At the same one you're going to. The one Stephanie invited you both to."

I looked at Emily, then back to my mom.

Stephanie Adler was one of my oldest friends. We'd lost touch when we were younger but had reconnected years later.

"I'm still not getting how you know about that."

"It's not a secret." Mom chuckled. "In fact, she reached out to your father and me a while back, asking if there was any way we could invite some influential people. Of course, after she told us about her mother's diagnosis, and thankfully, her remission, we told her we'd do what we could to help. I always liked Nancy. Such a nice woman."

I still had so many questions. "How did she get your number?"

"Emily."

I locked eyes with my twin. "How come you never told me?"

Emily shrugged before she stood up, grabbing our mom's glass and walking toward the kitchen. "I didn't think anything of it. It was after the conversation she had with you about not being able to come to our birthday shindig. She said she tried to call you but couldn't get a hold of you, so she tried me." I recalled seeing a couple of missed calls from Steph but figured I'd call her back when I had the chance. Then I just plain forgot. A certain moody and complicated bodyguard had stolen most of my attention.

"Are you going, too?" I asked.

"I'm planning on it." Emily walked back into the living room and handed our mom her refill. "Do you think you can create something for me to wear, as well? Would you have enough time to make it?"

I had no idea why I thought it was odd that not only my parents were going to the event, but that Emily was, too. During our last phone conversation, right before we left for California, my childhood friend did mention that she hoped both Emily and I could make it. But I must've forgotten to mention it to my sister, too focused on what we were all going to do to celebrate our twenty-fifth. Steph must've solidified plans when she called Emily to get our parents' number.

"It'll be tight, but I think I can make it."

"I don't want to wear anything too snug."

I sighed, then smiled. "I don't mean the outfit being too tight. I mean the timeframe is tight."

"Oh." Emily laughed, leaning to the side to rest against the armchair of the sofa.

"Is there vodka in that lemonade?" I asked. She never answered because I knew there wasn't, but she'd definitely just had a duh moment.

CHAPTER
SIX

Cara

Since the thought of making our outfits popped into my head—and the idea was solidified when I told our mom all about it—I became busy planning every step.

On Monday, I visited with Audrey Filip, the owner of Blush, one of my favorite boutiques, asking if she could hook me up with her manufacturer in Los Angeles. I told her of my plans, and she graciously gave me the number. I didn't know if her willingness to help me stemmed from me being a good customer, the fact the event was to raise money for cancer—the disease Audrey's mother passed away from two years prior—or because she was a sweetheart. It could be a mixture of all three, but whatever the driving force was, I happily accepted her help.

On Tuesday, I argued with the overnight delivery company about still not receiving my fabric, which should have been at my door by noon. By one o'clock I was giving them an earful. Luckily, more for their sanity of having to deal with me than mine, the doorbell rang two hours later. The truck had broken down and it took them that long to get it fixed. I breathed a sigh of relief once I was able to spread the material out on my bed, satisfied with the fabric choices I'd made.

By that evening, I finished the sketch of my outfit and

started on Emily's. All she told me was that she wanted a dress that came down to her knees and flared out at the waist. She didn't care about color, if it was strapless or not, or what type of material it was made from. She told me that she trusted my vision, and whatever I made for her she'd love.

By Wednesday afternoon, the sketches having been completed earlier that day, and the patterns cut, I'd finished my sister's dress. It took countless cups of coffee and a few minor cuts and pricks, but I'd done it.

Thankfully, I was able to work in the privacy of my bedroom, the overly large space accommodating the range of supplies I needed to work with, including the sewing machine I'd received many years ago as a birthday present.

I decided to call it a night, or morning, and go to bed. I never woke when I assumed one of the guys came into my room for early rounds, too lost to sleep and the dream that maybe my life could turn in the direction I'd wanted when I was young.

"I love it so much, Cara." Emily beamed, holding the dress up in front of her and twirling around in front of the full-length mirror. The vibrant azure blue set off her beautiful amber-colored eyes.

"Are you okay with the material?" I'd chosen chiffon because it was lightweight, a factor that made it challenging to sew. From the bustline on up, I added a deeper hue of blue lace, the combination of the two colors and fabrics complimenting each other nicely.

"I love it." Her bright smile filled my heart with pride for a job well done. "Can I try it on?"

"Of course. How else am I going to see what needs to be altered?" I returned her grin, anxious to see what my creation looked like on her. She disappeared from my room, only to return five minutes later, walking back through my door with an even bigger smile, turning around so I could zip her up.

"Put your arms out at your sides. Okay, now raise them up. Bend to the side. How does it feel? Does it give you enough stretch? Do you have enough room? The middle looks snug. Does it feel snug?" I circled her, scrutinizing every facet of the dress, tugging then releasing. The sleeveless part had been tricky because I wanted to give her enough room so the material wasn't digging into the underneath of her arm, but not big enough there was a significant amount of space. When I reached under her arm to test the stretch and space, she laughed. Ticklish.

After several more stretches and additional prodding, she playfully slapped my hands away. "It's perfect. Fits like a glove."

"Are you sure?" I asked, uncertain if the dress was perfect enough to be worn in public.

Emily saw the doubt in my eyes and drew me in for a hug. "It's perfect," she repeated. "Gorgeous. I'm going to be the envy of everyone there." Her words eased me, but a bit of skepticism remained. The age-old saying, *you're your own worst critic* slammed into me, and it couldn't be truer. "Even though I thought it was going to be longer, I love that it hits above my knee."

"I was hoping you wouldn't mind." I reached forward to touch the dress once more and she moved back a step, shaking her head before turning around and pointing to the zipper. She moved her chestnut colored hair to one side, making sure none of the strands became tangled in the metal teeth.

"I have the perfect pair of heels."

"You do or I do?"

"We'll see," she sang before disappearing again to get changed.

While I was still going over the look and feel of Emily's dress in my mind, deciphering if I loved how it fit, which I did, my cell chimed. Swiping the screen, I saw I had a message from Steph.

Steph: Can't wait to see you on Saturday. It feels like forever since the last time we hung out.

Mixed emotions plagued me whenever I spoke to or about her. I hated that what happened overshadowed our friendship, and I never had the time to process or deal with anything before her family moved to California. Then, as time passed, I dove headfirst into a life of reckless behavior and avoidance.

Me: Can't wait either. It's been too long.

Steph: Definitely.

Me: Can you send me the info again?

Steph: Give me a few. Last minute deets to handle.

Twenty minutes later she texted me the address, which happened to be on the Upper East Side of Manhattan. It would take us close to two hours to get there, and that was if traffic was light. I didn't care about the drive, but I wasn't sure how Ford would feel about the travel.

As I entered my closet to check to see if I could locate a pair of earrings I wanted to wear on Saturday, the thought I even considered how Ford would react to driving so far annoyed me. Why should I care all of a sudden? I most certainly hadn't before.

Locating the earrings in question, I rushed from my room, wanting to snatch Emily's dress back to make sure it didn't need any other alterations. As soon as I stepped into the hallway, I ran right into Ford. Literally. My forehead bumped against his chest.

Because of my surprise, I inhaled through my nose. He always smelled so good, and right then wasn't any different—a hint of the outdoors mixed with mint. I was sure it sounded like an odd combination, but it was intoxicating.

"Sorry," he mumbled, retreating until there were a few feet of space between us.

Every type of snarky response coiled in my head, ready to strike, but as I stood there looking at him, I didn't want to use any of them. *What is happening to me?*

He was dressed in his customary black slacks and white shirt, sleeves rolled up to the elbows. I never considered a man's forearms a point of interest, but his were sexy. His large hands disappeared into his pockets, something he seemed to have a habit of doing.

"I was actually going to come looking for you." I leaned against the wall, my body language foreign to me because it portrayed ease, and that was something I most definitely wasn't while in Ford's presence.

"What for?"

"We have a charity event to go to on Saturday. It's in Manhattan." I took a breath and let him digest the information. He didn't say anything, but did I really expect him to? What was he going to do, complain? Refuse to drive me there? No, he wouldn't do either of those things.

If I thought about all the times Ford appeared to give me a hard time, it had always been in response to something I'd done or said. I often lit the torch, hoping for an explosion, and sometimes my wish was granted when Ford reacted.

"Okay. What time?"

"It starts at seven. It'll take almost two hours to get there, but if we hit traffic, which we probably will because it's the weekend, it'll take us longer. So, I want to leave by four. If we're early, we can swing by someplace and grab a drink beforehand."

"I'll let Owen know." He brushed past me without another word and entered my bedroom, only to return several minutes later. Pesky rounds.

After I retrieved Emily's dress, hanging it up in my closet for safe keeping, I started working on my outfit. I had a little less than forty-eight hours to complete it. Talk about down to the wire, but I always worked best under pressure.

CHAPTER
SEVEN

Ford

The moment I caught sight of Cara descending the stairs, I wanted to make up any excuse I could think of as to why I couldn't accompany her to the event that evening. And the reason was simple. My dick would be hard the entire time.

Covered head to toe in black did nothing to diminish the glow she emitted, a beam of pride curving her lips with each step she took. She knew she looked good. Hot. She wore her blonde hair down and in loose waves. Images of me grabbing hold of her locks and spinning them around my fist so that I could anchor her to me assaulted my every thought.

When she cleared the last step, she stood there watching my reaction, a flash of uncertainty surfacing on her face, but it was gone as quickly as it appeared.

"You look very nice" was the only thing I could think to say that was appropriate. Anything else I wanted to blurt out would've gotten me slapped.

Her face brightened. "Thank you."

As she moved past me, I saw that the side of her silk jumpsuit was a nude lace material, her skin visible from her ankle all the way up to underneath her arm…on both sides. With my eyes glued to her, watching her every movement, it was apparent she wasn't wearing any underwear. No bra. No panties.

The absence of her undergarments wasn't in-your-face obvious, but to anyone who dared to take a longer look, it wasn't hard to figure out. And I had no doubt that Cara would have countless sets of eyes glued to her all night.

To say I was attracted to the woman was true. I wasn't about to deny it, never had, but that was as far as it went. I'd kept my thoughts to myself and never so much as shared them with Owen. Although, something told me he knew, just from the way he liked to tease me. He wouldn't say anything if he hadn't picked up on a hint that I thought she was beautiful.

I was aware Cara had made both hers and her sister's outfits for the night's event, having witnessed her creative process strewn around her room while I completed my rounds. For as little as I knew about her, I realized that the smile I now saw ghost across her face was a gift. To herself. She seemed happy. Driven.

My intention after I'd set up the faux kidnapping was to point out how careless her actions were, to try and make her aware that how she acted not only affected her but those around her. Initially, she hadn't taken it well, but I'd expected her reaction. What I didn't expect was the change I saw in her these past two weeks.

It was as if the experience shook her, jiggled something loose only to burst open. Maybe it was the jolt she needed to appreciate what she had. What she could have, if she stopped fucking around with her life and really started to live.

"Ready?" Owen appeared in the foyer, standing right next to me with the women behind him.

He'd been in the living room chatting it up with Emily,

complimenting her more than once on how beautiful she looked. And she did. Cara had done a great job on her sister's dress. And her own outfit, as well. Too good a job if my opinion counted because I could predict what kind of night was in store for me.

Fending off plenty of fuckers brave enough to try and get close to her. I only prayed the guys who were attending would respect the purpose of the event and behave themselves. Although, when alcohol was part of the scene, all bets were off. That much I knew.

A curt nod from me and we all walked out the front door.

We decided to drive together into Manhattan because it was pointless to take two vehicles. Besides, at least I'd have company in case Cara reverted into one of her typical moods. She'd been decent the past few days, our interactions not grating on my nerves like usual, but I remained on guard because that could all change in the blink of an eye.

With me behind the wheel and Owen at my side, the women sat behind us, Cara directly behind me. I caught her eyes in the rearview mirror every so often, staring longer than was safe. Not only was my focus pulled from the road, but I was giving her more attention than was appropriate.

"I hope traffic isn't a nightmare. You know how I get." Owen smiled, but he was serious. He hated other drivers almost as much as I did, but he often took it up a notch, honking when they didn't move out of his way quick enough.

"Why do you think I'm driving?" I reached over and turned on the radio, the satellite tuned into the Sinatra station. I glanced in the mirror and waited for Cara to roll her eyes or make a comment about the music selection, but her eyes were glued to her phone. Whatever she read had her biting her bottom lip and causing a deep crease between her brows.

Emily noticed her reaction, as well. "What's going on?" she asked, leaning over her sister to try and look at her cell. More lip biting from Cara followed by a deeper frown.

"I don't know why I'm considering it."

"Considering what?" Emily asked.

Cara turned her phone toward her sister so she could read it. *If I don't keep my eyes on the road, I'm gonna get us killed.*

"Yay," Emily cheered. "You should definitely do it. You never know who'll win."

"True," Cara confirmed, glancing up to look at me in the mirror.

"What are you talking about?" Owen had no qualms about being nosy, a trait which annoyed me most times, but right then I'd never been so grateful for his inability to mind his own business.

Emily was the one to answer, scooting forward to be closer to us. Well, closer to him.

"Stephanie, the one who organized the event, just asked Cara if she'd be willing to auction herself off to raise money."

"What does that mean?" I asked, trying to hide the disapproval from my voice, but Cara heard it loud and clear, an air of cockiness in her reply.

"It means I'll be auctioning off a date to help out."

"Like hell you will," I barked, gripping the wheel so tight my knuckles turned white.

"Hey," Owen warned, "calm down."

Choosing to ignore my brother, I kept my eyes on the road ahead so as not to have to meet her icy glare. Trust me, I knew she was throwing me daggers in the mirror. And if they weren't daggers, she had a haughty look on her face, an expression that would also piss me off.

"I won't calm down. It's not smart. Not with everything else going on. For all you know, the person who's been sending the threatening notes to your father could be the very same person to bid for a date with you. How much easier could it be?"

"I didn't think of that," Emily whispered, turning to look out the window.

"The likelihood of that happening is pretty slim. No one even knows I'm doing this. Besides, what are the chances the creep will be there? It's not like I publicly announced I was going."

"Your parents are going. Therefore, it's public knowledge. Everyone who needs to know does." Walter had called us earlier that day to let us know they would be in attendance, and to be on alert because it would be a highly public event. No matter if there were five people around or five hundred, Owen and I would do our job to the best of our ability. But I understood why he'd made the comment. These were his children. Enough said.

"You're overreacting. As usual."

"Listen, I don't think you shou—"

"Just do your job and I'll be fine." She moved closer to the window and out of my line of sight of the rearview.

CHAPTER
EIGHT

Cara

We arrived ten minutes before the start of the event. Traffic hadn't been too bad, and while the tension in the car quickly became stifling, there was no other outburst from me or Ford.

I supposed it was only a matter of time before we both reverted to the way we treated the other. He was an obtrusive pain in the ass, and I spoke my mind. Although, if you asked him, I was sure he could come up with a colorful way to describe me.

When Ford pulled up in front of one of the oldest hotels in Manhattan, I smiled. The old-timey feel of the brick and mortar, mixed with the modern touches of the time made it the perfect venue for the event. There was something about the building that allowed me to imagine it when it was first constructed, images of horse and buggies pulling up in front, people of the time dressed in elegant attire stepping down and onto the cobblestone, laughing and dreaming of what their stay would be like.

My rampant thoughts were cut short when Ford threw the vehicle in Park and exited, opening my door while his brother stepped back to open my sister's. I looked across and saw the smile on Owen's face when he looked at Emily, extending his hand to assist her. Then I turned to look at Ford, and all I saw was a scowl, and instead of him offering to lend me a hand, he shoved said hand in his pocket and took a step back.

Chivalrous. Not so much.

I pushed the door open farther before stepping out, tossing my hair over my shoulder and mumbling, "Such a gentleman."

Two steps later, his breath fanned across my cheek. "A gentleman wouldn't tell you that your nipples are hard. They're visible in that outfit. You should've brought a jacket." Heat swirled through me the instant he stopped speaking. I battled with the urge to flaunt my erect nipples and wanting to cover myself with my hands. In the end, I ignored him.

Ford walked past all of us but remained close enough to keep an eye on me. I couldn't say I was surprised by his comment, yet I was. Kind of. I realized he'd probably have some sort of retort, but I'd been unprepared for those words.

When I constructed the full-length jumpsuit, I made it with the mindset that I wouldn't be able to wear a bra or panties because of the sheer sides. I'd sewn in thin cups, but because of the unexpected chill in the air, my nipples pebbled. I was sure my body's reaction had nothing to do with Ford.

Walking toward the entrance, I was surprised there were no paparazzi. Ford had mentioned that people knew my parents were coming, therefore they probably found out that we were, too. The damn leeches were everywhere else I didn't want them to be. Of course, this would be the one time—when I was part of something worthy—they'd be MIA.

Once inside, we headed toward the largest ballroom, surprised by how many people were already gathered.

"I need a drink." I sauntered straight toward the large bar located on the other side of the room. While I realized Ford would be behind me, I prayed he would give me some space to try and clear my head. His comment about my nipples annoyed me, sure, but it was the disapproval in his tone that rattled me. Any other time I would've blown him off, not giving a second thought to his words, but right then I cared for some reason.

"It's early, so pace yourself," Emily warned, gifting me a tentative smile. "Just want to make sure you have your wits about you when it comes time for the auction. You don't want to get stuck with some old, fat guy, do you?"

"I don't think I have a say in who wins. I go to whoever bids the highest." Saying it like that sounded strange to my ears, like someone was purchasing me. Which, in a way, they were. They were buying time with me. No, wait, that made me sound like an escort. Anyway, it was all for a great cause, and if I ended up with a fat, old guy, I sure as hell hoped he was funny.

Ford was close by, as I suspected, and I heard him grumble, "Ridiculous," under his breath. While I wanted to goad him, make him explain his complaint, I ignored it and placed my order with the bartender. A handsome kid who practically tripped over himself when he saw me approach.

Once I had my drink in hand, I turned to face the growing crowd. I leaned against the lip of the bar and put the straw in my mouth, taking a healthy sip and hoping the night would be a fun one.

I loved to people watch, especially when I knew them and they had no idea I was paying attention. I found people's mannerisms quirky, their expressions telling if someone paid close enough attention, and their body language cinching the deal, exposing all their secrets.

In the center of the ballroom were a few of Hollywood's elite, and I had no doubt they were here because of my father. But whatever it took, right?

"There's Mom and Dad," Emily announced, pointing to our left. Our dad was dressed in a classic black suit and white shirt, but instead of a standard tie, he opted for a bow tie; a touch of difference for him was typical. Our mom had on a floor-length, pale-pink sleeveless dress, hugging her in all the right places. Her hair was down in big waves, similar to mine.

Clutching my drink, I followed Emily toward our parents. They beamed at us as we drew closer.

"Aren't you two lovely," Mom said, smiling big as she gave us each a hug.

"You don't look half bad yourself." I spun her around, to which she laughed and swatted my hand away when I rested it on her shoulder and wanted her to twirl again.

"I clean up well."

"You always look gorgeous," Dad said, leaning in to kiss her cheek. His hand disappeared behind her back, and if I wasn't mistaken, from the way she jerked away from him and laughed, he just grabbed her ass. I could be wrong, but he had been known to openly grope her in public. Nothing lewd, of course, but enough to have tongues wagging.

A faint blush tinted her cheeks right before she turned into him, whispering in his ear. She could've said something inappropriate or she could've chastised him for grabbing her, if that was indeed what he'd done. Regardless, he beamed at her words.

My parents loved each other fiercely and they hardly ever fought, but when they did, it was my mom laying down the law, my dad falling into place and apologizing for whatever he had or hadn't done.

As I contemplated whether I'd ever find someone who could put up with me enough to warrant as long of a relationship as my parents had, my eyes found Ford. He was not the type of man I envisioned myself being with, but there was no denying I was attracted to him. It took more than desire to sustain a relationship, however, and although I'd never had a real partnership with someone before, I realized that after the lust part of attraction faded, there had to be more for the connection to endure. I just didn't know what that would look like.

From my many interactions with Ford, he struck me as a no-nonsense type of guy. Someone who didn't have time for the fluff most people liked to engage in when trying to get to know each other. The niceties.

Our relationship, if that was the right terminology to use, had not been ideal right from the beginning. He was forced on me and I rejected his very presence, fighting the situation every step of the way. There were times he held his tongue, although, his expression told me everything. Then there were times he spoke his mind freely, most times in reaction to something I'd done or said.

But recently, we weren't as harsh toward the other. And by that, I meant my reaction toward him. Not his toward me since I seemed to have been the one who instigated most of our negative encounters.

I should still be furious with him for the stunt he pulled with his buddies, but being taken, and thinking I was in real danger, pushed away all my false bravado and terrified me. He made me see a side of myself I didn't want to confront. I'd tried not to show weakness, but my body told me to fuck off and took over, reacting in a way I believed most people would. Thankfully, it had all been a setup, but the happenstance was enough to jolt me into the reality that I should step outside my bubble, the one where I thought nothing bad could happen to me, and take a good look around.

I portrayed a woman who hadn't been affected by what Ford had done, but I truly had been. I'd never profess as much to him, however, because I thought that might give him a smidge of satisfaction.

"You two look beautiful," my dad complimented. "And I hear you made both of your outfits." His eyes were pinned to mine, and if I wasn't mistaken, I saw a shimmer of pride residing behind them. A look I hadn't seen from him toward me in longer than I cared to acknowledge. My heart swelled and I beamed, foolishly so, but I didn't care.

"She spent the past week working like a nut to get them done." Emily fluffed out the skirt of her dress. "She did an amazing job."

"She certainly did." My dad threw his arm over my shoulder and pulled me into him, planting a kiss on my temple before releasing me. "Well, now, if you'll excuse us, your mother and I have to mingle. I'm looking for my next lead, so I have to see if there are any viable candidates here."

"Always working," my mom grumbled but grinned, entwining her arm with his before they walked away.

The four of us were left standing by the bar, Ford and Owen a few paces to the side and talking amongst themselves. The younger of the two smiled as he chit-chatted, but his older sibling was straight-faced and looking right at me. For some inexplicable reason, the way he eyed me made me look down at myself in question. Was there something wrong with my outfit? I looked right at my chest first, thinking maybe my nipples were still hard, but they weren't. Then I glanced back over at the two of them and thought that maybe whatever Owen had said was the reason why Ford was staring at me. But even if I asked, he'd never tell me what they were talking about, so I pushed my curiosity aside and focused on having a good time, instead.

As I gossiped with Emily about all the people who'd showed up, I saw Steph walking toward us, talking to some man with salt-and-pepper hair. They were far enough away that I couldn't make out who he was; then they separated before I could get a better look. She proceeded walking our way and was next to us in no time.

"Thank you so much for coming." We embraced, and I hated it had been so long since we'd been able to connect in person. Her shoulder-length, chocolate-colored hair was styled down and straight. Steph had always had such a cute face, with a smattering of freckles across her nose. I had envied her trait but it was only as an adult that she had learned to love them, no longer choosing to cover them up.

As a grown woman, she was beautiful. Not the standard type of beauty plastered all over the magazines, but the small bump in her nose and the two-inch scar on her chin from a trampoline accident added to her appeal. I couldn't explain it, but those characteristics, mixed with the fact she was an amazing and giving human being, made her attractive. Inside and out.

Her rose-colored, strapless dress flared out at the waist, much like Emily's, but hit her below her knee.

"Love your dress." I reached forward and touched the material, fascinated with the way it shimmered at certain angles when she moved. "What is that made of?" I couldn't determine the exact fabric, and suddenly it was all I focused on.

"I don't know. I just saw it in the boutique and bought it." She laughed when my eyes remained glued to her dress, touching my shoulder to try and break my concentration.

"You two look stun—"

"Cara made our outfits," Emily interrupted, fluffing out her dress like she'd done earlier. Her pride in my work pumped up my confidence and filled my heart with even more love for my sister.

"You did?" Stephanie's eyes narrowed briefly before widening. "Really?"

"Yeah."

"She knocked them out this week. Both of them." Emily's enthusiasm was borderline embarrassing, but not quite there yet.

"Really." That time she hadn't posed her response as a question. She bit her lip and tilted her head. "I think there is someone you should meet."

"And who would that be?"

"James Hollen. Have you ever heard of him?"

"Uh… yeah." My face lit up. I wasn't easily starstruck, but the man was a genius, one of the greatest designers of our generation if my opinion counted for anything. I'd been following his collection for years, occasionally dreaming of being able to one day showcase my designs at Fashion Week, rubbing elbows with him and picking his brain about where he found his inspiration. His color palette never disappointed and his designs were on par for the everyday person, with a hint of flare for the extraordinary.

"You'll never believe this, but I ran into him last year when I took my mom to the doctor for her checkup. He was there with his father, and we got to talking while we waited for our parents. I had no idea who he was, but I knew he looked familiar. Coincidentally, I picked up a magazine during a lull in our conversation and there he was, on page ten, surrounded by gorgeous models." She took a breath and looked like she was lost in memory. Only when I nudged her arm, hungry for the rest of her story, did she continue. "When I showed him the article, he told me to toss it in the garbage. He laughed, but clearly he wasn't fond of the attention." She looked around the room, then back to me, like she was going to reveal her biggest secret. I leaned in close. "He's looking for new designers to work with."

"What do you mean?"

"He's looking for the new 'it' designer. He wants to branch out and help new up-and-comers. Wants to give back or something like that." She fiddled with the front of her dress, and something told me she wasn't telling me the entire story of their encounter.

"You know all this from your one meeting?"

She puffed out her cheeks before releasing her breath. "We had a few meetings." Before I could inquire more, she blurted, "He'll be here tonight. I could introduce you." Her tactic was a great way to redirect my sudden curiosity about the two of them and circle it back to meeting the man himself.

"That would be amazing." I swore if I didn't stop smiling, my face would be stuck in a constant look of glee. Not a bad look, I supposed.

Steph's attention was diverted, and after a quick hug, she flitted through the crowd to mingle, to schmooze and help raise as much money as she could for a cause that was unfortunately near and dear to her heart because of her mother.

After she was gone, I reached for Emily's hand and pulled her closer. "Did you hear all that?" I whisper-shouted, afraid if I projected my voice too much, I'd jinx myself and wash away the chance of meeting James Hollen.

Emily nodded emphatically. "That's amazing." My sister's enthusiasm was sweet. She didn't follow fashion like I did so she only recognized his name because I'd mentioned it on more than a few occasions.

I swore I was on cloud nine for the next hour, my only focus on meeting James and nothing else.

CHAPTER
NINE

Ford

I was vigilant with keeping my attention on Cara the entire time, only excusing myself for a brief stint when I had to visit the men's room. Owen had been by my side, both of us trying to blend in with the growing crowd. I'd been sporting my shades before we left the house, but Cara asked me to leave them behind, that she didn't want to draw unnecessary attention. And since she asked me without a hint of bitchiness, I tossed them on the entryway table.

Walking back across the large space, I recognized several famous faces, but most of the people were unknown to me. Not being someone who followed pop culture made my job easier. Being starstruck, like I had been when I first met Walter Dessoye, but thankfully hadn't shown it, interfered with my duties. If I met someone I was a fan of, I was fearful I'd ignore red flags, a trait that would hamper me being able to protect someone to the best of my abilities. Therefore, I steered clear of the tabloids as much as possible.

On my walk back toward my brother and the women, I couldn't help but be irritated at what Owen kept saying before I departed. "Cara looks gorgeous," and "Are you sure you don't want to pursue something with her when this is all over?" And my least favorite, "If you don't snatch her up, some other asshole will." So, not only was Owen trying to see where my head was at pertaining to thoughts of me and Cara, which there were none, but he'd essentially called me an asshole.

"All good?"

"Yup. Nothing much goin' on here except some ass kissing." Owen pointed toward Walter and the young guy standing next to him. I had no idea who he was, but my brother did. My philosophy of trying to remain as oblivious as possible when it came to well-known people wasn't something Owen adapted. He didn't purchase the magazines, but I often caught him watching *TMZ*. His excuse was that just in case our firm reached the notoriety where celebrities would search out our services, he wanted to be prepared. I'd brush off his pipe dreams, but it looked like his dream had come true. Having Walter as a client would open doors for Massey Security Inc., and I was still undecided if I was prepared for the fallout, or fortune as Owen would put it.

"Is that someone we should be concerned about?" I watched the interaction between the guy and Walter intently in case my brother answered the way I feared.

"You really have no idea who that is?"

"No."

"You really are oblivious." *Exactly.*

"All I care about is whether you deem him a threat in any way."

"Only if you had a woman here." Owen and his damn riddles.

"What the hell does that mean? And don't speak in more code because you're giving me a headache." I leaned against the wall and clasped my hands in front of me.

"That's Cody Caverly." I shrugged in ignorance. "He's only

the biggest womanizer in the business." Again, no acknowledgeable reaction from me. "He's in high demand and as such, he's worth big bucks."

"Why would I give a shit?"

"Because your woman is walking toward him." To be fair, I saw Cara headed toward her father, but my brother's comment about her being *mine* irked me. Not as much as when he laughed at me when I growled under my breath, giving him the illusion that I agreed with him calling her my woman. Because she most certainly was not. *Don't you want her to be, though?*

I shoved that asinine thought from my brain as quickly as it formed and moved toward Walter, Cara, and the bastard who leaned in to kiss Cara's cheek. I was next to them in seconds, startling Cara with how close I stood behind her.

"Is there a problem?" Walter eyed me with a frown, but before he freaked out over nothing, I shook my head, easing some of the tension from his face. "Good." He was going to say something else to me, but his daughter beat him to it.

"Do you mind?" Cara turned her head to the side, partially facing me. She kept her smile in place, but her tone belied her expression. The only reason I could think as to why she hadn't openly berated me for crowding her was because she was trying to either impress Cody or give the illusion that she wasn't a bitch. Harsh word, I realized, but Cara fit the trait when she wanted, although not as frequently as in the beginning.

I leaned in to whisper in her ear. "Only doing my job." When I stood up taller, she took a step back and bumped into me, that's how close we were.

"Will you excuse us?" she asked, touching Cody's upper arm before she reached back and smacked my leg. She never said another word as she walked away, each step she took purposeful

and hurried. I gave her father a shrug before I followed, silently scolding myself for overreacting to her being so close to the guy Owen referred to as a womanizer not moments ago. What did I really think would happen between them with her father standing there? And because I couldn't decipher why I acted like I did, I braced myself for the tongue lashing coming my way from one pissed-off socialite.

Cara waved to a few people as she passed but continued to head toward one of the hallways, reminding me of the last time we ended up in one. She'd kissed me. Then I kissed her back with eagerness before separating and telling her what a huge mistake it was.

But it wasn't a hallway we found ourselves in this time. It was a dining hall, dimly lit and empty. Not a good combination.

"Just what are you doing?" She folded her arms over her chest, and I couldn't help but look down at her tits, trying to see if her nipples were still hard. But I couldn't tell with her arms shielding them. Perfect placement. When my eyes found hers, she looked fit to be tied. "Don't you dare embarrass me tonight, Ford. I'm serious." Gone was the abrasive curl to her words, replaced with genuine concern I would somehow humiliate her. Her voice was softer, the look in her eyes worrisome.

"I don't know who that guy is." I closed my eyes after I spewed my pathetic excuse, but I didn't know what else to say.

Understandably, she called me out on my weak excuse. "Nice try, but that reason is getting old. You know damn well nothing is going to happen here tonight. There are too many people, and it's too open of a space. And I have no doubt you'll be following me whenever I stray from the herd." Sarcasm cut the edge of her words, and deep down I couldn't blame her. That didn't mean I'd change my ways, though.

There were a few things I could've said in response, but all of them would've evoked strong words from her, so I remained silent. A slight nod from me was all she needed to end our discussion.

I was thankful our encounter hadn't turned into something explosive, and while I should've been thinking of ways to avoid such encounters in the future between us, all I could focus on was the sway of hips and the plumpness of her ass as she walked away from me. The knowledge that there was only a thin layer of material hiding her nakedness riled me, and not in a good way. It was distracting as hell. It nipped at the corners of my control. I was sure anyone who looked at Cara knew that while the jumpsuit was classy and covered every bit of her private parts, seeing no hint of a bra or panties on the sides of her outfit only left one viable option.

"When do you think they'll start bidding on Cara?" Owen bumped my shoulder with his, his intention to piss me off landing right on point. I swore if he wasn't my brother….

As I opened my mouth to respond, to either tell him to fuck off or shut up, he jerked his chin toward someone across the room. When I turned to look, I saw a woman headed straight for us. She looked familiar but I couldn't quite place her. All thoughts of his idiotic question vanished, thankfully for him.

"Do you know her?" I asked.

"We met her when we went with Cara and Emily to that one club." He snapped his fingers, as if the action would help him recall. "I can't remember the name of the place. Anyway, she was the one who was looking to hire security, so I gave her a card."

I racked my brain to drum up the memory, but stopped when she stood three feet from me. What the hell was her name?

"Hi, Ford," she cooed, stepping closer before running her hand down my arm. *Oh, I remember her now.* And if my memory served me correctly, Cara didn't care for this woman. "It is Ford, isn't it?"

"Yes."

Moments passed in silence, making our encounter awkward, for me at least, so much so Owen jumped in. Otherwise I was set to walk away without so much as a goodbye. For some reason, it felt like I was betraying Cara on some level, which was ridiculous because I wasn't. So what if Cara didn't like her. I didn't like some people, but I'd never demand Owen not interact with them. Not that Cara had demanded anything from me. Oh Lord, my thoughts were running rampant and stressing me out unnecessarily.

"You remember Mrs. Dumont, don't you?" Owen gave me a look, one that told me not to fuck up the opportunity for a future client. And a famous one at that. Or used to be. I couldn't remember what Cara had rambled on about the woman.

"It's *Miss* and call me Heather." I swore if she came any closer, she'd be wrapped around me. Although, I had a hunch that was what she wanted. "You have the most gorgeous eyes I've ever seen. Truly, they're fascinating." Her compliment was genuine, one I often received, but when I didn't fawn back with gratitude, she stood taller and thrust out her chest before twirling a strand of her hair.

"What can we do for you, Miss Dumont?" My demeanor was strictly professional, even though all I wanted to do was pass her off to Owen, but I knew she wanted my attention and not his.

"What do I have to do to get you to call me Heather?" Her tongue darted out to wet her bottom lip. The woman was attractive in a girl-next-door type of way, but she did nothing for me. Besides, something told me she was a handful.

Speaking of handful, I looked over at Cara who was close by. I knew where she was at all times because it was my job. Her eyes were glued to every movement Heather made, and I swore she flinched when Heather ran her hand over my arm again. Because I didn't want anything escalating out of control, I excused myself and strode toward the woman who drove me crazy, leaving a potential client behind. No doubt reeling from my abrupt rudeness. But at that moment, Cara had my attention. She was all that mattered.

CHAPTER
TEN

Cara

After my brief talk with Ford, I returned to stand next to my dad and Cody, half listening to them discuss working together soon. Some movie about a long-lost love between two high school sweethearts who rekindle their relationship after the guy returns home from war. But I zoned out when I caught a glimpse of someone nearby. Someone I couldn't stand. Someone who went out of her way to try and hurt me, to destroy my reputation—not that there was much left of it to begin with. Someone who spread lies about me, simply for revenge.

Heather Dumont.

Just the sight of her boiled my blood. I'd been enjoying myself, trying to adopt a more optimistic approach toward my future only to be hauled back into the memories of the past—not as distant as I would've liked—as soon as I saw her saunter toward Ford and Owen.

How the hell was I supposed to move forward when I was reminded of the way I was before, shadows of memories cradling themselves around the edges of my mind, calling out for me to revert to my old ways? Not to get me wrong. I wasn't saying that I'd become sweet ol' Cara overnight, ready to jump into action and start doing good for the world, because I hadn't.

Rather, ever since my passion for creating a clothing line had sparked back to life, flashes of a more productive future swirled through the longing to party and laze about, dialing up my ambition a notch. Enough for me to see that if I put my mind to something, with hard work and dedication, I could achieve a goal I'd dreamed about when I was younger.

Anyway... I digressed.

Heather had expressed an interest in Ford when I'd run into her at the club we visited, No. 4, and I knew she'd somehow find an opportunity to sink her claws into him. I just didn't think it'd be this soon or that I'd care enough about it to want to intercede. But I did, and as soon as possible.

A burning sensation erupted in the pit of my stomach and at first, I thought it was from something I'd eaten earlier, but I quickly dismissed the thought when I recalled only having eaten half a bagel. Besides, the sensation deepened the more I watched the interaction between Ford and Heather, the brazen bitch running her hand down his arm. He looked to be disinterested, but he always looked that way, so I couldn't tell if he desired her or was annoyed with her.

When Ford hadn't removed himself from her touch, spots danced in my vision, images of the two of them rolling around naked tortured me, so much so that I lost all train of rational thought and missed the moment he walked away from her, his feet propelling him straight toward me.

When I looked back at Heather, her head swiveled to the side in order to watch Ford walk away, her flirty smile disappearing as soon as she saw me and realized the man she was just hitting on had left her to join me. I swore if no one else was around, she would've screamed and stomped her foot, much like I would react if something hadn't gone my way. Well, the old me. Although the old vs. new me hadn't been put to the test yet, so I couldn't say the prior version of myself had disappeared completely.

Small steps.

Before Ford reached us, I stepped closer to Cody and put my hand on his upper arm, just like Heather had done with Ford. I had no idea why I was trying to incite a reaction from the man walking toward me, but I did it just the same. Chalk it up to insecurity, or old behavior, or something else I didn't understand, but my hand remained on Cody's arm, the smile he flashed me when I touched him enough to make me feel ashamed for leading him on.

I saw the way the megastar watched me, and had it been a couple months prior I would've returned the attention. The guy was handsome with his thick, dark hair, bright green eyes, and a smile that could make any woman's panties disappear. Add to the list that he was filthy rich, famous, and talented in the sack. Or so I'd heard, not having experienced him myself, obviously.

"Well, if you two will excuse me," my dad said, "I have to go find your mother before she reads me the riot act for leaving her alone too long with those two." He pointed toward my mother, and sure enough, she was sandwiched between two uppity looking women. And from where I stood, they screamed plastic surgery addicts. Lord only knew what they were talking about, but as soon as she saw my dad approach, I swore her chest deflated right before she smiled.

Once we were alone, Cody opened his mouth to speak but didn't get the chance, because the same time Ford touched my lower back, Steph walked up next to me.

"Are you ready?" She wiggled her brows and grinned, reaching out to touch my arm.

"Ready for what?" Ford asked, standing so close I could smell the mint on his breath. The man barely gave me room to exist, let alone breathe.

"The auction."

"What auction?" Cody finally spoke, although I doubted that was going to be the question he would've asked had both of them not walked up on us.

"Cara has graciously agreed to auction off a date with herself to help raise money tonight."

"Really?" Cody's question wasn't posed as one, more of a surprised and exciting observation. I swore Ford growled, but I could've been mistaken. Not wanting to delve into entertaining his possible reaction to Cody's interest, I took one step toward my friend and away from the two men.

"Yes. So, you better be bidding." She pointed at the movie star before grabbing my hand and leading me across the room and toward the small stage.

When we finally stopped walking, I asked her something I should've when she first asked me to do this. "Is there anyone else auctioning off dates, or am I the only one?"

"A close friend of mine was going to participate but she came down with some sort of stomach bug at the last minute." She looked down before meeting my eyes. "So, you're the only one now."

Gone was my familiar air of assuredness, the need to be the center of attention and doing anything to keep people's focus on me. Out of nowhere, self-doubt took hold and shook me until my errant thoughts made me dizzy.

Did I look as good as I thought I did?

Would anyone want to bid on me?

Did anyone even care who I was?

Would they just see the daughter of Walter Dessoye, or would they see me?

Did they think I'd fuck them if they were the highest bidder?

Depending on who it was, would I do the deed?

How would Ford feel about all this?

Why did I care how he'd feel?

Emily pulled me into a side hug, surprising me enough I forgot all about my questions and appreciated her support. I hadn't seen her walk up to us, but was grateful she had.

"Are you okay?" She sensed I was nervous. I saw it in her eyes and the strained smile she gave me.

"Yeah. Just hoping I don't make a fool of myself."

"You'll cause so much of a bidding war, men will be fighting just to win the chance to take you out." Her words were appreciated even though the sentiment was an embellishment. She leaned closer, "Although, whoever does win won't get much time alone with you because if Ford acts the way he is now, I doubt the poor guy will stick around until dessert." She laughed, but I found nothing funny about what she said.

I zeroed in on Ford, who wasn't standing far from where we were. Not shocking. He looked like he was ready for a fight and not someone who was supposed to have blended into the crowd. Stoic expression and rigid posture didn't make for an approachable person.

While part of me tired of his outlandish reactions to almost every situation involving me, I kind of liked he cared so much. What exactly he cared so deeply about was still a mystery, however. Was he jealous over the attention I received from other men? Because that was what it looked like sometimes. Or did he only care that he had to follow me around so much? I was sure I wasn't an easy client. Not by any means.

Ford walked away from Cody to rejoin Owen. The two of them looked like they were holding up the corner wall, their focus solely on me and Emily.

Cody wandered through the crowd and mingled with some of his peers, laughing as if his safety hadn't just been in question, my shadow looking like he was ready to pounce on him given the right prompt to do so.

Ten minutes later, after I freshened up, Steph walked to the microphone in the center of the stage and called for everyone's attention.

Tamping down my nervousness, I forced a smile and took a deep breath.

CHAPTER
ELEVEN

Cara

" I want to thank you all for coming this evening to help support a cause that has unfortunately affected my family." Steph went on to retell the details of her mother's cancer, each word she spoke full of sadness but hope, as her mother had been in remission for quite some time.

Her speech hit me hard, the anguish in her voice reminding me to be grateful that my family and I were healthy. I often took for granted that my parents would always be there, that Emily would always be around. Assuming we would all die when we reached the age of one hundred. I realized life didn't work that way, but I ignored reality for as long as I could remember because I refused to face the possibility of the alternative.

Trust me, I knew bad things happened. I was proof, but how I chose to deal with the aftermath spurred the way my life unfolded. The partying. The drugs. The random hookups. The I-don't-care-about-anything-but-right-now attitude. Everything over the past decade had shaped the person I became, but the problem was I no longer wanted to walk that path.

"And now for some fun. My good friend Cara Dessoye has offered to auction off a date with herself to help generate even more money for cancer research." The sound of the applause spurred my brain to focus on the present. "Cara is the daughter of Walter Dessoye, our most favorite director of all time." My dad waved to everyone when she pointed to him across the room, his smile genuine and appreciative of her compliment. He received praises often and by many, yet he remained humble through it all. His fame and fortune had never gone to his head, much like it had to mine. My mom leaned in to kiss his cheek, her glow emanating the love she held for him.

"And while she takes after her father in the way of creativity, it is in a completely different realm." She waved me closer, clasping my hand in hers, a comforting gesture I didn't know I needed. "Cara is a gifted designer, one who is going to explode onto the fashion scene very soon." She released my hand, and with a gentle shove forward, she continued singing my praises. "She made the outfit she's wearing tonight." I heard a collective murmur of delight, the crowd's approval turning my cheeks pink. All eyes were on me, and for some reason, I wasn't prepared.

I loved to be the center of attention, often going out of my way to ensure I held the limelight, stole it from everyone around me. But right then, with my passion uncovered, I was exposed and vulnerable, an occurrence I wasn't used to.

Smiling, looking at Emily for encouragement and support, I tried to live in the moment. Soak it up for what it was, which was helping out a great cause, and assisting an old friend all at the same time.

"Cara is obviously gorgeous." A barrage of whistles assaulted my ears. "And smart," Steph continued, "driven and passionate. So, all you available men better play your cards right tonight and get out that checkbook."

Most of the people in attendance knew who I was. A famous director's daughter. A socialite. And whatever else they'd read or seen about me. I only hoped they didn't hold my past against me.

I grinned wider, and it had nothing to do with what was going on right then. It was because I was going to start making changes in my life to improve myself and to start living in a more positive and productive way. I wasn't delusional to think I'd change overnight, but I sure as hell was going to try to do better. My attitude wasn't going to disappear altogether, but I would attempt to curb it, to be more conscious of what came flying out of my mouth.

I searched the crowd for Ford, but didn't have to look long because he hadn't moved, standing off to the left, close by as was his protocol. His hand rested on the back of his neck, his gaze bouncing from me to Owen to my dad then back to me. I had no idea what thoughts ran through his mind, and my curiosity to find out should've annoyed me, but it didn't. When he caught my stare, I swore he stood straighter, lowering his arm to his side only for both of his hands to disappear inside his pants pockets. He did that a lot and his stance was yet another thing I wanted to ask about.

"Although time spent with Cara is priceless, we have to start somewhere." Steph walked up next to me, her closeness easing some of my anxiety.

What if no one bid? What if only one person did, and it wasn't for much money? I didn't have time to think of more what-ifs before my friend rattled off the opening price. "Let's start off with one thousand dol—" She didn't get a chance to finish her sentence before someone shouted a counter amount.

"Ten-thousand dollars." Everyone in the crowd, including myself and Steph sought out who'd made the offer. It was Alfred Nubble, a composer who'd worked on several of my father's films. He'd even won two acclaimed awards for his work. Thing was, Alfred was publicly gay, so his offer had come as a surprise, until I thought about the reason why he'd done so. If memory served me right, his sister had died of cancer a few years back.

"Okay." Steph laughed. "Ten-thousand dollars, it is. Thank you, good sir. Does anyone want to go higher?" We didn't have to wait long to find out the answer.

"Fifteen thousand." That bid came from a different male voice. Cody Caverly. He stood in the middle of some of his friends, who also happened to be actors. When I looked his way, he waved before winking at me, his smile infectious.

"Twenty thousand." There was no mistaking that voice.

"Um… Mr. Dessoye. I'm not sure that's how this works?" Steph was a good sport, ribbing my dad over his bid. I could admit it was odd, but I wasn't surprised he shouted it out.

"And I'm not so sure I want anyone here taking out my little girl." The crowd laughed, but I was mortified. Okay, maybe I wasn't so much mortified as I was slightly embarrassed.

I grabbed the microphone from my friend. "I'm sure whoever wins will be on their best behavior."

"They better be," he half threatened, all while smiling big and hugging my mom close. She smiled right along with him, and I had to admit that unfortunately, it had been too long since I'd seen them both relaxed and having fun, and all while I was present. My hope was for more of this kind of scene in the near future.

"Twenty-five thousand." That time the bid came from a guy named Blair Cooper, who just so happened to be one of Cody's buddies. Watching the interaction between them almost made me forget I was standing on a stage, auctioning myself off for charity. Blair was a few inches shorter than Cody and leaner, but his weight was due to a prior role he played where he'd had to lose thirty pounds to play a Jewish prisoner during World War II. He wasn't as handsome as Cody, but he was attractive all the same. I'd met him on a few occasions, and he was friendly and polite, so if he was the one to win that evening, I wouldn't be disappointed.

Okay, maybe a little disappointed, seeing as how Cody had thrown his name into the ring, so to speak. If I was going to go out with someone, he may as well be the man of the hour. The hotshot. The bad boy meets die-hard romantic. Sure, those were the characters he'd played, but wasn't it true that an actor poured a portion of their true selves into every character? If that was false, then at least he was nice to look at, and from the brief conversation we'd had earlier, he was charming and funny.

My thoughts about Cody made me inwardly cringe, as if I'd betrayed someone, when in reality, I realized it was just me overthinking a relationship that simply didn't exist.

I turned my head slightly to the side, looking down before briefly catching Ford's eyes. His attention flicked from me to the group of young men who were laughing and having a good time, Cody and Blair in the middle of them all, then back to me. If I didn't know any better, I could swear he was silently trying to tell me something, but I couldn't fathom what it would be.

"Thirty thousand," Cody countered, glaring at his friend before smirking.

"Looks like we have a healthy competition here. Keep it up, boys," Steph encouraged. "It's just more money for the cause." All eyes had turned to the two stars, waiting to see who would win in the end.

"Thirty-five." Blair tilted his head and smiled.

"Forty." Cody stood taller and raised his brow. The two of them faced each other and squared off.

Steph covered the head of the mic and leaned into me. "I should just tell them to whip 'em out so we can see who's bigger and let that be the deciding factor."

I choked on my swallow, her comment unexpected and hilarious.

"Forty-five." Blair looked to be a tad uneasy, frowning at the sight of his friend refusing to back down. I wanted to know how far they'd take it, and apparently, so did Blair.

"Fifty thousand," Cody said loud and with confidence, and we all knew he'd won as soon as Blair shook his head and slapped his friend on the back.

Several seconds of silence followed, everyone waiting to see if indeed Cody had won the auction.

"We have fifty thousand." More silence. "Anyone else care to bid?" A few more breaths passed. "Okay, then. Fifty-thousand dollars for a date with Cara Dessoye goes to Cody Caverly. Congratulations, and you better be a gentleman," she warned, shaking her finger at him.

An eruption of applause sliced through the air, but I didn't focus on the chatter or the winner, for that matter. Instead, I turned to look at Ford and witnessed him mouth "Fuck" right before he turned away from me and pulled Owen to another corner of the room.

CHAPTER
TWELVE

Ford

The moment I heard Cody bid on the date with Cara, I knew he'd end up being the winner. There was something about the guy, something I couldn't put my finger on, that I didn't trust. Then again, I didn't trust any guy around her, and I tried to convince myself it was because her safety was my concern, but my gut told me it was something deeper.

I pulled Owen farther away from the crowd while still being able to keep an eye on the women. I swore if my heart didn't stop beating so fast, the overworked organ would seize up. Then maybe I'd have an excuse to get the hell out of there.

I understood why Cara had agreed to the auction, and I realized it was for a great cause, but couldn't her friend have picked someone else to do it? Anyone else?

More than annoyed that I was going to have to accompany Cara on her *date*, a small sense of relief coursed through me because I realized nothing could happen between them. Not with me nearby.

A bead of sweat formed on my brow, and I swore my entire body had been lit on fire. My lungs strangled my breaths, and I could barely retain a thought long enough to speak the words.

At first, Owen's eyebrows squished together but after he looked me up and down, he grinned, slightly shaking his head.

"What?" My tone deepened, making me sound like I was possessed.

"I was just thinking the combination is cute."

"What?" I repeated, thoroughly confused.

"Cody and Cara." The bastard looked straight ahead, ignoring the fact I could barely breathe. "What do you think their celebrity name will be?"

"What the fuck are you talking about?" *Calm down. This isn't a big deal. It's one night. Then she'll go on with her life.* I thought my pathetic inner pep talk did the trick until I remembered that Owen had just asked me a question.

"Their celebrity name. It's when they mash up two people's names and spit out a nickname for the couple." He tapped his finger against his chin. "How about Codra? No, that won't work. What about Cocara?" He laughed when I closed my eyes and took two deep breaths.

No response came to mind. Not a "you're being an asshole." Not a "fuck off." Nothing. All I could do was consciously remind myself that my brother was getting his kicks by messing with me. That the date between Cara and Cody would be over with soon enough. That my jealousy toward the two of them together was ill placed and not professional.

"Well?"

"I don't give a shit about something so stupid. Talk to me again when you have something worthwhile to discuss." His laughter spurred me to walk away before he burrowed further under my skin.

Craving the taste of whiskey was unfortunate because I couldn't drink while on duty, and watching the bartenders serve shots freely was pure torment. Okay, maybe not so dramatic, but I would certainly welcome the relief the burn of the alcohol would give me.

"You know you can have one drink. I won't tell anyone." Cara had snuck up behind me, touching my arm to get my attention. I couldn't believe my focus had been off her long enough for her to surprise me. I blamed the distraction of my brother and my thoughts of her upcoming *date*. No excuse would be good enough for Walter, however, if something happened to either of his daughters under our watch.

"I'm working" was the only response I gave her, taking a step to the side so she had enough room to order a drink. The bartender practically ignored everyone else just to get to her. I rolled my eyes before looking around the large room. My keen observation told me I didn't have anything to worry about right then, but because our situation could change from second to second, I remained alert and focused, as much as I could while continuing to battle my inner distractions.

Twenty minutes passed, which meant we were closer to ending the evening, although we weren't quite finished yet. Various people, both men and women, approached Cara, either complimenting her on her outfit or applauding her for her generosity with the auction. I had to tune out the women when they fussed over the fact she'd be going out with Cody, and I had to bite my tongue when they referenced how lucky she'd be if she got to sleep with him. It was like they had no filter, no sense of proper social conversation, especially in front of people they didn't know, namely me.

Cara drank the last of her wine, but as she stretched her arm toward the bar to put the glass down, it slipped through her fingers and hit the ground, shattering on impact.

"Are you okay?" I asked, promptly moving her to the side so she didn't step on the shards, even though her feet were protected by her heels.

Cara didn't answer. Instead, a slight tremble shook through her. For the briefest of moments, I thought she was drunk and had somehow misjudged the placement of her glass, but my assumption disappeared when I looked at her face. Her complexion paled and her eyes widened. Whimpers fell from her lips, but I couldn't make out what she was saying, my concern turning up a notch when I saw her chin tremble.

Her breath burst from her body as if it pained her to release the air, only to be sucked back into her lungs in short and strained spurts. Her posture locked up tightly but not before she reached out to touch my arm. The whisper of her touch faded before I read too much into it.

"Cara, what's wrong?"

Her glassy eyes bore into mine until she diverted back toward someone who was directly in her line of sight. When I followed her gaze, the only people I saw walking toward us was her friend, Stephanie and a middle-aged couple.

"There you are." Her friend laughed before pulling her into a hug. "Thanks again for doing this. I'm not shocked you raised fifty-thousand dollars." Cara's distress evaporated, making me think I imagined the whole thing.

"You know me." Her comment was lighthearted, but her voice was shaky, at best.

Stephanie turned around and curved her arm over a woman's shoulder. "My parents wanted to thank you, too."

Her mother was petite with dark brown hair. She was dressed in a black, floor-length dress, a pink ribbon pinned near her heart.

"I can't thank you enough for doing this, Cara. It means so much to me. To us." Her mother embraced Cara before returning to whom I could only assume was her husband. Stephanie's father.

"I'm happy to do it. Besides, did you see who I'm going on a date with?" Cara joked, but it was strained, although I believed I was the only one who picked up on the tenseness of her tone. While I didn't like her comment, I said nothing, remaining still and looking on to see if Cara would reveal the reason for her odd reaction moments ago.

"He's the lucky one," Stephanie's mother rebutted.

"He sure is." The man standing beside Stephanie's mother flashed Cara a quick and reserved smile, the grin slipping from his face when she suddenly moved backward and smacked into me, her hand reaching behind her to find mine. She grasped onto my wrist and at first, I thought she may have stumbled and was trying to steady herself, but the tighter she squeezed, the more I knew her balance wasn't the issue.

"I know you haven't seen my dad in years, but surely you remember him, right?" Stephanie's expression faded into confusion when she glanced back and forth between her father and Cara, and had I not been paying attention so intently I wouldn't have seen the odd exchange because it happened so fast.

"I... I do." I swore if Cara squeezed any tighter, I would lose all feeling in my damn hand. What the hell was going on? Obviously, I couldn't ask her in front of the three of them, so instead, I placed my free hand on her waist, sensing she needed some sort of support from me. She didn't flinch at the gesture.

A wave of unease passed through the group, and that time I wasn't the only one to sense it. Tension-filled breaths mingled amongst everyone present before Stephanie cleared her throat.

"Well, I know my parents want to say hello to yours. So, I'll talk to you later on?" Stephanie's brows rose in wait.

"Of course." Cara's grip relaxed before eventually slipping away altogether.

"Oh, by the way, James called and told me that he can't make it tonight." Stephanie tilted her head down. "Maybe next time."

"Yeah, maybe."

After the three of them left, Cara signaled for the bartender, downing half her drink in three gulps before ordering another.

CHAPTER
THIRTEEN

Cara

"**D**on't you think you should slow down?" Ford's closeness gave me goose bumps, and while I'd clutched on to him for dear life, a gesture I wasn't about to explain any time soon, I needed him to back away and give me some space.

"Don't you get tired of butting into my business?" I asked, finishing off the rest of my drink and picking up the refill.

I should've been disheartened that the opportunity to meet James Hollen had fallen through, but I could only fixate on one thing at a time, and my past slapping me in the face unfortunately had flown to the top of the list.

The moment I laid eyes on Paul Adler, Steph's father, I thought I'd been in the midst of a nightmare, much like I'd been bombarded with years past. No one knew of the horrors that man put me through, and I sure as hell didn't want to relive any of that shit right then, which was why I signaled for the bartender to bring me another drink.

Two sips into my third glass of wine and Emily sidled up next to me. "Whatcha doin'?" I could detect the faintest smell of alcohol, but then maybe that was coming from me. "Are you excited about your date with Cody?"

I shrugged, playing off my enthusiasm for my future date.

Tonight was the first time I'd officially met the man, but I'd seen several of his movies and thought he was talented. I'd even seen him at a club last year, but ended up getting wrecked and had to leave before I caused a scene, something I'd done quite freely before. I wasn't saying my wild ways were behind me, because I wasn't a fortune teller, but I would at least make an attempt to behave myself. Although, depending on the amount of alcohol that passed my lips tonight, it would be hard to control myself.

Sensing I wasn't going to dive into the topic of Cody, Emily switched the subject. "Did you see Steph's parents?" She didn't wait for my answer before she continued to babble on. "I haven't seen them in forever. They look good. She looks healthy, especially for someone who has been through two bouts of cancer. And he—"

I never allowed my sister to finish speaking before I pushed off the bar, grabbed my drink, and walked away. She called after me, but I didn't turn around. I couldn't. The alcohol coursing through me only fueled my craving for numbness. I didn't need to brush elbows with the past. I'd lived there for longer than I cared to admit, and Emily's comments, although innocent, threw me into a tailspin.

Escaping to the ladies' room gave me the time I needed to try and compose myself. It'd been rude to walk away from my sister so abruptly, but I knew if I didn't leave then, I might've said something I'd later regret.

"You're a grown-ass woman," I whispered to my reflection. "You're fine." Lowering my head so as not to see the lie behind my eyes, I inhaled several times and continued giving myself a silent pep talk.

Two women walked up next to me and washed their hands, looking at me through the mirror.

"You're the one who's going on a date with Cody Caverly, aren't you?" the shorter of the two asked. I believed she knew the answer to her question before she asked it, but I supposed she wanted to make conversation.

"I am."

"You're so lucky," her blonde friend added. "He is so hot."

"He's the lucky one, ladies." I flashed them a smirk, hoping they bought the façade I tried to sell and exited the restroom, only to run right smack dab into someone. And it wasn't the person I would've thought.

"Pardon me." Paul retreated a step. I refused to refer to him as Mr. Adler because that acknowledgment meant I respected him, and that ludicrous sentiment was furthest from the truth.

Never before had I wished so badly for Ford to hover around, because I needed him right then, even though I hated to admit that to myself.

I attempted to sidestep the man, but he moved to block me. I tried once more, and he repeated his action. He was exactly how I remembered him all those years back, the increase in fine lines around his eyes doing nothing to detract from his good looks. To the world. But if they knew what he'd done, they'd see him for who he really was.

A sorry excuse for a husband.

A shitty representation of a man.

A bastard who preyed on his daughter's friend.

"Cara."

"Don't you dare say my name." I hated how he seemed to be unaffected by my presence when I was twisted up inside at having to see him, let alone be so close to him with no one around to save me.

Where the hell is Ford?

He cleared his throat several times, looking at me, then away, then back to me. Unease was the least of things he should feel.

Horror.

Shame.

Regret.

Fear.

I hoped all four feelings strangled him every single day of his miserable life.

"I never got the chance to apologize for what happened. I'm ashamed of the way I acted all those years ago." He leaned closer. Too close. "For what happened between us."

All I wanted to do was hightail it out of there, forget the past. Forget he existed. But my feet were anchored to the ground, my brain dillydallying in telling my legs to run. I wanted nothing more than to scream and shout, to tell him he stole my childhood and shoved me into a world of rebellion and destruction, but my words failed me, much like my instinct to flee.

I lowered my head briefly, driving myself insane with all the random thoughts and memories barreling down on me. I couldn't settle on a specific one, all of them melting together and making me dizzy.

"Please say you can forgive me." His hands disappeared behind his back, and for some reason, I read his body language as insincere. He looked like he didn't want to have the conversation at all, but since he'd run into me, he felt he should say something. "I'm really sorry, Cara."

I cringed. I hated the sound of those last two syllables coming out of his mouth. They were like acid to my ears. I remembered how he said my name when he backed me against the wall in his office. Drunk. Telling me how pretty I was and that all he wanted was a distraction from his life. I remembered how he shoved his hands between my legs and roughly cupped me, whispering my name in my ear, his breath hot and potent with whiskey.

Internally, I was a fucking mess. My stomach flipped every few seconds and my heart pounded inside my chest, aching from the sheer number of beats per second.

Trying to appear strong in front of him was difficult, but I didn't want him to view me as weak. I needed to take back control, even if it was but a sliver.

"What exactly are you sorry for?" My voice shook.

"For everything." He bowed his head for a moment before looking back to me. "I was in a strange place back then."

"A strange place," I parroted, the statement enough to warrant my uninterrupted attention. "A strange place?" My brain needed those few seconds to compute what he'd said. "I was only fourteen." Unshed tears blurred my vision, my chin quivering at the recollection. I retreated until my back hit the wall, my past and my present colliding to form the perfect storm.

CHAPTER
FOURTEEN

Ford

All sorts of bullshit distracted me from properly doing my job that evening. Owen's teasing about Cara and Cody together. Watching the way Cody visually devoured Cara when he'd been talking and how she appeared to love it. Projecting the outcome of their future date. Envisioning her trying to convince me to wait in the car while she spent time alone with him wherever they ended up.

Giving her a few minutes to do what she had to, I walked across the room before turning the corner into the hallway near the restrooms, stopping when I saw two people.

Cara and Stephanie's father.

Her back pressed against the wall while he stood in front of her, too close for my liking. I took a single step toward them and that was when Cara saw me. Her chest deflated the moment her eyes locked on mine. If I didn't know any better, I would've thought she was relieved to see me.

"Everything okay here?" I advanced closer until I brushed his shoulder with mine, an intimidation move that didn't go unnoticed.

The guy looked up at me and nodded before turning back to Cara. "I meant what I said."

She looked away briefly before looking back to me and not him, an expression flashing across her face I couldn't pinpoint.

Fear?

Relief?

Doubt?

Anger?

Several more tense seconds passed before he finally left, leaving me alone with Cara. I prepared for the backlash of interrupting them, but she never yelled. She never chastised me for breaking up their conversation.

"Where were you?" Her tone implied annoyance at my absence, but I had to be interpreting that all wrong. Why would she want me close when all she'd tried to do since the day I met her was to get as far away from me as possible?

"I was giving you time to sort yourself out."

"Perfect time for you to give me space," she mumbled before walking away, continuing to talk to herself as she pushed her way through the throngs of people in the main ballroom.

I followed but kept my distance for fear she'd start shouting at me for whatever reason she deemed warranted.

"What's with her?" Owen asked, appearing out of nowhere. Although, had I not had my eyes glued to the back of Cara, I would've seen him approach.

"I have no idea. But that's nothing new."

"True."

Cara stood next to her parents, smiling at something her mother said. But the way her eyes darted around the room and the way she shifted her feet made me think she'd rather be anywhere but here.

"We need to find out some information on Stephanie Adler's father," I said, keeping my attention focused on Cara.

"Why?"

"There's something there."

"What do you mean?" Owen shoved at my arm when I didn't respond right away, heightening my aggravation at the unknown to a whole other level.

"I saw him and Cara in the hallway." I stopped talking when Cody walked up behind her, wrapping his arms around her waist before kissing her cheek. She startled, but once she realized it was him, she smiled, and for the first time I wondered if she'd ever look at me like that. My thought surprised me, but thanks to my brother, I never had time to dwell on it.

"Hello?" Still I didn't respond, wondering why Walter would let some guy openly fondle his daughter in public, and in front of him to boot. Okay, maybe he wasn't fondling her, but I didn't like the way he looked at her.

"Ford!" my brother whisper-shouted. I averted my eyes to him without moving my head. "What were they doing in the hallway?"

"Talking."

"About what?"

"I don't know." I blew out a breath. "There's something there," I repeated. "Just get Hunter to look him up." Owen didn't argue, pulling out his cell and sending our buddy a text. He walked away a minute later and joined Emily.

Even though I didn't want to tear my eyes away from Cara and the famous bastard touching her, my attention was needed somewhere else. I glanced around the space for the man in question, wondering just what the hell his relationship with Cara was, if there was one at all. I spotted him alone near the bar. He finished his drink, then gestured to the bartender for another before cradling his head in his hands. His wife and daughter were busy talking to a group of people, laughing, oblivious there was something going on with the other member of their family.

I could be overreacting, taking my cue strictly from Cara, who'd proven to be dramatic. It could be nothing, and I would've loved to blame it on my overprotective nature, but my gut screamed for me to pay attention. However, I didn't get the chance to approach the guy. Something I warred with doing out of fear I'd end up causing a scene if he revealed something I didn't want to hear, because after he finished his drink, he approached his family briefly before abruptly leaving.

For the next half hour, I hung back and waited. Waited for Cara to come over and tell me it was time to go. Waited to hear back about Stephanie's father. Waited to come to grips with my unnatural feelings of jealousy toward the guy going on a date with Cara. Waited for the conversation I'd have to have with her about my role as her chaperone whenever they did go out.

I could stand there all night and ponder what would happen in the upcoming days, weeks even, but thankfully I was saved from my relentless thoughts when Cara strode toward me.

I tried to remain unaffected with the sway of her hips or the side view of her tit when she shifted slightly because someone called her name, the sheer material barely hiding her at all. I'd seen Cara's body before when I unexpectedly watched her masturbate. Maybe unexpectedly wasn't the way it happened, but at least I still bore the shame for being too weak to walk away from the cameras that spied on her in her room. She'd called on my baser needs and I'd given in like a moth to a flame.

"I want to leave." I thought she'd bark her demands and walk away, but she surprised me by standing there calmly. When neither of us spoke, tension built but I couldn't describe the nature of the unease. Was it sexual? Most likely, but something more existed.

Not being able to tolerate the odd exchange happening between us, I broke the silence. "What happened back there?" I hadn't planned on asking her that question right then, but I did, and there was no taking it back, my curiosity overruling my good sense.

"When?" she asked, tilting her head.

"In the hallway." In one breath, her shoulders tensed right before she looked down, closing her eyes for several seconds. "Nothing."

"It didn't look like nothing," I countered.

"Well, it was. Besides, it's none of your business." She whipped her head up and narrowed her eyes, challenging me, and while I'd love to push her for answers, this wasn't the place. "I want to go home," she repeated.

"After you." I extended my arm in front of me and waited for her to proceed. After Cara said her goodbyes to her parents and friends, we headed toward the exit, Owen and Emily five paces behind us.

If all of us hadn't driven together, I would've pushed Cara for answers on the way back to the house. There wouldn't be anywhere for her to escape, and although she could either ignore me or shout at me to shut up, there was a slim chance she might've revealed something.

CHAPTER
FIFTEEN

Cara

An old-timey crooner belted out tunes while we busied ourselves with idle chitchat on the way home. Owen and Ford held their own conversation while Emily and I talked about everything that happened at the event. Well, mostly everything. She asked me why I'd abruptly walked away from her, and I told her some bullshit lie about not feeling well, explaining it might've been something I'd eaten earlier. She believed me, or at least I thought she did, but I didn't dwell on the topic long before I switched to another. One that involved us both. Well, all four of us, to be exact.

"I saw you guys talking to our dad earlier. Did it have anything to do with the notes?" Ford caught my eyes in the rearview, the look he gave me unsettling, but I didn't believe it had anything to do with the threat toward our family.

"It did," Ford answered. Thankfully, I didn't have to probe him for more information. "He told us he hasn't received any more since the last one."

"So where does that leave us?" I asked, wondering what life would be like without the two men hovering around my sister and me whenever their services were no longer needed.

Emily shifted in the seat next to me, flashing me an odd look before peering out the window, fidgeting with the hem of her dress. Whatever her relationship was with Owen, I couldn't say for definite, but something existed between them. Beyond the scope of bodyguard and client, at least. Was she wondering the same thing I was? And did that make her sad to think about Owen no longer being around? I opened my mouth to ask her what was wrong, but Ford spoke before I could get the words out.

"In the same position."

As much as I tried to focus on Emily and my impending question, when Ford said the word *position*, I couldn't help but picture us in all sorts of them. Chalk it up to the alcohol or my wanting to forget about the encounter with my past, but I conjured up all sorts of filthy images of Ford and me.

Me pressed against him.

His hands exploring my body.

Our mouths fused together, our tongues dancing and dueling for dominance, to which I'd submit to his after a lengthy bit of teasing.

Before I could lose myself further into my fantasies, however, Emily leaned over and whispered into my ear.

"Owen told me that Ford asked him how much money they had immediate access to." She pulled back and smiled, expecting me to understand her out-of-the-blue comment.

"So?" I looked at her like she had three heads.

"So... he wanted to bid on the date with you, silly."

"What?" I said louder than intended, drawing Ford's attention, his eyes pinning me through the mirror. Heat bloomed in my belly while the ache between my legs intensified from the force of his stare. I turned fully toward my sister. "What?" I repeated, that time much quieter, the music drowning out our next spoken words.

"He wanted to win the date with you."

"Why would he want to do that?" Was it possible that Ford liked me? Like... liked me, liked me?

"So that no one else would." Disappointment swirled through me. The hope that he could truly have an interest in me disappeared as quickly as the thought had formed. Maybe it was delusion steering my dreams of having Ford want me, but my let down was real. "He told Owen it's going to be a nightmare tagging along on your date."

For some reason, part of me hadn't considered that Ford would be going with me on my date with Cody, although on another level, I knew he'd be there because I couldn't go anywhere without him.

Nerves took hold. How was I supposed to enjoy a night out with Cody with Ford hanging around? Watching every move I made and most likely interfering whenever he deemed Cody acted in a way he didn't approve of.

Ford was right... it would be a nightmare.

For everyone involved, but mainly me.

CHAPTER
SIXTEEN

Cara

Spending several days and nights locked away in my room was the only way I could remotely attempt to deal with what happened. I depleted my body of tears while I curled into myself, shutting out the world.

Coming face to face with the man who'd ruined me did more damage than I foresaw. I'd shoved those memories so deep down, I'd gotten good at the façade I showed the world, including my close friends and family.

I swore no one would break through my heavily guarded, barb-wire reinforced fence I had protecting me at all times. I never wanted to be that vulnerable again. Ever. But the second I'd laid eyes on him, everything shattered, and I was left exposed and raw.

Passing off my isolation due to sickness wasn't hard to do. I looked like shit, with my unwashed hair, my puffy eyes, and my blotched complexion. I swore I'd lost weight, too, refusing to eat most of the food Emily brought to my room for me.

But by day four, I started to emerge, and no one was any the wiser, believing I had indeed caught some sort of virus.

The night had arrived for my date with Cody. Or should I say his date with me? We'd exchanged numbers at the charity event last weekend and had texted several times over the past few days. He wanted to pick me up, but I told him I'd meet him at the restaurant because I had to have my security detail with me. He agreed, because he had no other choice, and told me we could figure out the rest of the evening when we met up.

Thoughts of what would happen after dinner plagued me, and not in the way I would've thought. I looked forward to meeting up with Cody again, and I found him extremely attractive and charming, but I was nervous about the possibility of sex. Not nervous in the realm that I'd be self-conscious because I'd heard of his reputation and didn't feel like I'd measure up. That wasn't it at all. I had my own reputation, some of it warranted, but since Ford would be tagging along, I'd feel on display. I wouldn't be able to let loose and fully enjoy myself as much. Not that he would be present if and when I decided to sleep with Cody. That's not what I meant.

I... hell, I had no idea what I meant.

Tiring myself out with the internal back and forth, I jumped in the shower, praying the hot water would rid me of my annoying thoughts. As the water cascaded over me, I knew there was no escaping the conversation that needed to happen between me and Ford. One where I asked him what his intentions were. Would he back off and give Cody and me the privacy we wanted, or would he barge into our date and be the proverbial third wheel? Would he have to sit with us, or would he sit nearby like he had when I went to lunch with Naomi? The impending talk with him made me tense, the hot water doing nothing to assuage my nerves.

I hopped out ten minutes later and started getting ready,

laying my outfit across my bed. Deciding to keep it casual yet sexy, I chose a black lace see-through shirt with a black bra. The top was revealing but not overtly. Not my normal sexy choice. Then I selected a pair of dark skinny jeans that hugged my ass. Compliments were in abundance whenever I wore them, and I thought they'd give me the extra boost of assurance I needed. Most people had the perception that I was arrogant and confident, the opposite of shy. And while sometimes that was true, that I owned my sexuality, even flaunted it on occasion, I possessed the same insecurities every other woman did. Would he find me attractive? Sexy? Interesting? Worthy of his attention?

As I asked myself those questions, it was Ford's face that popped into my head and not Cody's.

"You're being ridiculous," I berated to my reflection. "Who cares what he thinks about you?"

"About what who thinks about you?" Emily appeared in the middle of my room.

"You could knock, you know." She scared me, and for a second, I was angry, until the shock of her surprise wore off.

"Who were you talking about?" she probed, flopping down on my bed, careful not to sit on my clothes.

"Nobody."

"Come on. Was it Cody or someone else? Maybe a certain six-foot-three, tall, gorgeous creature? Or—"

"Stop."

She laughed, tucking her legs underneath her and leaning forward, watching me. I didn't know if she was waiting for me to tell her the truth or if she wanted to talk about something else altogether.

"What are you going to do tonight? Watch another documentary?" I smirked at her faux wide-eyed expression.

"I do have a life that doesn't revolve around docudramas."

"Oh, they're somehow dramas now, are they?"

"You'd be surprised how dramatic some of the women in history were." She opened her mouth to ramble on but, again, I cut her off.

"I love you, but I couldn't care less." Emily was used to my disinterest in the things she liked, and she rarely gave me shit about it.

As the curling iron glided through my blonde hair, twisting the strands into a bouncy wave, I watched my sister through the mirror. Her expression contorted every few seconds, the twitch of her nose indicating something was on her mind. She looked like how I felt most days. Confused. Conflicted.

"You okay?" I asked, turning around. "Anything you want to talk about?" She shrugged, her grin slowly fading until her expression morphed into a straight face. "Out with it, sis."

She opened her mouth but closed it before speaking. She did that a few time before shaking her head.

Selfishly, I was okay with her not talking right then. Getting ready for a date with a handsome movie star required mental energy. Then add Ford into the mix, and I had to remind myself not to become overwhelmed.

"Do you think Cody will try the move?" she suddenly asked.

"What move?"

"You know." I gave her a blank look. "The one he tried on Ella in *My Stolen Heart?*"

"You do realize that wasn't him. That he was playing a character in a movie?" She shrugged. "I'll tell ya what. If he tries the move on me, I'll let you know."

The famous move, the one that made every woman's panties wet when watching the film was when Cody's character,

Tristan, leaned in to whisper in Ella's ear but nuzzled her neck instead. He rotated from kissing to nibbling until he moved to her mouth, taking her bottom lip between his teeth and biting down. Then the kiss that happened afterward was epic. My nether regions tingled at the memory of that scene.

"Where is Ford going to be while you're with Cody?" Emily's question was one I'd asked myself multiple times but still had no answer to.

"I don't know."

"Well, you should probably figure that out. Seeing as how you have to meet Cody in an hour." She hopped off my bed and walked toward the door. "Besides, it'll give you another reason to talk to Ford."

Ford and I talked. Not often and not about much, but we talked.

After I finished getting ready, I left my room, but not before checking myself out one more time in the mirror. I looked good. Great, in fact. Then why did butterflies take flight in my stomach at the thought of going on a date with Ford? I meant Cody.

Fuck! This night was going to be harder than I anticipated.

CHAPTER
SEVENTEEN

Ford

As I paced the kitchen in the main house, I couldn't prevent the irritation from overtaking me. How the hell did I wind up being the one to have to escort Cara on a date with a known womanizer? A famed actor who allegedly fucked half of the Hollywood starlets, as well as countless models. There was no way he'd pass up an opportunity to get Cara into bed, although trying to do it that night would be impossible. Not unless he wanted me in the room with them.

The thought alone pushed my annoyance to anger.

"What's wrong with you?" Owen asked, entering the room and startling me. I'd been so consumed with projected images of what tonight would bring that I hadn't heard him come in.

"Nothing," I barked, reining in my temper because this was one time my brother didn't deserve it. Although, if he made a comment to compound my bad mood, then I'd have no issue letting loose on him.

"Oh, never mind. I know why you're all pissed off." *Here we go.* "Tonight's the night, isn't it?

"The night for what?" Playing stupid didn't sit well with me.

"Codra's date? Or was it Cocara?" He laughed, and the sound of his amusement plucked at my last nerve.

"What the hell are you babbling on about?" I yanked the refrigerator door open, and while I wanted to down a bottle of beer, maybe two, I couldn't drink while working.

"Cara's date with Cody Caverly." Owen leaned against the island, silently challenging me. But to do what? Admit my jealousy toward the famous fuck who'd be wining and dining Cara? Because the thought alone was laughable. Maybe not right then, but I'd find the humor soon, right?

"The last thing I want to do is go on a date." Owen's brows cinched together. "Shut up. You know what I mean."

His laughter rang out in the air behind me as I walked toward the steps. If I couldn't wallow in my frustration alone, then I'd try and refocus my attention. Besides, I had to see how much longer it'd take Cara to be ready.

The moment the thought of her entered my head, like she'd hadn't been there moments earlier, she appeared at the top of the landing. Without wanting to, I stared. Awkwardly long. Several seconds passed before she took the first step and I swore time slowed. As asinine as that sounded, it was true, like some sort of odd dream I was trapped in.

Her long hair hung loosely over her shoulders, the top she wore see-through, her black bra blending into the color of the material. She was covered, yet exposed. And those damn jeans of hers fit her like a second skin, her heels making her legs look like they went on forever.

"Are you going to move back?" she asked, looking up at me when she cleared the stairwell.

Not a word from me before I turned and walked out the front door, stopping on the porch so as not to appear completely rude. I waited for her to close the door and walk past me toward the vehicle.

Cara walked around to the passenger side as I approached the driver side.

"What are you doing?" I asked, confused about why she hadn't opened the back door.

"I'm tired of sitting behind you. I wanna sit up front this time." She folded herself inside before I could think of a reason why that wasn't a good idea.

After I started the engine, I glanced over at Cara, prepared to make idle chitchat but then thought better of it. Besides, she typed out a text to God only knew who and would probably make some sort of snide remark if I started talking. Best to stick to our normal routine of me driving and us keeping the conversation to a minimum.

I reached over and switched the satellite station to jazz, keeping the volume at a reasonable level so we could talk, if the opportunity presented itself.

"Do you listen to anything modern?" she asked while keeping her eyes glued to her phone screen.

"Jazz is modern music."

"If you say so." Her response wasn't sarcastic, which threw me for a loop. Cara appeared to be in good spirits, and there could only be one reason for her mood.

Cody.

Gripping the steering wheel, I took a deep breath. Then another. I'd been so distracted when she climbed into the front seat that I briefly forgot where I was taking her.

"You okay?"

"What?" I kept my eyes straight ahead.

"Your knuckles are turning white. You should let up on the wheel." Silence was my response, but I'd soon come to regret keeping quiet. "Listen, Ford." She stretched her seat belt wider so she could shift in her seat and face me. "I think we need to lay down some ground rules for when we get there." Cody had agreed to meet her at Bistro Bay, which was located along Three Mile Harbor overlooking the water. The restaurant was cozy yet upscale, and thankfully not far from the house at a twenty-five-minute drive. I had to respect that he didn't ask her to trudge back to the city for their date, but that's all the props I was going to give him.

"What ground rules?" My curiosity gave me a budding headache, and I hadn't even heard these "rules" of hers.

"Cody spent a lot of money to go on this date with me and I don't want anything to go wrong. Which means, I need you to be on your best behavior. No rushing over if you think he's getting handsy or interrupting us and shoving a glass of water in my face if you think I've had one-too-many drinks." She leaned closer, and even though I kept my eyes on the road ahead, I could feel the weight of her stare. "I mean it, Ford. Oh, and you have to keep your distance."

"I'm gonna be close. I have to have an eye on you at all times."

"I know, but I need you to sit far enough away that you don't make me uncomfortable."

"Don't you mean so that I don't make *him* uncomfortable?"

"Both of us." Her words were clipped, and I knew if I pushed, we'd end up arguing, and I didn't think I had enough emotional reserve for another one of those.

"I'll give you privacy, but I'm gonna be close enough to interfere if I feel I should." I heard her gasp, so I made the clarification before she threw a fit. "I'll try not to overstep." It was the best I could give her.

"You better try hard," she warned, situating herself back in her seat so she faced forward.

We arrived not long after, and Cara hopped out before I could hand the keys to the valet, Cody waiting for her by the entrance. If I wasn't in such a shitty mood, I could've appreciated the large covered patio that overlooked the bay. Or how cool the sunset looked that evening. But I didn't allow myself to fawn over how nice the place was because the only reason I was there was to chaperone Cara's date.

And try not to strangle someone tonight.

CHAPTER
EIGHTEEN

Cara

"You look beautiful," Cody greeted, pulling me in for a quick embrace before planting a lingering kiss on my cheek. His compliment helped to erase some of my nervousness.

Stepping back, I looked him over from head to toe, much like I'd done when I walked up to him seconds ago. He wore black jeans and a long-sleeved gray shirt. A simple enough outfit, but he looked amazing.

"So do you."

There was a reason Cody was one of the hottest men in Hollywood right now. With his thick, dark locks, his piercing green eyes, and a killer smile, the man was unstoppable. Add to that list his incredible talent, his ability to play any character wonderfully, and I should be the happiest woman in the world to be on a date with him. And while I conjured up the mood to try and enjoy myself, I couldn't fully appreciate the experience because of the man following closely behind us.

Ford dressed all in black. Inconspicuous wasn't what he was going for, and I had to argue with him to leave the shades in the car. It was bad enough Cody knew there'd be another guy on our date, I didn't need Ford drawing constant attention to himself. Although, he drew unwanted attention wherever he went, shades or not.

Cody wrapped his arm around my waist and escorted me inside. The place was crowded, but we didn't have to wait to be seated. Looking around, I didn't see a place for Ford to sit, other than at the bar, which had two empty seats. But that would mean, he'd be ten feet from our booth, and I didn't think that would be a good idea.

"Can we see if there is a place outside on the patio?" I asked, first to Cody, then to the waiter as he led us toward our seating.

"We're all full out there," the waiter answered, placing our menus on the table before stepping to the side. I looked over at Ford and swore I saw a smirk on his face, but I didn't look at him long enough to determine if it was true.

"Are you okay with sitting here?" Cody stood by the edge of the table, waiting for my answer.

"Of course. I just thought it might be nice to get some fresh air." I scooted into the booth before looking back at Ford. He sat too close for my liking, but there didn't seem to be a damn thing I could do about it now.

We placed our drink orders, and I swore I heard Ford mumble something, but thankfully the sound of the other patrons drowned him out.

"So, have you had your detail long?" Cody asked, tilting his head toward Ford. "He looks thrilled to be chaperoning our date." He laughed, but there was a twinge of edginess behind his words when he glanced back over at Ford.

"Not long. My father got paranoid so he hired him to watch over me." Our waiter brought our drinks, and I grabbed mine before he had a chance to put it on the table. I took a mouthful, then another. Cody remained silent, watching the way I licked my lips, tasting every drop of my wine. Waste not.

"You in some sort of danger?"

"Yes. No. Well, maybe." I couldn't figure out which answer was the truth. Deep down, I didn't think anything would come of the threat, but if there was a chance some lunatic was out for revenge against my father, Emily and I being the real targets, then I'd learned my lesson when Ford set up my kidnapping.

While I'd been livid at him for doing it, I hadn't tried to ditch him since. And trust me, I wanted to take off on him the first chance I got just to get back at him. Rebel and all that shit, but I didn't. Was that called growth? Or fear?

"I don't know what that means, but if there is something going on, a chance you could be hurt, then I'm happy you have someone to watch out for you." He took a sip of his beer. "He looks intense." He snickered when I rolled my eyes. "What? You don't like him?"

We both looked over at him, and sure enough, he was watching us. Not a raise of his brow, or a nod, or a glimmer of a smirk. Nothing. Typical.

"It's complicated." If Cody had asked me that question a few weeks ago, I would've shouted, "No, I don't like the surly bastard." But now my answer wouldn't be as cut and dry. It was difficult to wrap my head around, but Ford had grown on me, and our interactions weren't as harsh as they had been. We still had our moments, but I couldn't hate someone who'd given me their support when I needed it most.

The second my eyes landed on Steph's father, I thought I was going to pass out. But instead, I reached behind me and grabbed onto Ford. He hadn't flinched. He hadn't pulled away. He had no reason to support me in any way, yet he had.

Cody clapped his hands, pulling me out of my own head.

"Let's get to know each other, shall we?" He leaned back in his seat and flashed me a genuine smile. He was boy-next-door-meets-sexy-as-fuck movie star.

"Well, you're enthusiastic." I laughed, the sound bitter-sweet to my ears. Cody had a charm about him that put me at ease in his presence all while doing strange things to my body. And while I was attracted to him, and truly wanted to make the effort to get to know him better, he didn't hold a candle to the man sitting too close for comfort.

Ford didn't put me at ease. In fact, the opposite was true. Every time I was around him, my limbs tingled, and my insides quivered. My breathing would accelerate, and a flush would overtake me. He didn't seem affected by me, but I most certainly was by him. All the damn time. I hid my reactions to him and believed that for the most part, I pulled off the illusion of indifference.

"Why waste an opportunity to connect with each other?" I must've unknowingly made a face because he spoke again quickly. "I didn't mean for that to sound weird. It's just that growing up in a small town, I didn't get the chance to meet a lot of different people. I went to school with the same group, from grade school to high school. All the same people partied together, worked together." He took a sip of his drink. "It was a rarity that anyone new came to town, so when I have the opportunity to meet someone new, especially a beautiful woman such as yourself, I want to genuinely find out more about them."

I narrowed my eyes and studied him. Was he telling the truth or was this just his shtick? Make the woman believe he's truly interested in her, therefore making it easier to get her into bed. I'd ever cared about their intentions in the past with the guys I dated, not that this was a real date. The only reason I was out with him that night was because he'd had the highest bid. Although, a small part of me thought that maybe he would've asked me out, even without the auction. Maybe I was delusional or maybe it was a gut feeling. Either way, I'd never know for sure, and I wasn't going to ask him, because no matter what answer he gave me, I could never be sure it was the truth.

"Too much?"

"I'm not sure yet." I smiled before bringing the edge of my drink to my lips. After a small amount slid down my throat, I mirrored his body language and relaxed against my seat. "Small town, huh? I would've never guessed. You seem so... what's the word?" I asked, snapping my fingers two times.

"Hollywood?"

"Yeah, but there's something else about you that screams the opposite of small-town boy."

He leaned forward with intrigue. "Oh, this should be good."

"It's nothing insulting," I replied. Several seconds passed while I contemplated what to say next. "Damnit! If I figure out the word, I'll let you know." I swallowed another sip of my drink, careful not to overdo it. I'd thrown caution to the wind when drinking way too many times to count, but I wanted to have my wits about me tonight. Not only did I want to enjoy myself, but I also didn't want to give Ford reason to feel he should interfere.

Speaking of, I turned to look at him again and sure enough, his eyes were still glued to us. To me.

"Man, he's watching to make sure I don't put the moves on you." There was amusement in his tone.

"What?" My eyes swung back to Cody. "I think he's just making sure I don't drink too much, or that you overstep and get handsy." I winked at him, to which he smiled big.

"I would never think of it."

"Really?"

"You sound disappointed." He chuckled, running his fingers up and down his bottle of beer. Before I could think of a comeback, our waiter approached and took our order. While Cody spoke to our server, I nonchalantly glanced over at Ford. He remained in the same position, only this time a woman sat next to him, chatting away, oblivious that he wasn't paying attention.

"So, what were we talking about?" Cody's voice startled me. "You okay?"

"Sure." A few breaths passed my lips before I spoke again. "Now tell me all about this supposed small town you grew up in." Some things about Cody I knew. Which movies he stared in. Whom he'd most recently dated, and I used that term loosely. That he was known as quite the ladies' man. That he had a thing for fast and expensive cars. What I didn't know was anything personal, including where he grew up.

"Blowing Rock, North Carolina." He drummed his fingers on the top of the table and watched for my reaction.

"You made that town's name up," I challenged, pursing my lips and waiting for him to fess up.

"Nope. I'm serious. That's the name of the town I grew up in. Population… not many." I laughed, caught off guard when he widened his eyes and stuck his tongue out.

"Wow. The town's name says it all, I suppose."

"It does." He took a swig of his drink, the bottom of the glass clinking on the wood when he placed it back down. "I had a great childhood, though, and had a lot of fun there. Even though boredom was often my best friend. But I had a close-knit group of friends and a cool-ass family. So, I can't complain. Not too much, anyway."

"Did it take you long to get used to the life you have now?" I asked, riddled with genuine curiosity. "Do you go home often?"

"I don't allow myself to get used to the notoriety part of my career. To be fair, my brothers said they'd kick my ass if I ever let it all go to my head. So, there's that. And yes, I go home as often as I can. My dad's sick, so I want to spend as much time with him as I can."

I reached across the table and put my hand over his. "I'm sorry to hear that." My dad and I had our issues, but I loved him fiercely and didn't want to think about what I'd do if something happened to him.

Cody placed his free hand over mine and gave it a squeeze before pulling back and placing them in his lap. Clearly, the topic of his father was sensitive, so in order to lighten the mood, I switched the topic to one of his brothers. If they looked anything like him, I was sure the Caverly brothers were the talk of their small town.

"How many brothers are we talkin' here, and do they look like you?"

"I'm the ugly one, if you can believe that."

"I don't."

The waiter approached and placed our food in front of us. The Cobb salad I ordered was huge. Whatever doubt I had at just ordering a salad, fearing I'd be hungry afterward, was erased by the sheer size.

"I hope you're hungry. Damn," Cody said, shaking his head.

"Your meal isn't small either." A part of his steak hung off the edge of the plate, his baked potato the biggest I'd ever seen.

"I'm a growing boy. I need to eat like this." He rubbed his belly and wiggled his brows.

"Growing boy? I think you hit your last growth spurt a decade ago."

"True enough," he confessed, looking at me expectantly.

"What?"

"Are you going to eat?"

"Yes."

"Okay, then." Cody placed his hands on the edge of the table and stared at me.

"Why are you looking at me like that?"

"I'm waiting for you to start eating. It's rude for me to start before you." He reached for his fork and steak knife after I reached for my utensil.

"Is that Southern charm?"

"I suppose so."

We dug into our meals, my stomach growling as soon as I brought a forkful to my lips. So as not to be rude and talk with my mouth full, I finished the first bite before asking, "Why don't I hear an accent? A drawl. Or do people in North Carolina not have one?"

He took a sip after swallowing a piece of his delicious-looking steak. "We do. Some are thicker than others. Mine was in the middle, I suppose, but I worked with a dialect coach to get rid of it. Mostly." He shrugged. "Whenever I go home, it comes back."

"Say something for me," I urged, leaning forward and lightly tapping his forearm. "Lay some of that sexy accent on me." I found most accents appealing, from Southern to British. If you spoke differently than me, I was intrigued.

"Ya'll fixin' to go ridin'?" The lilt of his words tickled my ear, and I immediately pictured him in nothing but a pair of faded jeans and a piece of straw hanging out of the corner of his mouth.

"I like it."

"Thank ya, ma'am."

"Let's not get crazy." I laughed, bringing another forkful of my food to my lips.

Over the next hour, our conversation flowed from how he got into the business to my goal of creating a fashion line. Cody turned out to be a genuinely nice guy. I had formed my own preconceived notions, mostly from what I'd read or heard about him, and while he could be all those things, he was much more.

After dinner, he excused himself to visit the men's room. As I watched him walk away, I noticed that Ford was watching Cody, as well, turning back toward me when Cody disappeared into the hallway underneath the Restroom sign.

The woman who'd been flirting with Ford had disappeared soon after he refused to acknowledge her. When she walked away in a huff, I couldn't help but be pleased, even though I had no room to feel any sort of way toward their situation. I was on a date with another man. I had no right to give in to jealous tendencies. The thought alone was ludicrous.

Ford walked toward me, his hands folded in front of him when he stopped by the edge of the booth.

"You ready?"

"No."

He huffed. "How much longer?" His frown was indicative of his mood, but because I could never get a good read on him, he could either be bored, annoyed, or even jealous. The slight tick of his jaw did nothing to pinpoint any one of those emotions specifically.

"I'm not rushing out of here just because *you* want to leave." I pulled a small mirror from my clutch and checked my face, making sure I looked okay. Snapping it closed, I put it away just as Cody walked up behind the impatient man standing next to me.

Ford blocked the end of Cody's seat, and for a second, I didn't think he was going to move, but when he sensed the other man approach, he took two steps to the side, allowing Cody to sit back down.

Cody opened his mouth to speak, but Ford abruptly turned around and left, his shoulders tense as he strode back toward his barstool.

"He seems pissed off," Cody acknowledged, tipping his bottle of beer toward his lips and swallowing the remaining alcohol.

"He's always like that."

"So, I shouldn't take it personally, then?"

"Well...." I laughed before finishing the sentence.

"I think he likes you." A small smirk appeared on Cody's face, and I couldn't tell if he was messing with me or not.

"Trust me. He doesn't. Not in the slightest."

"And trust me. As a guy, I know these things." He reached across the table, turned my hand over so my palm faced up and ran his finger over the sensitive skin. "And I don't blame him one bit."

Cody's flirtation was more blatant that time, and while I should've been flattered, my eyes darted to Ford. The flare of his nostrils and the heave of his chest screamed he didn't like Cody touching me.

Because we had no privacy from prying eyes, I decided it was time for us to leave. And while a part of me wanted to continue the date somewhere else, I knew Ford would never allow Cody and me to be alone, so it was pointless to suggest dragging out the night.

After Cody paid the bill, he ushered me toward the exit, his hand placed on my lower back until we walked outside, the evening air refreshing but doing nothing to tamp down the sudden heat that swirled through me. He handed his ticket to the valet, and while we waited, he pulled me away from the three other people outside, one of them being Ford. He made a move toward us but stopped when I threw my hand in the air. The motion had been behind Cody, so my date never saw what happened.

"I had a really nice time tonight. Do you think we can do it again?" I never indicated to Cody that our time together should end, but he was smart enough to pick up on the tension Ford gave off.

I nodded and smiled.

"Is that a yes?"

"Yes."

With my affirmation, Cody stepped into my personal space and placed his fingers under my chin.

Without thinking, I blurted, "My sister asked me if I thought you were going to try the move on me." Clamping my lips together out of mortification, I widened my eyes and leaned back.

"What move?" A deep crease formed between his eyes.

"I don't know why I said that."

"Now you have to tell me. What move are you talking about?" My silence gave him the time to think. "The one my character Tristan pulled on Ella? Is that the one you mean?" The amusement behind his eyes had me shaking my head.

"Forget I said anything." I didn't embarrass easily, but right then I prayed for the ground to open and swallow me.

"I can tell you this." He placed his right hand on the back of my neck and stared into my eyes. "If we were alone right now, I'd attempt *the move*. But seeing as how we have an audience, I don't think that'd be wise."

"Me either," I agreed.

"But I would like to give you a kiss goodnight, if that's alright."

"Of course." I couldn't remember the last time a guy asked if it was okay to kiss me. They'd assumed it was okay and dove in. Most times, I'd been as drunk as they were, so formalities like that weren't even thought of, let alone spoken.

Cody's mouth covered mine, the tip of his tongue drifting over my bottom lip. The kiss wasn't short and sweet, but it wasn't drawn out either. As our breaths mingled together, I couldn't help but compare it to when Ford and I had kissed, the two occurrences worlds apart. While the kiss with Cody was good, it was nothing like the way Ford and I had connected.

Ours had been filled with passion, an animalistic need that overtook both of us, even though he'd broken away too soon and had said it'd been a mistake.

Several heartbeats later, Cody retreated, squeezing my hand before heading toward his car.

"Cultured," I shouted, remembering the word I was at a loss for earlier.

He stopped as he reached for the door handle, frowning until he figured out why I'd shouted after him.

"I'll take it." He laughed, disappearing inside his car.

With a smile on my face, I swung my glance toward Ford, and the look on his face made my grin disappear.

CHAPTER
NINETEEN

Ford

Throughout their dinner, whenever she laughed at something he'd said or whenever they briefly touched, I wanted to storm over there and put the guy in his place. Put a damper on their date, so much so Cara would insist we leave because I'd embarrassed her. But I held back. Barely. Besides, I'd never hear the end of it, and quite frankly, Cody didn't do anything to deserve my fury. He didn't overstep like I envisioned he would. Damn Owen for getting in my head.

When their date was finally finished, I breathed a sigh of relief only to amp myself up again when the thought they might want to go somewhere else barreled in. But thankfully, Cara called it a night. I kept my distance when they kissed, but it was a struggle not to rush toward the bastard and kick the shit out of him for daring to put his lips on hers. And now all I wanted to do was go back home and pass out. Too many emotions to deal with left me exhausted and eager to end the evening.

I bounced between wanting to inquire if she was going to see the guy again and keeping my mouth shut. Such questions should remain unspoken, and even if my curiosity pushed its way to the forefront, there was no guarantee she'd indulge and answer me. Either way, I'd be setting myself up for unnecessary aggravation.

Switching through the radio channels, I came across a Sam Cooke classic and turned it up. "You Send Me" sounded through the speakers, and I looked to see if she was rolling her eyes or opening her mouth to complain about the choice of music.

But she was busy typing into her phone, the corners of her mouth turning up. My pulse pounded in my ear and a warmth flushed through me. Was she texting Cody already? Or was it someone else? Emily, perhaps? Was Cara going on and on about how wonderful her date was and that she couldn't wait to see him again? Had they even discussed going out in the near future? My brain concocted all sorts of scenarios, but none of them were known, and she sure as hell wouldn't tell me.

"Now this song I like," she said, glancing over at me at the same time I looked at her.

"What?" It took me several seconds to compute what she'd said.

"This song. It's Sam Cooke, right?" I nodded. "My dad used to play this all the time when we were kids. He likes this singer." I remained silent, not knowing how to respond, or even if it was a statement worth a response.

Ten minutes into the drive back to the house, I couldn't stand not knowing any longer. I told myself that the next time I caught her looking at me, I was going to ask her about Cody, or at the very least, whom she was texting. But she remained glued to that goddamn phone of hers.

Baffled as to why I cared so much, and why my thoughts had become consumed with Cara as of late, I tore into the driveway going a little faster than I should have.

"What the hell, Ford?" she shouted, reaching for the door handle to steady her.

"Sorry," I mumbled, but I didn't think she heard me before she hopped out a second after I threw the vehicle into Park.

Walking in behind her, I noticed all was quiet, several of the downstairs lights left on. I had no idea where Emily or Owen were, but her BMW was outside so they couldn't be far. I glanced at my watch and saw that it was just shy of eleven o'clock, probably a record end to an evening for Cara.

Speaking of, where the hell did she go?

Rounding the corner, I entered the hallway, stepping into the kitchen twenty paces later. "There you are," I blurted, shaking my head at my impulsiveness. Why was I speaking at all? My job was done for the night. I'd accompanied her. She'd been safe. And now we were home.

"Don't worry, Ford. I won't take off on you again. I learned my lesson. You made sure of that." Her reminder of what I'd done came out of nowhere. "Besides, we're home. Where would I go?" Her question was rhetorical, and even if it wasn't, it'd be pointless for me to answer.

She opened the refrigerator door and leaned in, and I couldn't stop myself from checking her out. The way her jeans hugged her ass made my dick twitch, and if she didn't stop swaying her hips while she mindlessly looked for something in that damn fridge, I wouldn't be able to stop myself from getting hard.

"Ford!" Cara shouted, pulling me back from the devious images I'd concocted in my pervy brain. I hadn't noticed she faced me until she yelled my name.

"What?"

"Were you just staring at my ass?"

"Of course not. Don't be ridi—"

Her phone chimed with an incoming text, her attentiveness moving from me to her cell. For as much as I hated being caught ogling her, I hated it even more that she smiled when she opened her phone, mumbling something to herself as her fingers flew over the keyboard.

"Who is that?" Not only had I not meant to ask the question, but the tone in which I asked it was surly. Accusatory. Which was ill placed and certainly inappropriate. Why, then, did I not retract my question and walk out of the room?

"Nobody."

"Is that Cody?" I stepped around the island and closed in on her. She looked up at me, clutched the device to her chest and retreated, but not fast enough. I grabbed the phone and looked at the text, realizing the entire time I was making a huge mistake.

"Give it back," she demanded, tugging at my arm, but her efforts were useless. "Ford! Gimme back my phone. It's none of your business." She tried to grab her cell again, but I moved before she made contact.

Scrolling through her texts, I saw it was indeed from Cody. He told her what a great time he had. How he couldn't wait to see her next Saturday. I tossed the device on the island before I became even more incensed.

If I didn't get a hold of my temper, I was going to explode, and while my reaction didn't make total sense to me, it would make even less sense to Cara. But I couldn't stop myself, the words flying out of my mouth before my brain could stop them.

"You're not seeing him again. I'll make sure of it."

Her eyes widened so big I thought they were going to pop out of her head. "Are you kidding me? You can't stop me from seeing him. You don't have the authority or the right," she shouted.

"Oh, but I do." My absurd demand that had come out of left field, had been fueled by jealousy but was justified when I remembered that Walter had told her and Emily they couldn't date until the threat against their family ended.

"The only reason you were allowed to go on this 'date'," I said, using air quotes, "was because it was the direct result of the charity auction. But you're not allowed to go on any more, with him or anyone else, until further notice. Your father will back me up wholeheartedly, seeing as how it was his idea in the first place."

"It was *your* idea for us not to date," she accused. And she was right. I'd made the suggestion, but their father was the one who enforced it.

Cara snatched her phone off the island and pushed past me, and for some reason I thought it was a good idea to trek behind her.

I should've kept my mouth shut and walked out the front door.

I should've let her cool off for the night.

And I certainly should've kept my distance and not followed her up the stairs, down the hall, and into her bedroom.

It was one of the biggest mistakes I'd made to date.

CHAPTER
TWENTY

Cara

"I don't know who you think you are," I shouted over my shoulder as I crossed the threshold of my bedroom. "You can't throw your weight around and forbid me from doing anything. You're not my father."

I heard Ford walking behind me, or should I say stomping behind me, his anger billowing off him and choking me. What I couldn't understand was why he was so angry.

I spun on my heel only to knock right into him, he was that close to me.

"All it'll take is one phone call from me. Then you can expect one from your father. Plain and simple."

"Oh my God!" I tugged at the strands of my hair in frustration and disbelief. After my outburst, we stood toe to toe, quite literally, and stared at each other. It was the first time his gorgeous eyes hadn't distracted me. "You need to leave." I threw my hands on my hips and challenged him.

"No." He refused to budge a single inch.

"No?"

He shook his head and arched his left brow. If ever a look was condescending, it was the one he threw me right then.

Infuriated beyond belief, I trudged toward my bathroom

and just as I attempted to close myself off from him, he appeared, his hand the barrier stopping the door from shutting.

"What are you doing?" My bathroom was big but suddenly felt tiny, his presence domineering and stifling. My breath hiccupped in my chest while the ache that bloomed between my thighs, the one that had been on a low simmer since the day I laid eyes on Ford, intensified. My conflicting reactions were just that… conflicting.

Unreasonable.

Confusing.

He moved farther into the room, essentially backing me against the vanity. I had nowhere to run, and I wasn't sure if I even wanted to. My thoughts became jumbled, and as words formed on my tongue, I choked on them, never giving them life.

Ford reached out and put his fingers under my chin, the same way Cody had done earlier, but the look in his eyes was different than what had been in Cody's. Ford's was predatory. Full of want, and that wasn't me reading into something that wasn't present.

"What are you doing?" I breathlessly repeated, not daring to make a move for fear I'd break whatever this was happening between us.

He rubbed his thumb over my bottom lip. "I hate that he kissed you," he admitted, licking his lips while his eyes pinged from mine to my mouth and back again. Over and over. "I wanted to beat the shit out of him for touching you." Ford's free hand squeezed my waist before pulling me impossibly close. "I hate when anyone touches you because I can't." I had no idea what he was talking about because he was touching me now.

"Wha—" The air left my lungs before I could finish speaking. His breath mingled with mine as his mouth descended, his eyes searching mine, waiting for me to tell him to stop. But I refused to speak those words. The memory of our last kiss consumed me often, and I wasn't about to ruin another one, needing to see how long our connection would last before he backed away, claiming it was yet another mistake. Even though the possibility of his denial was imminent, I threw caution to the wind and engaged, leaning up on my tiptoes and snaking my hands behind his head, brushing my chest against him.

Our kiss turned into a frenzied one, each of us trying to savor the taste of the other, our tongues dueling while our lips suckled, and our teeth nibbled. My constant ache exploded and traveled up my body, the need to be ravished by Ford uncontrollable.

He broke from my mouth and sucked my earlobe into his mouth, his warm breath fanning my neck and driving me crazy. Goose bumps broke out all over my body, and I shivered with the intensity of my passion for this man.

It drove me crazy.

It scared me.

"Tell me to stop," he whispered, running his tongue up the side of my neck before first kissing my jaw, then the corner of my mouth. "Tell me to leave." He placed his hands on my face and pulled back so he could look into my eyes. "Cara, tell me to go," he pleaded, his breathing choppy and ragged. His bottom lip disappeared between his teeth while he waited for me to tell him to stop. To leave. To go.

But I would never utter such a stupid request no matter how much he wanted me to.

I leaned back into him and attacked him with an intensity I didn't even know existed within me. Gone were the memories of all the fights we had. All the times he'd overstepped and all the times I'd been rude to him. Gone were the feelings of him judging me and me lashing out at him in response. In defense. Gone was the fear he'd leave before I got the chance to explore my lust for him.

Everything faded away, leaving only the desire to give in and chase the attraction that pulsed heavily between us.

Without a word, Ford grabbed my waist and hoisted me on top of the vanity, spreading my legs so he could fit in between, the heat from his body overwhelming. Before every touch, he silently asked for permission. He arched a brow before drawing my shirt up my body and over my head. Before he unbuckled my belt, he tilted his head, his fingers resting on the metal before working it free. Before he removed my jeans, he narrowed his eyes, proceeding when my head slanted downward.

While I sat there in only my bra and panties, I felt more exposed than I ever had before, and it had everything to do with Ford still being fully dressed. My fingers played with his top button before moving to the second, then the third. When the sides of his shirt fell open, I ran my hand over his warm flesh, starting at his waist and moving up. His muscles twitched when my nails trailed over him, but he stiffened when I drifted over the scar on his lower right side.

Ford moved my hand upward and away from his healed wound, all with a slight shake of his head and a resolute expression. I never spoke as I continued to explore, the silence heightening the experience. He made the sexiest noises as my hands traveled over him, pushing his shirt from his body when I reached his shoulders. He stood before me, shirtless and glorious. I'd seen his body several times before, but not like this. Not when I was able to touch him, be this close to him. Not when I'd been able to inhale his scent while looking deep into his piercing, different-colored eyes.

The necklace he wore hung between his defined pecs, and while I wanted to touch it, I knew better. He became angry the last time I attempted to do so, and even though we found ourselves in a completely different scenario this time around, I hesitated to reach for it. In the end, I left the pendant alone, deciding to focus on removing his pants, instead.

Ford shifted his weight while he removed his shoes, kicking them to the side to join mine, which he'd removed right before he took off my jeans. He leaned back into me and captured my mouth with his once more, reaching around and unhooking my bra in seconds, exposing my breasts before my next breath.

"You're gorgeous." To hear him tell me such a thing was odd. And I realized that statement sounded weird, considering the position we found ourselves in right then, but his compliment rattled me. I wasn't sure if it was a good or bad thing, so while I battled which side to land on, I fumbled with the button on his pants, practically popping the damn thing off in my haste.

When I drew the slider through the metal teeth, he gasped. When I placed my fingers beneath the fabric of his boxer briefs and pulled them, along with his pants, down and over his ass, he groaned. When I wrapped my hand around his thick cock, he bit his bottom lip before tipping his head back.

Ford was the gorgeous one. Every movement he made was sexy. Every twitch of his muscles, every lick of his lips, every entrancing stare he flicked my way hyped my craving for him.

I wanted to taste him, but the position I was in didn't allow for it, so instead, I stroked the full length of him, his thickness making it near impossible for my fingers to meet.

"You're gonna be the death of me, woman," he growled, grabbing underneath my knees and pulling me forward. His swift movement made me jerk backward, but his hand was behind my neck to steady me in seconds. "Sorry." He smiled but his grin disappeared when I pushed my chest forward.

"Bite me." I pushed my breasts farther into him. "Make it hurt." I tried to spread my legs wider, but it was hard to do so close to the edge of the counter.

"We can only do one thing in this position, and I want to play with you before that happens." I pointed toward my room, not wanting to waste one more second.

"I have a bed right over there."

Ford removed his pants completely and lifted off the vanity. But instead of putting me down, he carried me into the bedroom and tossed me on top of the bed, coming down on top of me before I could move back toward the middle of the mattress. His necklace hung in the small space between our bodies, the tip of the metal cool against the heat of my skin. He leaned in close, and just as I closed my eyes, expecting him to kiss me, he hopped up and stood at the edge of the bed. Naked in all his glory.

He looked at me but didn't say a word, instead hooking his fingers into the waistband of my panties, slowly drawing them down my thighs until I lay bare for him.

Without a single word, he sank to his knees and pulled me toward the edge of the bed. The silence was both a blessing and a curse. The lack of words allowed me to focus on what he was doing, but the quiet played on my insecurities.

Did he want to do this, or was he reacting out of jealousy? Would he regret sleeping with me directly afterward? Would he ask to be reassigned because things could get weird between us? Another question popped into my head, but the moment he positioned my legs over his shoulders, my mind went blank. He trailed a finger through my pussy, and I held my breath.

Waiting.

Wanting… everything.

"Ford." I pushed myself up on my elbows so I could see him. His thick, dark hair was messed in spots, his disheveled look intensifying his sexiness. He met my eyes, smirked, then licked his lips.

"What?" he answered.

"I don't know."

"Do you want me to stop?" Concern flashed across his face and he attempted to move back, but I dug my heels into his shoulders to stop him.

"No," I eagerly replied, silently screaming for him to take me already. The wait was torture, but I realized he'd do what he wanted, in his own time.

"Then lean back. Unless you want to watch me." Ford winked and it was the most casual thing. So unlike him. Ford wasn't a casual type of guy. He wasn't relaxed. He wasn't easygoing. In fact, he was the exact opposite of all those things. Therefore, to see him in this light just proved there was more to him than met the eye.

I could only hope he felt the same about me.

CHAPTER
TWENTY-ONE

Ford

Every thought I had screamed for me to stop what I was doing with Cara and run from her bedroom. Never mind the fact there was a camera capturing every moment. But I couldn't. I wouldn't. I'd envisioned this very scene so many times I was embarrassed to admit it, but here we were, and there was no going back now.

It sounded so clichéd, but everything happened so fast I was powerless to do anything but what my instincts told me. Perhaps not instincts so much as a baser need that roared to life within me.

Last I knew we were arguing over her not being able to date anyone, and the next thing I knew she was naked and lying on her bed with her legs anchored over my shoulders.

She'd told me to bite her, to make it hurt. Was she a woman who enjoyed rough sex normally, or was her desire for me pushing her over the edge, budging her outside her comfort zone? Of course, as a man, I'd love to believe the latter, so I didn't voice my question. Maybe that'd be a topic for the future, if ever we found ourselves in this scenario again. Even as the possibility occurred to me, I realized that not only was it wrong for us to be here together like this but to do it again in the future would be a huge mistake. I could only imagine what

Walter would do if he found out about us, never mind the shit I'd get from Owen.

A soft moan fell from Cara's lips, her sounds eliciting the beast that hid inside me to rise from his slumber. Drawing on some semblance of control, though, I placed my hands underneath her delectable ass and pulled her closer, my mouth inches away from her pussy.

I smelled her desire.

With a flick of my tongue, I tasted her passion. She arched her back and tried to close her legs, and there wasn't a more enticing sight than seeing this woman start to lose control because of me.

I repositioned my hands to her inner thighs and spread her as wide as I could, all while keeping her legs strewn over my shoulders. Control was what I was after, what I thrived on, and if she didn't fight me on it, I could show her the best time of her fucking life.

The moment my lips covered her clit I thought she was going to shoot off the bed, and while her movements were a testament to how good I was making her feel, I wasn't going to go easy on her.

Every time my tongue lapped up her juices and every time my lips sucked her clit deeper into my mouth, the more satisfied I was that she'd come undone quickly. At first, I wanted to tease her unmercifully, pulling back when I thought she was close, but the more I tormented her, the more aroused I became. However, if I wanted to last longer than five minutes while fucking her, I had to stop and collect myself.

Pushing two fingers inside as deep as I could, I crooked them until I touched the one spot inside her that would drive her crazy.

"Yes," she groaned, rotating her hips and grinding against my face. "Right there." I couldn't help but smile. For as much as Cara acted like she didn't like me, and for all of the torture this woman had put me through since day one, all I had to do was get her beneath me and she crumbled. Like putty in my hands. I had no doubt, I'd react the same way if her pretty little mouth was all over me, too.

Our attraction to each other was evident, but our perception of each other had stood in the way before. I viewed her as spoiled, bratty, and someone who couldn't see past tomorrow. And I was sure she saw me as an overbearing, inappropriate at times, stubborn, pain in the ass. And why wouldn't she? I admittedly was all those things.

But something shifted between us in the past several weeks. I started to view her differently, mainly because she appeared to emerge from herself, talking about starting a clothing line bringing light to her eyes I'd never seen. Granted, I'd only known her a short time, but from what Emily had told me, her sister hadn't shown that kind of enthusiasm for anything other than partying in a very long time.

The second Cara grabbed her tits and pinched her nipples, I thought I was going to tip over the edge. Then she reached down to grab the back of my head and pushed my mouth closer, as if that was even possible.

I pumped my fingers faster.

I licked her from hole to clit and back again. Slow then fast. Switching speeds without warning.

But when I grazed my teeth over her most sensitive area, she moved with lightning speed, scrambling to remove her legs from over my shoulders. She flipped over on her belly and crawled up the bed until she was at the other side.

She moved so quickly she almost kicked me in the face, and at first, I thought I'd hurt her. But from the way she looked at me over her shoulder, lust dancing behind her blue eyes, I knew I hadn't done any such thing. Whatever she felt was simply too much for her to remain still.

Cara raised her ass in the air while she looked at me, her right hand disappearing underneath her. When I saw her touch her pussy, I shook my head right before I smacked her left cheek. Hard.

"Oww," she complained, but the corner of her mouth lifted.

"Stop touching yourself," I ordered, "and let me finish what I started."

"I can't. It's too much."

"Did I hurt you?" I asked the question, but I already knew the answer. Nevertheless, I wanted her to clarify.

"No."

"Then remove your hand and turn over." I leaned back on my haunches and waited for her to do as she was told, silently counting to five. She shook her head. I didn't even make it to three before I jumped up and flipped her over. I dragged her down the bed, spread her legs with mine and pinned her arms above her head, holding them both with my right.

"I can't do it, Ford. It's too much." She struggled to release herself from my grip, but her efforts were futile.

"Did I hurt you?" I repeated.

"No."

"Then I'm gonna continue and I don't want you to move. Got it?" I sucked her bottom lip in my mouth and gently bit her. She gasped, but when her tongue met mine, I knew she liked it. After all, she had told me to do it earlier.

When I was confident she wouldn't move, I released her

hands and traveled down her body, all the while keeping her spread wide. I didn't waste any time, eager to make her come as soon as possible so I could finally fuck her.

My mouth worked her to the edge.

My fingers disappeared inside her, coaxing her to come undone.

And when I thought she was close, I bared my teeth and clamped down on her clit once more, careful to apply the perfect amount of pressure so that pain wasn't the result, but instead heightened pleasure. The kind she apparently didn't think she could handle.

Cara struggled to move away from me once more, but I anchored her to the mattress with a firm yet gentle arm over her belly.

"Ford!" She shouted my name right before her upper half rose off the bed. "Fuck! I ca... I can't." She grunted. She cursed. She struggled. But in the end, her fingers gripped my hair and she tugged. Hard. The prick of pain fueling me.

Cara's body locked up tight, and she didn't breathe. My eyes pinned hers, and her coming on my tongue was the most beautiful sight I'd ever seen. When the wave of pleasure subsided, she flopped back down on the bed, throwing her arm over her eyes, struggling to control her breathing.

"What the hell just happened?" She peeked out from beneath her strewn arm and laughed. "I've never felt... I don't even know what that was."

"You're welcome." She threw a pillow at me before moving to dangle her legs over the side of the bed, but before she could push herself to her feet, I blocked her from standing.

"Where do you think you're going?" I asked, curious as to what she was thinking. Then something dawned on me. Maybe she didn't want to have sex. Maybe her orgasm had knocked some sense into her, and she saw what a mistake it was for us to sleep together. "Are you rethinking this?" Part of me cringed in preparation that she'd say yes, and the other part hoped she said no. Then I flip-flopped, hoping she would say yes so that we could put the brakes on this before anything else happened. Then my brain fucked with me some more.

"Why? Are you?" Her eyes traveled the length of me, pausing when she reached my cock. She licked her lips, and I doubted she even realized she'd done it. It was only when I cleared my throat that she looked at my face.

Wanting to erase the doubt in her voice, and the uncertainty behind her eyes, I placed my hands on her shoulders and pushed her back down on top of the bed.

"Move back." She did, her tits bouncing while she situated herself. All I wanted to do was pounce on her and wrap my lips around them. The need to dominate her overwhelmed me, but before I lost control, I needed to get one thing out of the way first. "Do you have a condom?"

She pointed toward her nightstand. "In there."

I walked around the bed and opened the drawer, two foil packets staring me in the face. Grabbing one of them, I put it between my teeth and tore the side of it open. My eyes never left her face as I approached and sheathed myself. I studied her, wanted to be sure there was no hesitation on her part. I'd like to say that once we had sex, there was no going back, but how could that possibly be true? Deciding not to dive into the countless what-ifs and should haves, I wanted to enjoy the moment.

Cara lay on her back, watching me as I took the final steps toward her. She bit the corner of her lip, spreading her legs for me as I crept closer, and I knew as soon as I laid in between her thighs that whatever I'd thought seconds earlier was utter bull-shit. Once we slept together, I knew I'd never want to go back to just being the guy who was hired to protect her.

I'd want more.

I'd want her.

Question was, would she feel the same?

CHAPTER
TWENTY-TWO

Cara

The way Ford watched me should have been unnerving, like he was trying to see inside my soul, searching out my darkest secrets. Instead, I was entranced by him. I wanted to spill all the dirty details of my past if only he would be the one to save me.

But I knew that wasn't possible. No one could save me. What's done was done, and I had to find a way to move on, and how I'd chosen to do that for the past decade wasn't working for me any longer.

"Cara?" Ford's voice interrupted my wayward thoughts, sounding deeper, raspier. Only when he saw he had my full attention did he cover my body with his, licking at my lips, but pulling back before I could kiss him properly.

Before I could demand he kiss me once more, he rubbed the head of his cock over my clit, all the while observing me. Whenever I'd had sex with someone, I barely made eye contact. I was either on my stomach, on all fours, or my lids were closed for most of the interaction. I'd never wanted to be that intimate with anyone, and for as odd as that sounded, connecting with someone through eye contact took it to a whole other level.

But with Ford, I wanted to see him, to look into those gorgeous eyes of his and be seen, as well.

He continued teasing me but never attempted to push inside. "What are you waiting for?" I reached down and grabbed his ass, pushing him harder against me, running my tongue over his lips like he'd done to me.

"I think I'm just waiting for you to change your mind." His lips parted as if he was going to say something else, but then thought better of it.

"I've never wanted it more," I admitted, not surprised by my confession. Any reservation that remained had disappeared. Not about having sex with him, but about connecting with him on a deeper level. For as much as I wanted our interaction to be just about the physical act, it was more for me. But what I couldn't keep from wondering was… was it the same for him?

"Go slow. You're kinda large." I meant for my comment to be lighthearted, but I must've twisted my expression because he stroked the side of my cheek in reverence.

"I won't hurt you." My gut told me that his words had a double meaning. Seconds later, Ford pushed inside me, stretching me, slowing as I took a deep breath. "Are you okay?"

"Yes." Wrapping my legs around the back of his thighs, I urged him to go deeper, and thankfully he didn't stop until we were fully connected.

A moment passed before he started to move, rotating his hips then thrusting forward, latching on to my mouth when his speed increased. Then, unexpectedly, he slowed down.

"Faster," I groaned, pressing my heels into his thighs.

"I can't."

"Faster," I repeated, closing my eyes and grabbing his hips to try and move him. But the man was a mountain and no amount of feeble attempt on my part would change his mind.

"Cara." I opened my eyelids. "I haven't had sex in quite a

while. If I go any faster, it's gonna be over too soon." The corner of his mouth lifted, but fell when I grabbed his ass and squeezed.

"Then we'll just have to do it again."

On my suggestion, he pulled back then thrust forward, giving me exactly what I wanted. What I needed. He clenched his jaw and the muscles in his arms locked up. The sight of Ford barely composed was glorious, and knowing I was the reason he barely held on to his restraint was a boost to my ego.

"Again," I pleaded, unhooking my legs from around him and placing my feet on the bed, all the while keeping my hands in place on his backside.

"Fuck," he grunted, slamming into me over and over, any reservation he had about fucking me fast vanishing with the swivel of my hips and the sounds of my pleasure mixing with his.

We moved together.

We writhed together.

We moaned and grunted together.

"I'm so close," I cried, moving my hands to clutch the covers, arching off the bed as much as I could while his weight held me in place.

"Not yet. Don't come yet," he growled, bending his right leg forward and throwing my leg over his hip. The force with which he fucked me pushed the boundary of pain, but my pleasure was so much more.

He nuzzled his head into my neck, licking and sucking at my skin, baring his teeth and grazing them over my collarbone before nipping me.

"Ford... I'm... I'm gonna..." I lost my breath as my vision blurred, every cell in my body electrified. He tortured my body with his own, digging his fingers into my thigh while he teased me with his mouth. His tongue. His teeth.

His grunts turned into groans, his cock pulsing inside me while he thrust deep and hard. In the blink of an eye, he pulled back before pushing my legs toward me so he could go deeper.

"Am I hurting you?" he asked, all the while never breaking his stride. He derailed my orgasm with the switching of my body but brought it back to life in seconds.

I shook my head in response, the ability to speak too much for me.

"Good. Because I don't think I can stop," he confessed, licking his lips and flaring his nostrils. He looked possessed, but in the sexiest way possible.

Missing the heat of his body, I placed my hands on his chest, the drum of his heartbeat matching my own.

The familiar pull started in my belly and spread through my pussy; the anticipation unbearable. When the first wave hit, I threw my head to the side. When the second pulse vibrated through me, I screamed, and when a third explosion surprised me, I reached for Ford to pull him closer.

He swallowed my cries as I rode out the rest of my orgasm, his body detonating seconds later and joining me in the aftermath.

CHAPTER
TWENTY-THREE

Cara

Snuggled into his side with my head resting on his chest seemed like the most natural thing in the world. But it was us. Nothing about us was easy and expected.

His heart rate slowed with every controlled breath, and I couldn't stop myself from wondering what he was thinking. I wouldn't dare ask, however, for fear he'd tell me something I didn't want to hear. Possibly the truth. Maybe my own insecurities were clouding my thoughts, but I just couldn't take the risk of Ford telling me that what we'd done was a mistake. Much like he said after our kiss on my birthday.

Both instances had come out of left field. Although, this time allowed for a clearer head on both our parts, so for him to say or act like us having sex was a slipup, would wound me more than I'd ever let on.

Instead of risking a rejection, I trailed my fingers over his heated skin, his muscles twitching every time I moved over a sensitive spot. When I made my way toward his lower right side and touched his scar, he grabbed my hand and stopped breathing.

"What happened?" I tried to touch him again, but his grip was too tight. "Ford."

"Don't, Cara. I can't."

Against my better judgment, I pushed. "Does it have anything to do with Julia?" Gut instinct told me that his wound was somehow tied to his sister, and not from his time spent in the service.

The entire time we laid there, we didn't look at each other, but that changed when he shifted his body away from me, hopping off the bed before I realized what he was doing. He faced away from me, his posture rigid while he clenched his hands at his sides. Over and over.

"Why won't you talk about her?"

"I'm not having this conversation with you." Something about the way he said *with you* I found partially offensive.

"Oh, so I'm good enough to have sex with but not good enough to talk to about anything personal?" My voice rose an octave, my defenses locking up tightly.

Ford spun to face me. For as much as I wanted my attention to remain on his face, my eyes roamed his body, stopping a few seconds longer on his lower half than I intended. And even though I could appreciate the sight of him, I was upset.

"That's not what I meant." He offered nothing further, crossing his arms over his chest and looking like quite the pissed-off specimen.

"That's how it sounded," I replied. "I'm sure her death was hard on you and Owen, but it might help to talk about it." His skin flushed and a vein in his neck strained against his skin, bulging and making him appear like he was set to explode any second.

"Hard? It was hard on us?" he mocked with gritted teeth. "You have no idea what you're talking about and I suggest you drop it before…"

"Before what?" I just had to push.

He didn't answer my question, instead disappearing inside my bathroom, reemerging with his clothes. He hastily pulled up his boxer briefs, then his pants, zipping them but leaving the button undone.

"Where are you going?"

"I need to leave. I don't want to say anything I'll regret." Instead of throwing on his shirt, he stood before me, motionless and quiet.

"I just think if you're able to share with me a little about her, about—" I stopped speaking when he took a threatening step toward me, his eyes wide and full of disbelief. I should've listened to him and kept my mouth shut about his sister because he went from irritated to beyond angry.

"About what, Cara?" he spat, tossing his shirt to the floor. "Do you wanna know that the night she died she came to me for help? That she needed me, but I turned my back on her? Do you want to know that I turned to my baby sister, while she was high, and told her that if she didn't get her shit together once and for all, that she was dead to me?"

Ford threw his head back and covered his face with his hands, his chest rising and falling with ragged breaths. Every muscle in his body strained from the emotion, and I could only imagine the pain he felt right then.

A moment of silence passed before he dropped his arms to his sides and schooled his expression. He advanced closer until his knees hit the edge of the bed. His voice was dangerously low when he spoke again. "Do you want to hear that she left crying, got in her car, and sped away? That she crossed lanes into oncoming traffic and died on impact?" Ford closed his eyes for several seconds before opening them again and pointing at his scar. "That I sliced open my side when I tried to get her out of the car? Are those the types of things you want to hear about?"

By this time, I'd moved farther across the bed to put some distance between us. Not because I thought he'd physically hurt me, but to give him the space he needed.

"I'm sorry," I whispered. Unshed tears had pooled in his eyes, but he managed to keep them at bay. He ignored my apology as he leaned down and placed his fists on the bed.

"Since you're so gung-ho about wanting to talk about all things personal, why don't you tell me what the story is between you and Paul Adler." His words were like a slap to the face, a punch to the gut. I hiccupped my next lungful of air, vigorously shaking my head. So much so, I made myself dizzy. "Why don't you want to talk about it?" he taunted. "Huh? Is it because maybe you had an affair with your friend's father? Did he dump you after you gave it up? Did you think he'd leave his wife for you?"

"No," I cried, clutching the sheet to my chest to shield me. His words tore me apart, ripped me open so wide I didn't think I'd ever heal. "Stop."

"Stop what? Stop asking you about your past? About something you clearly don't want to tell me?"

I scrambled off the bed and retreated until my back hit the wall, shaking because of the confrontation. He walked toward me with purpose, stopping when he was but a foot away.

"I didn't want it," I mumbled, but he didn't hear me.

"How does it feel to be pushed?" he asked, continuing to berate me.

My head was hung low and I trembled standing there before him. "I didn't want it," I repeated, that time a little louder.

"You didn't want what?" Anger clipped every word he spoke. "You didn't want the affair? You thought he'd leave his wife? Was that it?" Ford had no idea what he was talking about, deriving assumptions of the nature of my involvement with Steph's father, driving home what he truly thought of me. But he was wrong. So unbelievably wrong.

Something about the tone of his voice forced me to raise my head and stare him down. The sneer on his face shoved me toward expelling all the pain and shame I'd carried inside me for the past eleven years, and before my brain could shut down the impulse, I released the words. Words I'd never said out loud before, not even to myself.

"He raped me," I yelled.

I saw the moment my words hit their target, the muscles in Ford's face relaxing right before his brows knit together and his mouth fell open. "What?"

"He raped me," I shouted louder, shoving at his chest. "I was only fourteen when he forced himself on me." I didn't want to do it. I tried to hold them back as best I could, but the tears flowed down my cheeks in rivers, my vision blinded by grief and humiliation.

I hit Ford's chest again and again, needing a place to focus the plethora of emotions raging through me. Over and over he allowed me to use him as a punching bag before he finally grabbed my wrists and pulled me into him, wrapping his arms around me and holding me impossibly close.

I'd never felt more raw and visible in my life. Yet, I'd never experienced such a sense of relief before, either, the opposing emotions sparring inside me.

"I'm so sorry," he said, kissing the top of my head to try and console me. Soon enough, I found myself exhausted but calm. Not wanting to separate from him yet, I wrapped my arms around his waist and held on for dear life. Before I knew it, my anguish resurfaced, and I sobbed once more. "Shhh... I know."

We stood in the middle of my bedroom, me weeping against his chest and him rocking me until every one of my tears dried up. When I moved to back away, he released me but reached for my face, placing his hands on my cheeks. The bedsheet I'd been holding fell away and I stood before him completely naked in every way.

"Cara..." His sympathetic tone tugged at my heart, but I'd done enough crying for one night. I didn't have it in me to do it again. All I wanted to do was forget... about everything.

Forget it happened all those years ago.

Forget I blurted it out to Ford.

Forget he now knew I'd been violated.

"I can't." I shrugged away from him, folding my arms inward to cover me.

"Who knows about this?" He walked the few feet toward the chair in the corner of my room and retrieved a robe I had thrown over the side. When he was next to me, he helped me put my arms through before cinching it shut with the belt. I was like a wandering child, lost and unaware of what to do or say next.

"No one."

"You never told anyone?" He lifted my chin toward him. He repeated, "You never told?"

I shook my head.

"Not even Emily?"

Fresh tears emerged as my chin quivered. "She doesn't know."

"She knows something happened," he offered, removing his hand and placing it on my upper arm.

"What do you mean?"

"That night, after the first incident with Kurt at the club, when I drove your sister home and Owen drove you, Emily told me what you were like as kids and that one day you just changed. And the timeframe matches up," he concluded, flashing me a sympathetic smile.

"Why are you being so nice to me?" I blurted, baffled by his sudden and overwhelming show of support. "After I pushed you about your sister?"

"You upset me. A lot. And while the subject of Julia triggers me, especially now that you know why, you telling me that that bastard raped you…" He lost his words, but he didn't have to say anything else. I knew what he was getting at. That me telling him I was raped trumped whatever anger he had about his sister.

"You believe me." I uttered the words without realizing they were sitting on the tip of my tongue.

He tilted his head and leaned in close. "Of course, I do."

Here come the tears again.

Ford pulled me in for yet another embrace and I let him. I'd been carrying around my secret for many years and I was tired.

Tired of the burden.

Tired of acting out because of what happened.

Tired of excusing my behavior as rebellious and impetuous.

Tired of the loneliness that accompanied the shame.

"Will you stay with me tonight?" I asked, realizing how much I needed him. If he left me alone after I'd showed him a piece of my broken soul, I didn't know what I'd do.

Ford was silent as he guided me toward my bed, pulling

back the covers and helping me under them. Afterward, he walked around to the other side, removed his pants, and climbed in next to me, repositioning me so that my head rested on his chest.

Much like we'd been right before everything turned to hell.

CHAPTER
TWENTY-FOUR

Ford

As I lay there, restless but not daring to move for fear I'd wake Cara, I couldn't help but replay everything that happened between us.

When I accompanied her on her date with Caverly, as if I had a choice in the matter, I was man enough to admit that my jealousies took over and got the better of me. Which was apparent when I started an argument with her when we arrived home, reminding her that she wasn't allowed to date anyone until the threat against her family was abolished.

Then I followed her upstairs and into her bathroom where everything came to a head. I'd lost mine when I rubbed my thumb over her bottom lip, wanting like hell to erase any trace of that bastard's kiss.

I warred with myself, knowing what I was about to do would complicate the dynamic between us, but I did it anyway.

I kissed her.

We had sex.

She pushed me about Julia and I lost my temper.

Then she revealed a secret she kept hidden from everyone.

My blood boiled when I thought of what that bastard did to her, and when she was a kid, no less. The thoughts that ran through my head made my heart speed up, and I had to remind myself to calm down. There wasn't a damn thing I could do about what happened. Since Cara never told anyone, she wouldn't want me to tell anyone either, which tied my hands in what I could and couldn't do. Hunter hadn't found any substantial dirt on the guy. Nothing more than a couple of speeding tickets over the years. So, either Cara had been his only victim, or the others had been too afraid to say anything, as well.

I drifted in and out of sleep over the next several hours, waking with a start, more than once, because of the dream that often plagued me.

Julia's accident.

Her death.

Sometimes, the dream was a true account of what happened that fateful night, and sometimes she was alive inside the car, pleading with me to help her. Other times, I'd been the one driving, my sister buckled into the passenger seat. I'd survive the wreck, but she never would.

I lived with guilt over her passing every single day, and when Cara wouldn't stop pushing me about her, I'd erupted. Owen often told me that it didn't do me any good to keep shit bottled up inside and I suppose he was right.

Waking with a start once more, I looked over at Cara, who was still sound asleep, then at her bedside clock. It read 7:30.

"Shit!" I grunted, gently removing my arm from underneath her. I needed to leave before Owen started morning rounds and if he caught me in her bed, I wouldn't hear the end of it, especially after all the shit I gave him about him and Emily.

Gathering my clothes, I dressed quickly before taking one last look at Cara. She'd rolled over on her stomach, her blonde hair fanning all around her. The covers shifted lower and rested halfway down her back. All I wanted to do was crawl back into bed and wake her up, see if she was up for another round, but I couldn't. Not only would that not be a good idea because my brother would catch us, but after what she revealed last night, I didn't want to push her to do something she now might have reservations about.

When I was fully dressed, I closed her bedroom door behind me and descended the staircase, rounding the corner and heading toward the kitchen.

I was halfway across the room when a cell rang, vibrating on top of the counter. The rush of sound startled me because I'd been wrapped up with the memory of the prior evening. The phone finally silenced only to ring again. When I approached the device, I saw it was Cara's, but the call ended before I could see who it was. I didn't have to wait long to find out, however, because a few seconds later, her screen lit up again.

Stephanie's name flashed across the screen, and instantly I tensed. Did she know what happened all those years ago? I remember Cara said she'd never told anyone, but did her friend have an inkling about what her father did? Had he possibly done the same to his own daughter? My thoughts pinged from one to the other, concocting all sorts of possibilities, but the truth was, I may never know for sure.

I swiped the screen before the call ended for the third time. "Hello," I answered, attempting to sound casual and not pissed off.

"Hello? Is this Cara's phone?"

"Yes." Short and to the point.

"Who is this?" Stephanie sounded confused, and I couldn't say I blamed her.

"Ford."

"Oh. Ford. Why are you... you know what? Never mind

because it doesn't matter. All that matters is that you give Cara a message ASAP. I don't care if she's sleeping or not, which she probably is." Her speech was rushed, and I couldn't help but be nosy.

"What is this about?"

"Tell her that James Hollen is leaving the country for the next three weeks and if she wants a shot at meeting with him, she has to do it today. Otherwise, she might miss out on the biggest opportunity of her life."

"James Hollen?" I sounded bored even though my curiosity had been piqued.

"Ford!" Stephanie shouted. "Just tell her. Go wake her up and give her this message. I told James she'll be calling, but she has to do it within in next half hour. Do you have a piece of paper? I'll give you the number." I didn't answer while I searched for something to use to take the message, but I supposed I wasn't quick enough. "Are you ready?"

"I'm trying to find a paper and pen. Give me a second." She huffed into the phone and I almost *accidentally* hung up on her, but I realized the importance of this call, so I didn't do something so childish.

I rooted through two drawers before I found a pad and pen. "Okay, give me the number."

Stephanie rattled off the information and hung up after reminding me once more how important it was for me to give Cara the message as soon as possible.

As I held the paper in my hand, prepared to walk back upstairs and wake Cara, Owen walked in the back door and for some reason, guilt bombarded me.

I hated hiding things from my brother, but Cara and I never discussed the ramifications of what happened last night.

Revelations came to light from both of us and we didn't have the emotional energy to dive into where to go from there. I suspected that conversation would happen sooner than later.

"Hey," he said, looking at me with his brows slanted inward. "When did you come over here?"

"Just a few minutes ago."

"Really? 'Cause I was in our kitchen for the past twenty minutes and you weren't there." He tilted his head and deepened the crease between his eyes. That was the one thing that got under my skin about my brother. He was a dog with a bone, so before he asked me a million-and-one questions, I threw him a correction.

"Then it must've been a half hour ago," I lied.

"What time did you get home from your date last night? Sorry, I mean Cara's date?" The corner of his lip twitched and had I not ended up in bed with her last night, his comment would've got under my skin.

"Late."

"How did it go?"

"Fine."

"What did you do afterward?" he asked, leaning against the corner of the island, hell-bent on driving me crazy with his incessant questions.

"Retired for the night."

"I don't recall hearing you come in."

"Are you done now?" I had no patience for twenty questions so early in the morning, especially when I was trying to hide shit from him. I'd been told I was a hard man to read, but if Owen kept digging, he'd uncover the truth, or a part of it, at least.

"For now." He smiled, but his expression fell when Emily

walked into the kitchen. He glanced from her to me then back again, a mix of worry and guilt plastered on his face.

"I'll take the upstairs this morning. You can check down here and then we'll both do the perimeter." I never waited for his answer before I headed back up the stairs and down the hall toward Cara's room.

CHAPTER
TWENTY-FIVE

Cara

Stretching my arms above my head, I sensed I was alone even though my eyes were still closed. The moment I opened them, everything would become too real, and I needed those extra seconds to live in my bubble, wrapped up in the notion that my life could take a turn for the better.

I never intended on telling anyone about what happened to me when I was younger, hoping to take that devastating secret to my grave, but it all happened so fast I was powerless to stop the words before they left my mouth.

Rolling over onto my side, I pried my lids open and looked out the window, the blinds resting several inches from the bottom. Slivers of light filtered into the room and each steady breath I pushed from my lungs promised hope. Or at least I wanted to believe that. The dawn of a new day. Wasn't that what people meant when they used that phrase?

Lost in the memory of last night and what would happen going forward, I never heard anyone enter my room. But my body tingled, and I knew he was close. When I turned to face the other side of the room, Ford stood in the doorway, watching me, still wearing the clothes he had on last night.

"What time did you get up?" I sat up, my robe opening and

revealing most of my breasts. Ford looked behind him quickly, then closed the door before diminishing the space between us.

"Not too long ago," he answered, his eyes traveling down my body before landing back on my face. He smiled more with his eyes than he did his mouth, and all I wanted to do was grab him and pull him on top of me. It was too risky, though, and if his brother or my sister walked in and caught us, we'd have to explain. I wouldn't know where to begin, and I doubted Ford did either.

"Do you regret what happened?" he asked, shifting from one foot to the other. His uncertainty alleviated my own, but I didn't know how to answer. Was he talking about the sex or me telling him about the rape? Or both?

"If you're talking about us sleeping together, the answer is no. But if you're talking about..." I shrugged my shoulders and tilted my head from side to side a few times. There was only so much my brain could handle and I didn't possess the mental strength to think about what I'd told him. To deal with the implications of all that it entailed. "I don't know yet." I nodded. "Do you?"

"Do I regret having sex with you?" Ford sat on the edge of the bed and touched my arm. "Not one bit."

"What about telling me what you did about your sister?"

"Yes and no. I'm still overly protective of Julia, and to talk about her and what happened, especially revealing my part in the whole damn thing... it hurts. Too much."

"So, where do we go from here?" I asked, uncertain if I wanted to know the answer just yet.

"Not sure. Our situation is a little complicated right now."

"I know." Ford moved his hand and I saw he held a piece of paper. "What is that?"

He looked down before handing me the note. "Sorry, it was the whole reason I came up here."

I gave him a nod, not wanting to showcase my insecurities by asking him if it was the only reason he'd come to my room. But he must've sensed my doubt because he put my mind and ego at ease.

"The message wasn't the only reason." He rose from the bed. "Your phone kept ringing, so I answered. Stephanie was the one calling. She said it's imperative you call him right away so you don't miss out."

"Call who?" I looked down at the paper in my hand and saw a name scribbled down but couldn't make out what it said.

"James Hollen."

"What?" I shouted, lowering my voice when I realized how loud I'd been. "When... what...when?" I repeated, flustered with excitement and forgetting about everything else. Nerves shook me while I tried to regain an ounce of composure.

Ford turned around and walked toward the door. "Let me know when you're ready and where we're going." He left before I could ask him anything else.

I continued to sit on the bed in a daze. I was about to call one of the most renowned designers of my time, and it was all due to my friend. The same friend who'd unknowingly been mixed up in one of the most disastrous times in my life. My friendship with Steph had been affected by what her father had done to me. I'd cut ties with her over the following days and weeks after it happened, blaming my absence on other things, and while guilt ate at me for doing it, I couldn't tell her the real reason.

I'd been fortunate enough to maintain contact with her over the years, and thankfully so, because she'd just done me one of the biggest favors of my life. And even if nothing ever came of it, I'd be forever grateful she'd tried to make my dreams come true.

I searched my room for my cell, but then realized Ford must have it since he was the one to take the call. I rushed into the hallway and down the stairs, barreling into Emily when I turned the corner into the living room.

Her eyes were red and puffy.

"What happened?" I asked, hoping it wasn't anything serious because, for as much as I wanted to talk to her, I needed to make this phone call.

She shook her head and hurried past me without a word, giving me the opportunity to deal with what I had to before searching her out to talk about what was going on.

I walked into an empty kitchen, and for a moment, I was disappointed Ford wasn't there. But my upset was canceled when I spotted my phone on top of the island.

Grabbing my cell, I swiped the screen and dialed the numbers on the piece of paper. I swore I held my breath during the time it took for the call to connect, and three rings later I heard a man's voice on the other end.

"Hello?" His tone was deep.

"Hello? Is this James Hollen?"

"It is. Who's this?"

"My name is Cara Dessoye. I'm a friend—"

"Yes, of course. I've been waiting for you to call."

"You have?" I asked, surprised.

"Stephie couldn't stop going on and on about how talented you were, so I figured it couldn't hurt to see what you got. Can you meet me in the city at noon?"

"Absolutely." I glanced at the clock above the sink and saw it was 8:45. If I hurried, I could get ready and have enough time to make it to our meeting on time, barring any issues with traffic.

"Just bring what you have."

"I don't have anything professional put together, yet. I just have a sketchbook. But I can bring along two outfits I recently made." I tried not to stumble over my words, my nerves rattling me the more I spoke.

"Great. See you then."

I raced outside and into the guesthouse, surprising Ford who was in the middle of taking a drink. At seeing me, he spilled the water down the front of him and I couldn't help but think that I'd love for him to remove his shirt so I could take a quick peek before I had to get ready.

"Woman," he grunted, brushing off the pellets of liquid from his shirt. "You have to stop rushing in here like that."

"The last time I did it, I was in a much different mood." I swore my cheek muscles were getting sore from smiling.

"Did the call go well?" he asked, taking a few steps closer. Owen walked into the room before he was able to touch me, and because there was a respectable distance between us, I doubted his brother thought anything inappropriate was going on.

"It did. He wants to see me at noon. In the city."

"Okay. I'll be ready to go."

As I was about to turn and leave, I locked eyes with Owen. "Do you know why Emily is upset?" I intended to ask my sister that very same question but was curious if he knew anything, and if he'd tell me.

He shook his head and flashed me too quick of a smile. Owen also cleared his throat before answering. "No, I don't." He averted his eyes for a moment, and I knew right then that whatever my sister was upset about had everything to do with him.

Problem was, I didn't have enough time right then to get to the bottom of whatever happened.

While I showered, I couldn't help thinking that my life could change after my meeting with James. Maybe I was being presumptuous, but I believed that something good was fated for me. Not that I'd done anything to deserve it, but I still wished, nonetheless.

Rushing through my normal routine because time was an issue, I got ready in record speed. Minimal makeup, a purposely half up-do, one of my favorite, simple yet classic black dresses, and a pair of red peep-toe Jimmy Choo's, and I hurried from my room and into the hallway. Emily came out of her room the same time as I passed by and we almost smacked into each other, narrowly missing by inches.

"Where are you off to?" she asked, rubbing at her still puffy eyes.

I looked her up and down before answering, worried about her. "I have a meeting with James Hollen in the city at noon."

"When did this happen?" She smiled big and grabbed my shoulders. "Oh my God!" she exclaimed, looking down at my hands. "Aren't you going to take anything with you to show him?"

"Holy shit! I completely forgot to grab the outfits and my portfolio." I shoved my purse at her and ran back to my room. In my haste to leave, it'd completely slipped my mind to bring the very things I needed to showcase, the entire reason why James wanted to see me in the first place.

Gathering my book and the outfits I'd made for the charity event, I reemerged into the hallway and headed toward Emily, careful not to drop anything. She tucked my purse under my arm.

S. NELSON

"We're gonna talk as soon as I get back. I want to know what's going on with you." Emily looked down at her feet and closed her eyes. I swore she was about to cry again, but when she looked back up, the glassiness of her eyes was gone.

"And I want to hear all about your meeting. I know he's going to love you."

"I don't need him to love me. I need him to love my designs," I joked.

"You know what I mean." She leaned in and kissed my cheek, and I wanted to remain in that moment for a few seconds longer. When I looked at Emily right then, I saw the mirror image of myself. Not the physical attributes, because we were fraternal twins, but the longing to be seen, and understood. That was the reflection I referred to, something we intimately shared standing there in the hallway.

Ford walked halfway up the staircase and took the outfits from me, interrupting my unspoken time with my sister. "You won't make it if you fall on your face."

"Thanks." I smiled but it fell away when I realized I was grinning at him a little too long, and Owen was standing at the foot of the steps, watching us.

When we made it outside, we put the clothing and the portfolio in the back. Then I walked toward the passenger side. Ford didn't say a word as I sat beside him. He just gave me a look before turning over the engine. When he looked at me again as we drove away, I was curious as to what he was thinking.

"What?"

He shrugged. "I'm just surprised you're sitting in the front seat again."

"Well, considering we had sex last night, I think I can sit

156

next to you, don't you think?" It was a joke, but he didn't laugh or even smile. "Should I not have said that?"

"You didn't say anything wrong."

"Then, what is it?" The hairs on the back of my neck stood at attention, and I couldn't decide if my reaction was because of unease due to the nature of mine and Ford's relationship or my upcoming meeting. Or maybe it was a mixture of both.

"It's nothing."

"Ford." He looked over at me, then back to the road. "What is it?" I repeated, growing impatient with his silence.

"I was just thinking that I'd love to hike up your dress and fuck you right where you sit."

Okay, I didn't see that one coming.

CHAPTER
TWENTY-SIX

Ford

I meant what I said, even though I should've kept that to myself. Now all I'm going to fixate on is what she has on underneath her dress and how wet she'd be if I put my hand between her legs.

Cara shifted in her seat more than once, bouncing between looking out her window and turning to look at me. We didn't talk for several minutes, the last thing I said resonating between us both.

"I probably shouldn't have made that comment. Sorry." I had no idea what else to say. The mounting tension was enough to strangle me if I let it continue building. I'd never been in this sort of predicament before.

I'd protected high-powered people before.

I'd been put in precarious situations in the past, some requiring split-second decisions to ensure the safety of the person I'd been assigned to.

But I'd never slept with a client before, much less one I was still employed to watch over.

"I like what you said. But yeah, it is awkward, especially when I'm trapped behind this damn seat belt." She laughed, something she hadn't done often since I'd known her. At least, not with me. "Now, if you said that while we were still in my room, then the outcome would be a whole lot different." Cara reached over and put her hand on my thigh.

"You shouldn't do that."

"Why?" She moved to face me.

"Because you'll definitely be late for your meeting."

"Oh." She wasn't sure if I was toying with her or not, so she placed her hand back in her lap.

There were so many questions I wanted to ask her, but I didn't want to rile her or turn our calm situation into a hostile one. Stress was the last thing either of us needed, especially her.

I didn't know much about the fashion industry, but I'd looked up James Hollen as soon as Stephanie gave me his name. Not being able to find any scandals involving him put my mind at ease, but when I clicked on a picture of the guy, my gut tightened. I was man enough to admit that he was good looking, and for as much as I hated to admit to myself, I knew Cara would find him attractive, as well. What if he propositioned her? Enticed her to sleep with him and he'd in return give her a shot? Would she take it? Before last night, I would've said it wouldn't surprise me at all if she slept with someone solely to further whatever agenda she had. But now? I wasn't so sure. Maybe that was just me being egotistical, thinking since we had sex, she couldn't possibly want anyone else, but the reality was Cara and I weren't involved. Other than me being her protection detail.

"Your knuckles are turning white," Cara pointed out, tapping my hand on the wheel. "What's the matter?" Her tone was one of concern, but there was no way I would ever tell her where my thoughts were. So, what did I say instead?

"I'm thinking about what you told me. About what happened to you. I think you should tell your family." As soon as the words were spoken, I knew I'd made a mistake.

Her entire demeanor had changed in seconds, from her breathing to the tension she now held in her posture.

"Cara…."

"No." She kept her eyes away from me. "No," she repeated. "I can't."

"But you have to deal with it. You can't just pretend like it never happened."

"You should take your own advice," she threw back at me. "And besides, I've been dealing with it for eleven years by myself."

"Yeah, how's that working out?" The words left my mouth before I could snatch them back.

"Why don't you tell me?" Her tone was a familiar one. We could go back and forth all day long, but it wouldn't get us any closer to resolving either of our issues. So, I kept my mouth shut and my attention on the road.

So much for not wanting to create a hostile situation.

No traffic delays meant a smooth ride into the city. After twenty minutes of silence, I turned on the radio.

The melodic sounds of Nina Simone drifted from the speakers, and with each tune she sang, the rigidity of my muscles relaxed.

"Okay, I have to know. What's with the old-timey music? Is that all you listen to?" Cara asked, sounding genuinely interested, not like the other times when she'd been annoyed by my choice of the genre. I certainly thought she would still be upset with me, but I supposed this was how she'd gotten through the years, ignoring the past and moving on to something else.

"It soothes me."

"I think there's more to it. Did an ex-girlfriend like it and convinced you it was good music?" She smiled when I shook my head and rolled my eyes.

"No."

"Then, why?"

"Only because you're not making fun of me this time, at least, I don't think you are, I'll tell you. My parents used to listen to Sinatra and Simone and Cooke and Stafford and Bennett. The list goes on and on. They used to dance in the kitchen, then make their way into the living room and interrupt whatever show we were watching and make us dance with them, too. My mom would alternate between me and Owen, and my dad would dance with Julia." The memories made me smile, remembering a time we were whole and happy.

"Are your parents still alive?" she asked with reservation.

"My mom is, but I haven't seen her in a little while. She went to stay with her sister in Florida a few months ago." Cara remained silent, so I purged the rest of my story. "My dad died of a massive heart attack when I was twelve and Owen was eight. Julia was only two. Of course, we were all devastated, and because my mom wasn't the type of person who could be alone, especially with three young kids, she remarried two years later. Steve, our stepfather, was nice enough and provided what my mom needed, so we accepted him as much as we could. But after dealing with Julia for so many years, he decided enough was enough. They were married just over twenty years when he left my mom, coincidentally two months before my sister died. At first, I was angry with him, but there's only so much someone can take, I suppose. I'm not saying I agree with his decision, but my sister was a lot to handle, and she got worse as she got older, stealing money from them, as well as their car, which she wrecked more than once. She left home when she was eighteen but always came back to repeat the same patterns."

My fingers curled tighter around the wheel at having to talk about a painful time in my life, but when I remembered I wasn't the only one present who'd lived through a tragedy, I relaxed some. And while talking about Julia was difficult, it was a little easier the more I did, which I never thought was possible.

"I'm sorry about your sister. And your dad." Cara comforted me, reaching over and squeezing my leg.

"Thank you."

Over the next hour we talked about lighter subjects, places we'd like to visit, our favorite foods and go-to movies, ones we'd seen too many times to count. Funny thing was, Cara and I had a lot in common. We both wanted to visit Egypt someday, we loved to gorge on mac and cheese, and every time *Jaws* came on television, it was like all the other channels didn't exist.

Distracted with the flow of the conversation, I almost missed our exit but veered off the highway at the last minute. It wasn't much longer afterward that I pulled into a parking garage underneath a large stone building on Madison Avenue.

As we rode the elevator to the twenty-second floor, I couldn't help but feel like I was going to be tested in some way once we reached our destination.

CHAPTER
TWENTY-SEVEN

Cara

A flutter erupted in my belly as the elevator climbed higher and I couldn't remember the last time I'd been this nervous. Confidence was something I prided myself on, whether it was forced or not, but to have self-doubt wasn't something I allowed myself too often. Although, the notion was popping up more recently now than ever.

"You'll do great," Ford encouraged, gifting me a smile when I looked at him. The outfits I'd brought were slung over his left arm—his right hand tucked inside his black pants. Even with my nerves rattling me, I couldn't help but appreciate his masculinity.

Ford was a man's man, his roguish good looks drawing the attention of everyone around him, men and women alike. From his height of six three to his thick, dark hair to his broad shoulders and slim yet powerful build, there weren't many men like Ford. Add in his unique and piercing eyes and the mysterious persona he played up well, he was one of a kind for sure. And it was best to not get me started on his talent in the sheets or the way his scruff tickled the inside of my thigh, or… I could go on and on.

The ding of the elevator startled me from my lustful longing, and I took a step closer to Ford without realizing. "Sorry," I said, bumping into him.

"You don't have to apologize for being so close," he teased, and I had to admit I enjoyed this side of him. Seriousness was still his main objective, but other sides of his personality emerged the more we got to know each other on a deeper level.

When we stepped out of the car, I stumbled, catching my heel on the grate of the elevator but instead of falling forward, I was stopped with a firm yet gentle grip on my shoulder. And it wasn't Ford who touched me. When I picked my head up, I looked directly into a familiar pair of eyes.

"Nick. What are you doing here?" Nick Costa was a good friend of mine who also happened to be a well sought-after model. His chiseled good looks bordered the line of masculine and pretty, a perfect mix for the fashion world.

"James Hollen asked to meet with me for an upcoming show he has. What are you doing here?" Nick briefly looked behind me at Ford and gave him a quick nod.

I could only imagine what Ford was doing behind me. Hopefully, he wasn't snarling at my friend, remembering his reaction to him the last time he saw Nick at the club where he accosted him.

"I have a meeting with James, too," I confessed, biting my lip in the process. Nick looked at the book I held, then to the clothes flung over Ford's arm.

"Are you serious?" His smile was infectious. "That's amazing. How did I not know you designed clothes?"

"Because it's sort of a newer adventure for me."

"Well, if James wants to see you, then you must be talented."

"She is," Ford interrupted, placing his hand on my shoulder.

"I don't doubt it," Nick agreed, leaning in to kiss my cheek. If Ford intimidated him, Nick didn't show it. "I have to run to another meeting, but I'll talk to you soon, okay?"

"Of course." We said our goodbyes, and once the elevator doors closed, I looked up at Ford. "Thank you for not causing a scene."

"Why would I cause a scene?" I swore the corner of his lip twitched.

"Because of your last encounter with him."

"I don't know what you're talking about." That time his lip kicked upward into a smug grin.

I rolled my eyes before walking toward the receptionist desk at the far end of the hallway. Once I approached, I gave the red-headed woman my name, then took a seat and waited. Twelve o'clock came and went, amplifying my nerves the longer I waited. When the clock read twelve twenty, I thought maybe James had changed his mind about meeting with me, fully expecting to be told to go home, that the appointment had been set up under the guise of a favor to my friend, and after thinking about what he'd promised, he reconsidered. All sorts of doubt entered my overactive brain and messed with me.

"Can you please sit down?" Ford paced the room instead of sitting next to me. "You're making me more nervous."

"I think it's best—"

"Cara," the receptionist interrupted. "Mr. Hollen is ready for you now. If you'll follow me, please."

Ford grabbed the outfits he'd placed over the back of the seat before I could.

"I can take those," I offered, stretching out my hand but he held on to them. "You can wait here. I'll be fine."

"Not a chance," he said incredulously, looking at me like I'd gone crazy. "You know the deal." He extended his arm and waited for me to concede, which I did right away because I didn't want to keep James waiting.

But when we walked up to the receptionist, she placed her hand on Ford's arm to stop him. The woman was attractive, her red hair pulled up into a tight bun, showcasing her elegant bone structure. Her voluptuous curves surely drew Ford's attention, the thought alone pricking at my newfound jealousies.

"Sir, you'll have to wait out here."

"That's not gonna happen. I'm hired to protect her, so where she goes, I go."

Her arm fell to her side. "I see." She batted her eyes at him before licking her lips. *Brazen bitch.* And just like that, there was no way I was going to leave Ford behind, even if I could, and allow that woman to flirt with him.

I cleared my throat and she finally tore her eyes away from Ford long enough to look my way. "Sorry. Follow me."

"Uh-huh," was all I managed to say, keeping some distance between her and me. She led us down a short hallway before rounding a corner, James's office the first one we came upon. She knocked, opened the door, and disappeared inside. I took the opportunity to turn toward Ford.

"You should've worn your shades," I grumped.

"Why? You hate when I wear them."

"Because maybe then she—"

The receptionist appeared before I could finish my gripe, standing to the side and allowing Ford and me to enter.

"Miss Dessoye," James greeted right before he extended his hand. "It's a pleasure to meet you."

"Cara, please," I instructed, taking his hand briefly. I'd seen pictures of him online and in magazines, but the images didn't do him justice because he was much more handsome in person. He wore his dark blond hair short, the style drawing attention to his light green eyes. With his clean-shaven face, I could see the slight dimple in his chin clearly, and while I wasn't particularly drawn to that feature in men, he pulled it off well.

"Of course. Please have a seat." He motioned toward the large leather sofa across the room. For as big of a deal as he was, his office was a moderate size, comfy. Nothing fancy, but sophisticated all the same.

After I sat, James looked at Ford. "You can have a seat as well, sir. Or if you chose to stay standing, that's your right." He gave him a smile, and Ford's only response was a curt nod before he stood next to the door, his hands clasped in front of him.

"Well," James said, sitting on the couch next to me. "Let's have a look." He reached for my sketchbook, silent while he looked at page after page. I hated that I couldn't tell what he was thinking while he gazed at my drawings. Did he like them? Did he regret taking the meeting? Would he laugh in my face and tell me there was no way in hell I'd ever make it as a designer? I glanced over at Ford in my nervousness and saw that he was staring intently at James. When he sensed me looking, his eyes connected with mine, and he flashed me the faintest of smiles.

"Okay, you definitely have talent. More so than Stephie let on." Again, with him referring to my friend as Stephie. I'd never known anyone to call her that, which only affirmed some of my suspicions that the two of them were closer than she let on. "Can I see the outfits you brought with you?"

"Of course." I handed him the blue chiffon dress I'd made for Emily and the black silk and lace jumpsuit I made myself for the event.

James rose from the couch and walked toward the corner of his office, opened a cabinet, and pulled out a rod that housed a large steel hanger. He draped the blue dress over it first, inspecting my handiwork for several moments, then replacing it with my jumpsuit. When he finished, he headed back toward me.

"You did a great job. Plain and simple. And kudos for choosing the chiffon. That fabric is a bitch to sew." He laughed, putting me at ease with his intricate scrutiny of my work.

"Thank you so much, Mr. Hollen. Coming from you, that's quite the compliment."

"Call me James. Mr. Hollen makes me feel old."

I nodded. "James, it is, then," I said, smiling so big I was sure I looked deranged.

He rose from the couch and extended his hand to help me to my feet. "Can you send me these designs digitally along with any others you have?"

"Absolutely."

"Okay, great." He handed me his business card, which had all his contact information. "Just email me the file as soon as you can. Then we'll go from there."

"Thank you so much for taking the time to meet with me. I appreciate it more than you know. I've been a huge fan of yours for as long as I can remember."

"It can't be that long, seeing as how you're, what, barely twenty-five, if that."

"Just recently twenty-five, to be exact."

"Wait and see how fast time goes. You'll be my age in no time. Enjoy your youth while you can," he said, staring off into space with a grin. "I tease Stephie all the time about—" James suddenly snapped his mouth closed and pulled his cell from his pocket. Looking at the screen then back to me, he said, "Well, I have to get ready to leave. We'll talk soon, Cara. It was a pleasure to meet you." He shook my hand, but before he released me, he leaned in close and whispered in my ear. "He's interested in you. Just so you know." He pulled back and winked before showing us to the door.

With my book and garments in my hand, I left his office with Ford closely behind me, passing by his receptionist soon after.

"Have a good day, sir." Then, she looked at me and her flirty grin faltered a bit. "And you, Miss Dessoye."

"You, too," I sang over my shoulder, her blatant perusal of Ford doing nothing to hamper my excitement.

CHAPTER
TWENTY-EIGHT

Ford

"How old is James?" Cara asked, opening her phone and bringing up the Internet once we were back in the elevator. "He doesn't look to be that much older than me."

Her comparison of their ages annoyed me, and let's not forget that he whispered something in her ear right before we left. And because I hadn't heard what he said, I conjured up all sorts of possibilities. Instead of staying silent and fuming about it, though, I decided to just ask her. Hopefully, she'd tell me the truth.

"What did he say to you?"

"When?"

I gritted my teeth and stepped into her personal space.

"When he whispered in your ear?" I asked, choking on my jealousy. *Rein it in, man.*

"Huh. I don't remember." At first, I thought she was serious, but when she smiled and backed up against the wall of the car, I realized she was messing with me. "Something about clothes?"

"Funny." I grabbed her waist and pulled her into me, towering over her even though she wore heels. "Tell me what he said or else."

"What are you going to do if I don't?" she breathlessly

replied, her eyes glazing over while her bottom lip disappeared between her teeth.

"You'll just have to imagine." I paused for a moment to collect myself.

"Oh, I can imagine all right." Cara ran her fingers down my chest, then rested them on my belt buckle, all the while keeping her eyes pinned to mine.

"Don't make me imagine the worst. Did he ask you out? Because I saw the way he looked at you when we walked in. Not that I can blame him."

Moments of silence passed while she kept me in suspense, adrenaline pumping freely through my veins the longer she made me wait.

Then she leaned up and kissed me, whispering against my lips, "He didn't ask me out. He told me that you were interested in me." As we reached our floor, she removed herself from my space and clutched her belongings tightly.

Relieved the guy hadn't made a move on her, I was conflicted with another issue.

Us.

The thought of us.

The prospect of us.

The reality of us.

She had to *know* I was interested. We'd had sex, for Christ's sake, but maybe that didn't mean anything to her. Maybe it was just sex, nothing more.

But was it? I know it wasn't for me.

As we settled in and drove out of the parking garage, I gave her a tidbit of information on James Hollen, one I was surprised she didn't know, seeing as how she was a fan of his.

"He's thirty-eight."

"Who?"

"Hollen."

"How do you know that?" she asked, then threw her hand up to stop me from answering right afterward. "Never mind. I'm sure you researched him before our meeting."

"You know I did."

"By the way," she started, turning in her seat as much as her seat belt would allow, "what did you mean you saw the way he looked at me?"

"Why?"

"Just curious." She tried to hide her smile, but I saw it. Plain as fuckin day.

"You like him?" I asked, regretting my question as soon as it left my mouth.

"He's nice." She smoothed out the bottom of her dress. "With him behind me, I could achieve a lot."

I hated the image that filtered in with Hollen literally behind her, fucking her. What could I say? Apparently, I loved to torture myself. I started mumbling to myself, but then Cara reached over and put her hand on my forearm.

"Calm down, Ford. I'm not interested in James. And he's not in me, either. In fact, I think there's something going on between him and Steph."

I relaxed, but not enough to stop my heart from continuing to slam against my chest.

"What makes you say that?"

"From the way she talked about him at the event. And twice he referred to her as Stephie, which is a nickname I've never heard used for her before. Just makes me think I'm right about this."

"Hopefully."

"Why hopefully?" She laughed.

"No reason." My heartbeats lessened and fell back into a steady rhythm. I swore since last night, further back if I was being honest with myself, I didn't know which way was up when it came to the woman sitting next to me. One minute I wanted to rip her clothes off, and the next she'd say something to piss me off, making me want to be as far from her as possible. Of course, sleeping together turned everything upside down and I scrambled to make heads or tails of how to move forward.

Cara's phone dinged with an incoming message, and as she dug through her purse to find her cell, she looked over at me before pulling it out. Her fingers flew over the keys with lightning speed, replying to a few more texts, then tossing the device back into her purse. She looked out the window, and I couldn't help the sneaking suspicion that she was going back and forth with a guy.

"Who was that?" I asked, trying to be casual about it but failing miserably.

"Cody."

My heart picked up its pace at the mention of his name. "Yeah? What did he want?" Again, my knack at subtlety failed.

"He wanted to know if we were still on for Saturday."

"You're still going out with him?"

"Sure, why not?"

"Because... you know." I shrugged, not knowing quite how to verbalize my thoughts so that they made a lick of sense.

"Because you and I slept together?"

"Fine," I conceded. "Yes, because we slept together. Are you happy?"

"Very. But we can't be together, Ford. Not now. It's weird, don't you think?"

"Weird?" When I looked at her, she raised her brows. "I suppose," I huffed. "But I don't think you should go out with him. Besides, your father won't allow it anyway." That argument was the catapult that led to us sleeping together in the first place.

"Don't start," she warned, folding her arms across her chest and turning to watch the world pass us.

As the miles flew by, I was at a loss for how to continue our conversation, of how to handle whatever it was going on between us.

CHAPTER
TWENTY-NINE

Cara

The word conflicted didn't even begin to describe the way I felt about Ford and me, so I chose to keep things casual, stupidly saying we couldn't be together. Which, in essence, wasn't all that impractical to say because he was still employed to watch over me.

Refusing to allow my mood to be dampened, to have my euphoria snatched at having just had the opportunity to meet with James freaking Hollen, I bit my tongue the rest of the way home.

"Cara." He threw the vehicle in Park and grabbed my wrist before I could jump out. "We need to talk." Now I knew why men hated those four dreaded words. Whatever Ford wanted to talk about probably wasn't good, and I didn't have enough mental energy to deal with it because I was confused... about everything.

"Look at me." I kept my focus ahead and away from his eyes. "Please."

Finally, I relented. Big mistake. I saw so many things in his eyes. Confusion. Desire. Doubt. Hope. Or maybe I was simply reflecting what I felt onto him.

"I don't want to argue with you anymore."

"That's something we can agree on then," he said, releasing my arm.

"Can we talk later?" We had a few things to hash out, and I tried to be an adult about our situation, but all I wanted to do was run into the house and tell Emily all about the meeting with James. Then call Steph. Then call Naomi, whom I hadn't seen in more time than I cared to admit.

Between her new job as a personal assistant for a CEO of some hedge fund company, or something like that—honestly, I zoned out when she tried to explain the details to me—but between her job and her budding relationship with Benji, mixed with what I now had going on, we hadn't been able to squeeze in the time. But I would make sure to change that. Besides, I needed to celebrate, and I needed my girl with me.

"Sure."

I hopped out and walked ahead of him inside the house, calling out for my sister as soon as I hit the foyer.

"Emily!" I shouted, throwing my stuff on the couch. "Emily!" Still nothing. I rushed up the stairs, the memory of my meeting exciting me all over again. I checked all the rooms, hers being the first but I couldn't find her. "Emily. Where the hell are you?" Barreling back down the stairs, I saw Ford standing in the foyer reading something on his phone. "Where's Owen?"

"I have no idea. But he's here somewhere because Emily's car is out front." I walked through the kitchen and out to the patio. Maybe she was by the pool, although it was cloudy outside.

Two steps onto the patio and I saw it was empty. No Emily. Unless she and Owen went for a walk, which wasn't uncommon, she had to be inside the guesthouse. Without knocking, I turned the handle to the smaller house adjacent to ours and entered. And there she was sitting on the couch, crying. Owen had his arms around her as he consoled her.

"What happened?" I asked, startling them both. "Is it Mom

or Dad?" My heart thumped against my rib cage and I suddenly found it hard to catch my breath, all sorts of awful thoughts running through my head. My sister witnessed my reaction and rose from the couch to come stand next to me.

"Calm down, Cara. No one is hurt. Nothing happened," she lied, the evidence of her fib trailing down her cheeks.

"Then, why are you crying?"

"Uh… just hormonal." She stepped back and looked down. She was a horrible liar and we both knew it. Something was going on and I would get to the bottom of it, but I needed to get her alone. Grabbing her hand, I pulled her behind me, no resistance on her part, confirming some of my suspicions.

We passed Ford in the kitchen, and while he was still engrossed with whatever he read on his phone, he looked up briefly as we walked by, his eyes pinging from me to Emily and back again. I shook my head before he parted his lips to speak and disappeared upstairs, all the while keeping a strong hold on Emily.

Once we were inside her bedroom, I shut the door and gestured for her to sit down, taking a seat next to her.

"Out with it," I demanded. "What's going on?"

She hopped off the bed and started pacing, gripping the strands of her hair tightly. When she looked at me, I saw so much fear behind her eyes I became more concerned than I was initially.

"I don't know."

"What kind of answer is that? Of course, you know." The last thing I wanted to do was yell at her when she was clearly distressed. She'd shut down altogether and we wouldn't get anywhere. "Does it have anything to do with Owen?" Her head popped up at the mention of his name and she answered me without words. "What happened? What did he do?"

S. NELSON

"Nothing. Everything." Now she sounded like me whenever I failed to put my emotions into words.

"Come sit down," I said softly, reaching out to take her hand. My sister and I had been extremely close when we were younger, and we were finding our way back to the way we were. It was slow but promising. I needed to put everything else aside and be there for her because she needed me. Plain and simple.

Emily accepted my support and sat next to me once more, burying her head in her hands before bursting into tears again. I allowed her time to purge her sadness and pulled her close to show her I was there for her.

"It's okay. No matter what happened, you'll get over it." I threw out generalizations because she still hadn't revealed the issue.

She pulled back. "That's just it, you can't get over a baby," she blurted, and it took me several seconds for my brain to compute her words.

"I'm sorry... what?"

If she bit her lip any harder, she'd draw blood. Her chin quivered, and her eyes filled with fresh tears.

"I'm pregnant." Once those two words flew from her mouth, she rambled. "I don't know what I'm going to do. I'm not ready to have a baby. I'm not married. I'm not even in a relationship, not in the traditional way." The more she talked, the less sense she made.

"Who's the father?" I knew the answer before I asked, but I needed her to confirm it. Emily gave me an are-you-kidding-me kind of look. "Say it."

"Owen." With hunched shoulders and a despondent demeanor, she flopped back on the covers and threw her arm over her eyes. "I can't believe this is happening to me. Not only will

178

Mom and Dad be disappointed in me, they're going to fire the guys. I won't ever see him," she cried, rolling on to her side.

"I'm assuming he knows about the baby?"

"Yes, I just told him right before you dragged me out of there." For a split second, I felt bad, but then my regret morphed into protectiveness over my sister.

"How far along are you?" She remained silent, so I asked her again. "Emily, how far along?"

"Five weeks."

"Jesus. Did you sleep with him the first night you met him?"

"Like you're one to talk," she shouted back before crawling off the bed.

"I'll let that slide because you're upset, and not totally off base, but we're not talking about me." I approached and pulled her into another hug. "Everything will work out."

She held on to me, and for as much as I hated to see her so upset, I was comforted that she'd confided in me. Not that I gave her much of a choice.

Moments later, Emily composed herself, wiping away her remaining tears.

"It was a week."

"What was a week?" I asked.

"It was the week after I met Owen that I slept with him, but we wanted to keep that a secret. Both of us realized it should've never happened."

"You only slept together that one time?" Emily shook her head. "So, you knew it was a mistake, yet you did it again?" If anyone looked up hypocrite in the dictionary, they'd see my smug expression right next to the word. Ford and I hadn't slept together but that one time, but I'd thought about doing it again, and again.

"I love him," she whispered and at first, I didn't hear her, but when she repeated those words, all I could do was sigh.

"Emily," I started, "you don't love him. You hardly know him. I think you're confused."

"I know what I feel," she responded angrily, her sudden defensiveness a sign I needed to back off before she shut down completely and stopped telling me anything.

"Did you tell him you loved him?" She nodded. "Did he tell you he loves you?"

"He said it's complicated."

"Oh, I'm sure it is," I fired back, angry about the situation. My sister was a good person, and she didn't deserve to be treated like an afterthought. Granted, I didn't know a thing about their relationship or what they'd talked about, and Owen didn't get much of a chance to react to the news of her being pregnant because I basically barged into the guesthouse and dragged her out of there. But still, the fact she was this upset riled me. Emily was the better person out of the two of us and she only deserved good things, not for some guy to tell her "It's complicated," even though that was probably the case.

I flip-flopped from one side to the other, trying to see both points of view, but I always landed on my sister's.

A knock at the door interrupted my internal back and forth, the door handle turning before either of us could open it. Owen stood in the doorway, his left eye reddened, and looking like someone killed his dog. Ford stood close behind him.

"Emily, can I talk to you?" Owen was pushed to the side when Ford walked into the bedroom. He headed straight for me.

"Let them hash this out," he muttered, reaching for my hand but I pulled back before he touched me. "Cara."

"No. I'm not going anywhere. Not unless Emily wants me

to." I stepped closer to Owen, prepared to do God only knew what, but instead of asking him anything related to the current situation, I asked him something else, curiosity getting the better of me. "What happened to your eye?"

"He fell," Ford barked, grabbing my hand and dragging me from the room. Before I crossed the threshold, I saw Emily look down at our clasped hands, raising her brows before the door closed behind me.

"What are you doing?" I yelled, struggling to break free. Ford pulled me down the hallway and into my room, releasing my hand when he closed and blocked the door.

"They need to figure it out. Besides, there's nothing either of us can do about it now."

"Fine. But they better figure it out quickly or I'm marching back in there." I paced the room, all my thoughts consumed with Emily. What was Owen saying to her? Was he flippant about the baby? About her? The prospect that he could be saying something that would hurt her angered me all over again.

CHAPTER THIRTY

Cara

"What really happened to your brother's eye?" I asked, walking next to Ford as we approached the top of the stairs. As we passed Emily's room, we heard them talking, but because the door was shut, we couldn't make out what they were saying, not unless we pressed our ears against the door. He stretched his arm in front of him and stepped back, allowing me to go first.

"I punched him when he told me."

"Are you serious?" In my surprise, I stumbled on the step but caught myself by grabbing on to the railing.

"Jesus, Cara. What are you trying to do? Kill yourself?" His worried tone receded when he saw I was fine. When we reached the bottom, we disappeared into the living room. At some point, Emily and Owen would have to emerge and we'd be waiting.

Getting back to my question, I pushed Ford for more information. "Why did you hit him? It wasn't like we didn't sleep together, too."

He leaned forward on the sofa. "Yeah, but I didn't get you pregnant."

"How do you know?" I retorted, realizing the premise of my argument was both rational and asinine.

"Because we used a condom." He ran his hands through

his hair before leaning against the back of the couch. "Besides, this isn't about you and me. It's about them and what's going to happen once your parents find out."

"You're right."

"Holy shit," he blurted.

"What?"

"You agree with me," he said, a disbelieving smile spreading over his gorgeous face.

"Don't get used to it." I rose from my seat and had intended to grab a drink from the kitchen, but when I heard the click of a door upstairs, I refused to move. "I think they're coming down."

Sure enough, Emily and Owen appeared at the bottom of the steps ten tense-filled seconds later, both looking like they'd seen better days.

Would my sister tell me what they talked about or would she take a page from my book and keep everything secret?

"Everything okay?" Ford asked, standing, as well.

"No," Emily and Owen replied simultaneously.

"We better figure something out because once Dad finds out, he's going to fire these guys," I said, throwing my hands on my hips.

"I don't want anyone else watching over you," Owen uttered, pulling Emily into a hug. Apparently, their talk hadn't gone as badly as I feared.

My sister kept her hands at her sides and her eyes averted from everyone. She mumbled something under her breath before putting some distance between her and Owen.

"What did you say?" I asked, taking a step closer so I could hear her better.

"I said…" She took a breath, then another. "There won't be any reason to."

"To what?" Owen asked, seemingly just as confused with her rambling.

"To watch over us."

"You know damn well Walter is going to hire a replacement until the threat is gone for good," Ford interjected his two cents that time.

"Well… that's the thing." Emily looked more uncomfortable than she did moments ago.

"What's the thing?" The corners of Emily's mouth kicked up, forming a tentative and unnerving faux smile right before she slowly raised, then lowered her shoulders. "Oh my God. What did you do?" I asked, having no idea what she was going to tell us. She clamped her mouth shut and took a step back, away from the three of us. "Emily, what did you do?" I repeated, breathing deeply to prepare for what would fly out of her mouth.

"I sent them."

I swore the three of us tilted our heads to the side at the same time.

"You sent what?" I asked, more confused the longer this conversation went on.

"I sent the notes."

I repeated her words over and over in my head, each time distancing myself from their meaning. I heard what she said, but it took my brain time to understand, and as soon as my comprehension clicked, I ran through all the ramifications of what she'd done, starting from the very beginning.

Not only had she lied to our parents and caused them unnecessary fear and worry, but she'd been the sole reason Owen and Ford had come into our lives in the first place.

I tied everything that happened back to her deceit.

Feeling trapped because I had someone watching my every move.

Going out of my way to rebel because of it.

Being confused whenever Ford was near me. Hating being around him but craving his attention, his approval in some twisted way.

Him fake kidnapping me to prove a point and scaring me half to death, a point which was now moot.

Having sex with him.

Wanting to have more sex with him.

Contemplating some sort of relationship with him going forward, but at odds with that thought due to our circumstances.

Revealing the secret I wanted to take to my grave.

And the biggest ramification was that Emily was now pregnant.

Fury shook me to the core. I could only imagine how our parents were going to react.

I hadn't realized I was walking backward until I bumped into the corner of the end table. My anger had morphed into bewilderment.

"Why?" One word left my mouth while I continued to make sense of everything she'd said.

"Because I—"

"WHY?!" I shouted that time, never giving her time to finish her answer.

Emily cautiously drew closer and reached for my hand. I gave it to her, wanting to understand, and if she felt that touching me would help, then I let her.

"I was so worried about you. Every day that passed, you slipped further from me, and I feared that one day you wouldn't be able to come back. That you'd eventually end up dead."

Again, I heard her words, but I didn't understand.

"What the hell are you talking about?"

"I sent Dad those notes because I knew he'd do something. Whether it was enforcing a curfew or insisting maybe we go stay in California at the house there, I'm not sure. But him hiring bodyguards to watch over us didn't dawn on me."

I jerked my hand from hers. "I still don't understand why?"

"Because you were partying all the time, hanging out with people who were dragging you down. You drove drunk too many times to count, I'm surprised you didn't kill yourself or anyone else. You slept with anyone, didn't matter that you just met them, and you had no reservations when it came to drugs. You took them, from anyone."

Every word out of Emily's mouth was the truth, but that didn't stop the anger inside me from bubbling over. My palm connected with her cheek before I realized I'd raised my hand.

Ford and Owen rushed toward us, separating us before the situation worsened.

"Okay, I think everyone needs to take a breath," Owen said, trying to calm the both of us, although his comment was most likely directed more toward me.

"I can't believe you did this," I yelled at my sister. The only argument I had worth any salt, the one point that would dig at her the way her intrusion into my life dug at me, was to speak the truth. "I hope you're up for raising a baby on your our own because Owen won't be around anymore after Dad finds out."

Of course, our parents would be upset, but in reality, neither of them could stop Owen and Emily from being together, if that's what they chose to do. There would just be some tense family dinners for a while, I was sure.

Ford forced me out of the room before I could continue

my tirade, but I heard Emily's cries as he guided me into the kitchen and out onto the patio before entering the guesthouse.

"You need to calm down," he instructed, leaning his hip against the doorway after I'd entered.

"Calm down? Were you not just in there when she told us that she was the one behind the threats? Then to give the absurd reason that she did it because I was out of control? She took it upon herself to turn my life upside down for nothing." I barely had time to suck air into my lungs before I rambled on. "She was always jealous of me, and this was her way to get back at me. I know it."

"Don't you think you're being a little overdramatic about this? Yes, what she did wasn't right," he agreed, "but it seems to me she did it out of love for you."

"How can you justify what she did?"

"I'm not. What I'm saying is that from the time I came on this job, I witnessed some of the things Emily pointed out. Not the sex but—"

"Except for with you."

He sighed. "Except for with me."

The last thing I needed to do right then was reminisce about our time in bed. Therefore, I pushed all memory from my mind. Or at least, I gave it my best effort.

"It's my life and she had no right to butt into it."

Two long strides put Ford right next to me, placing his hands on my shoulders before tipping my head up. "No matter what I say, I'm going to be wrong, so I won't butt in. However, your sister loves you. Even I know that. So, at some point, you're going to have to forgive her. I truly believe what she did was with the best intentions even though sending fake threatening notes to her parents was a little unorthodox." He smiled, but his lips flattened into a straight line when I tried to back away from him.

"So much for you not butting in," I griped. "God! I need a fucking drink."

"Probably not a good idea."

"I need *something* to take the edge off." I backed up a step and looked him over from head to toe, more than once.

Ford looked down at himself, then back to me, frowning. "What? Why are you looking at me like that?" I smirked, then shrugged. "*I'm* the something that'll take the edge off?"

"Sure. Why not?"

I couldn't think of anything better than an orgasm to relax and numb me all at the same time.

CHAPTER
THIRTY-ONE

Ford

The look in Cara's eyes sparked my intrigue and I would love nothing more than to give her exactly what she wanted. But right then, I didn't think sex was the best idea. Not only was Cara using me as a distraction, much like she'd used drugs, alcohol, and I hated to think it, sex with other men, but she refused to deal with the issue with her sister. Much like she refused to deal with what happened to her all those years back.

She snaked her arms around my neck and leaned up on her tiptoes, kissing me before I could back away. All I wanted to do was throw her on the couch, hike up her dress, and rip her panties off before driving my cock so deep inside her, every neighbor she had would hear her screams. And there wasn't anyone around for miles.

"Cara," I whispered against her mouth, "we can't do this right now." I unhooked her fingers and lowered her arms to her sides, regretting it immediately. My dick was painfully hard, and because of my hasty rejection of her advances, I'd be taking care of it myself.

"Why? You don't want to fuck me?" she asked, raising the bottom of her dress so I could see the sheer lace panties underneath. She turned around before I could answer, and I saw she wore a thong, her round ass begging for either my hand or my mouth, or both.

"You know I do." I stood stock still. "What if either of them comes in here? What, then? Besides, we don't have a condom, and seeing as how Emily is pregnant, I doubt my brother has any in his room."

Cara lowered her dress, and a mixture of disappointment and relief spiraled through me. Seconds later, though, she grabbed my hand and pulled me into the downstairs bathroom, shutting the door before I could react.

"Then we'll do it in here and be quick and quiet."

"What about the condom?"

"I'm on the pill, and before you say anything else, I'm clean. I may have done some stupid shit in my past, but I wasn't that reckless."

"I can't believe I'm saying this, but I don't think—"

Cara unbuttoned the top button to my pants and yanked them down along with my boxer briefs before I finished speaking.

"Are you clean?" she asked, wrapping her fingers around my cock and squeezing.

With hitched breath, I replied, "Yes." I'd never been that reckless before either. The last time I had sex with someone without a condom was with my high school girlfriend, Jessica. And she'd been a virgin.

"Then stop overthinking this and fuck me," she demanded. She removed her hand and turned toward the mirror, leaning over and resting her forearms on the counter. With her heels still on, she was at the perfect height. "Any day now, Ford." She pushed her ass against me. Enticing me. Driving me insane.

When I caught her gaze in the reflection, I faltered. Unshed tears pooled in her eyes, and although she tempted me, my God, how she tempted me, I realized having sex right then would be a mistake. A Band-Aid for the real issue.

Cara was furious and hurt, as was apparent when she struck Emily. A part of me understood her anger, but a part of me also understood why Emily felt she had to go to such lengths. She tried to protect her sister, and although she chose to go about it in one of the most extreme ways, I couldn't fault her for her concern for Cara. Maybe if I'd gone to such lengths, Julia would be alive today.

After I pulled my pants back up, I turned Cara to face me. "I don't want to have sex like this."

"What do you mean?"

"You have a lot going on right now and you need to deal with it. In the right way. Not by sleeping with me just because you want to forget about what your sister told you, or about...." My words trailed off, hesitant to say the word even though she was smart enough to understand what I was leading up to.

"Or... what I told you last night? What you forced me to tell you?"

"I didn't force you to tell me anything."

"Yes, you did," she shot back, reaching for the handle to pull the door open.

"I can't do this anymore with you." I followed her out of the bathroom, almost slamming into her when she whipped around to face me.

"Then, leave. No one is holding a gun to your head, Ford. You're not here against your will. Besides, my dad is gonna fire you anyway, so you may as well beat him to it." She rambled on and her sudden attitude confused me.

I reached for her, but she backed away. "I meant the back and forth we get ourselves caught up in. Tit for tat. It's too much. It's exhausting. Aren't you tired?"

Cara didn't answer; instead, she plopped down on the couch. After a tense filled moment, she blurted, "I feel like I'm stuck. I can't go back over there because I don't want to see Emily right now."

"Then, just stay here," I offered.

"Why?"

"What do you mean why?" I took the seat beside her, angling my body so we faced each other.

"You just told me I exhausted you. So why would you want me to stay with you?" *This woman.*

"What I said was that the constant back and forth between us is exhausting. You throw up this barrier whenever you feel like it and there's no getting through. And before you say anything, I know I do the same thing. Although, I don't think as bad as you," I mumbled, half grinning when her eyes widened.

She crossed her arms and leaned back. "What am I gonna do?" Her question seemed more rhetorical than not, but I answered, nonetheless.

"You'll hang out here until you decide." She looked at me, a fresh batch of unshed tears waiting to be released, but she managed to keep them at bay for the time being.

There was something I wanted to talk to Cara about, and even though I knew the topic wasn't going to be well received, I had to bring it up again. While I couldn't imagine the horror she lived through and continued to deal with today, I truly believed that if she was able to lean on her family, their support could make all the difference.

"You look like you want to say something." She bumped my leg with hers, having no idea that her somewhat relaxed expression would twist into something else in a few short seconds.

I debated on whether to move closer or move back to give

her more space. In the end, I couldn't decide so I stayed put. "I think that if you tell your family what happened to you, they'll understand."

In a flash, she shot off the sofa and was across the room before I could blink. "Understand what exactly?" Her tone was calm but her expression was pained. "Why I'm such a fuckup?"

I stood but never moved, hoping the space gave her some sort of solace. Or maybe delusion had become my friend. Either way, I stayed frozen in place.

"You're not a fuckup, Cara. But if they knew, then they'd understand why you've acted out all these years."

"Are you some sort of psychiatrist now? Because the last I knew, you were just my security detail." Her words hit a mark I wasn't sure she intended. Or maybe she did. I was man enough to admit that they stung a little, being reduced to nothing more than the hired help, which in essence was true. But I refused to snip back or get angry and say something just as callous because that wasn't the point of our conversation.

"I'm the only person you've told, right?" I asked, choosing to ignore her harsh comment. I took a tentative step forward, against my better judgment. "Right?" I repeated when she re-fused to answer. If I wasn't staring so intently at her, I would've missed the slight nod she gave me. "That's an unbelievable bur-den. A weight no one should carry alone."

If ever I witnessed another person's anguish before, it was nothing compared to Cara's. With slumped shoulders and the look of despair hiding behind her beautiful blue eyes, all I wanted to do was take back my words. Erase any trace of the past whatsoever.

Right in that moment, between the past and the future, the space where all decisions lay, I realized I needed to follow my own damn advice. I stood in front of Cara and dished out advice, telling her she needed to deal with what happened, lean on her family for support. But what had I done after Julia died? I blamed myself. I refused to lean on my family, the same people who were hurting just as much as me. I should've been there for my mother, who'd lost her daughter, and for Owen, but I'd been selfish, wallowing so deeply in my own grief I couldn't see past the tragedy.

A lonely sob sliced through the air and tore me away from my revelation.

"I can't," she whispered, the tears she'd managed to keep contained slipping down her cheeks. There was no hesitancy on my part as I rushed forward and pulled her close, kissing the top of her head right before she wrapped her arms around me.

I couldn't take away her pain.

I couldn't erase the memory of what happened.

I couldn't force her to move past the rape, if that was even at all possible.

All I could do was gift her my strength and comfort.

We stood in the middle of the living room for the next several minutes. Quiet except for the sounds of Cara's gripping sadness.

Her uncertainty.

My support.

As we pulled apart, and my mouth opened to dive back into trying to convince her to talk to her family, Owen pushed open the door and walked in. His eyes bounced from me to Cara, coming to rest back on me with a question laced in his stare.

Cara stood close enough that my fingers brushed hers right before she walked past my brother to leave.

"I'm going to shower and get ready," she said, leaving before I could ask where we were going.

Once she left, I glared at my brother, although the only difference between what he and I did was that he somehow managed to get Emily pregnant. Not only would there be no denying their relationship, but once Walter found out they'd been sleeping together, almost the entire time, he'd be furious, and rightly so. Never mind the kind of shit he could rain down on our business.

"Where are you two going?" he asked, attempting to be casual when I knew damn well he wanted to either talk about what was going on with Emily or yell at me again for punching him.

"Do I ever know?" I snarked, heading into the kitchen for something to drink. A nice shot of whiskey would've been a blessing right then, but I needed a clear head. Besides, I was working, although I wasn't sure for how much longer.

CHAPTER
THIRTY-TWO

Cara

"I know, I'm still kind of freaking out over the whole thing." Lying on my stomach, I positioned my cell phone close to me, the device on speaker so I didn't have to hold it. "Thank you again for telling him about me."

"You can stop thanking me, woman." Steph laughed. "I'd be doing the world a disservice if I didn't tell James about you. Besides, you're the one who impressed him enough for him to want to see more."

"I suppose." I repositioned myself so I laid on my back, placing my cell on my chest. "I'm just nervous he'll second-guess himself and just forget he even met me."

"He's not like that. If he told you he likes your stuff, then believe him." I heard someone in the background, but the voice was muffled, almost as if she had put her hand over the phone.

"You know a lot about him, don't you?" I sat upright, as if being in that position would make my friend spill all the dirty details. Silence was her only response, and when she remained closemouthed, I suspected she wasn't telling me the whole story. Or even a fraction of it. "Are you two together?"

"No," she blurted. "Well, not really." An exaggerated sigh from her, and she then said, "I don't know."

"I'm glad you could clear that up." I laughed, feeling good I was able to take my mind off everything that happened earlier. My friendship with Steph had always come easy, and even though we'd lost touch for a while, it was like no time had passed. I would've thought that her being the daughter of my rapist would make me cringe every time I heard her voice, or read her texts, or even saw her in person, but somehow, I was able to separate the two. I didn't dive into the reasons why, but I refused to allow that bastard to steal one more thing away from me.

"We enjoy each other's company."

"I'm sure you do. He's a hottie."

"Yes, he's attractive," she agreed. "But he's so much more. I've never met anyone like him before." Her voice trailed off, and again I heard someone speaking in the background. Then it dawned on me that James might be the someone who was there with her.

"Are you with him right now?" I asked, lowering my voice as if he could possibly hear me.

"Yes. He's in the other room so I'm gonna get off the phone. But we'll catch up when I'm back in town, okay? Maybe grab something to eat? I want to hear everything."

"I'm sure your boyfriend can fill you in," I teased.

"Oh Lord." She chuckled before telling me she'd call me soon. The moment our call ended, Naomi's name popped up on my screen. I answered on the second ring.

"I was just going to call you," I said, needing to talk to her. "Can you grab a drink tonight?"

"That's why I called. Well, one of the reasons."

"What's going on?" I detected something in her voice, but couldn't determine if she was upset or not.

"I'll tell you when I see you. I'm actually in Long Island. Do you want me to come there, or do you want to meet here?"

"I can come there. Just text me where you want to meet."

"Will do. There's this restaurant I really like. Do you mind if we go there instead of a club? I'd like to hear myself think for a change."

"Only twenty-five and already you're getting old."

"I'm twenty-six, and yes, I certainly feel much older."

"Next you'll be saying you have to get to bed early because you have a busy day coming up." What started off as a joke on my end ended up being her reality.

"Wait till I tell you all about it."

"Can't wait."

Hanging up the phone, I tossed it on the bed next to me and closed my eyes. Even though it was barely six in the evening, I was suddenly exhausted. My day had been filled with nerves, anticipation, excitement, shock, betrayal, anger, sadness, and every other freaking emotion known to man.

I must've fallen asleep, because the next thing I knew, Ford was next to me, tapping my leg to wake me.

"I thought you were taking a shower." He looked me over from head to toe, his eyes stopping on my upper thighs. The skirt of my black dress had ridden up when I'd laid down and I'd never bothered to fix it.

I cleared my throat, and he looked up at me, smirking because I'd caught him staring. He shrugged before walking toward my bathroom, closing the door once he was inside. I heard the water running, then the flush of the toilet. He re-emerged moments later, drying off his hands before tossing the towel onto the sink behind him.

"You all good now?" I asked, sitting up and dangling my legs over my bed.

"Yeah."

"Do you need to take a shower while you're at it? Cause I can wait while you use my bathroom again," I said with a straight face.

"Does that bother you?" He frowned.

The need to rile him had morphed from trying to get under his skin to teasing, and I had to say that I preferred the latter. Less ramifications involved.

"Relax." I hopped off the bed and headed toward the same place he'd just came out of. "I'm not serious." He swatted my ass as I passed him, and I squealed. Before I could shut the door, he pushed me inside and up against the vanity, much like we'd been in the guesthouse restroom.

"What are you doing?"

"What I wish I could whenever I wanted." He coaxed my lips open with the tip of his tongue, and I lost myself to his kiss. All the events of the day faded away as our breath mingled, and our mouths melded together. Before we took it further, however, he pulled back and leaned against the wall.

"Why did you stop?" I reached for him, but he grabbed my hand before I could touch him. He wore an odd expression, and for the life of me, I couldn't read him, but then again, I never could.

The way his eyes penetrated the tough exterior I showed the world made my heart skip a beat.

"I'm conflicted," he confessed.

"About?"

"About you. I just can't stop thinking about what happened to you."

"I'm not going to break, Ford. I've lived through it." I pulled my hand back from his, curled my fingers into my palm, and rested my fist in the middle of my chest. "It's over."

"But it's not," he argued, running his hand through his hair.

"Why do you care so much? What happened to me doesn't involve you in any way." I waited for his answer, but it never came. Instead, his teeth worked over his bottom lip and his shoulders slumped.

Then the missing piece slid into place.

The topic had proved to be sensitive, a source of pain and hurt whenever it had been broached, which because of his reaction had not been often. Placing my palm on the side of his face, I stroked my thumb over the trimmed hair on his jaw.

"You're thinking maybe something similar happened to Julia. That's why she got involved with drugs in the first place." His pupils darkened at the mention of the possibility, but he didn't pull away from me. He didn't yell, and he didn't deny anything.

My past collided with his. Too many unanswered questions that would never be resolved. And that was one of the hardest parts of all this. The not knowing why or blaming oneself for not handling the situation differently in the first place. So many what-ifs, a person could drive themselves crazy if they allowed them to fester for too long.

"Maybe if I pushed her for answers, I could've saved her." His sullen voice filled with regret, each syllable he spoke heartbreaking.

"Maybe. Or maybe it wouldn't have made a bit of difference. The shitty thing is that you'll never know." I removed my hand from his face only to squeeze his hand. "I can only imagine how hard this is for you, but I'm not your responsibility."

"Technically, you are."

"You know what I mean."

He released a sigh. "I know."

We stood there staring at each other for what seemed like an hour, but in reality, it was mere seconds. There was so much more I wanted to say, but never had the chance to voice because my phone dinged with an incoming text.

I walked away from Ford and into my bedroom to retrieve my cell. Glancing at the screen, I saw that Naomi had messaged me the restaurant name and address, along with the time she'd be there, which was an hour and forty minutes from now.

Rushing back into the bathroom, I turned on the faucet to warm up the water. "I only have forty minutes to get ready." I flitted about the small space, but Ford didn't move a muscle. "Are you going to watch while I shower?" While the thought thrilled me, I knew it wasn't a good idea.

He looked like he wanted to respond, but instead just left, closing the door behind him.

It seemed that every time Ford and I discussed anything, there was no resolution. No end. No final decision.

Being in limbo had become my new norm.

CHAPTER
THIRTY-THREE

Cara

"Sorry I'm late." I scooted into the booth Naomi had chosen and placed my purse next to me. "Were you waiting long?"

The ride there had been mostly silent, idle chitchat about the weather breaking up the quiet. I wanted to say much more, and I got the feeling Ford did, as well, but neither of us took the lead. He walked off toward the bar after I sat down, and in true Ford fashion, he situated himself where he could keep an eye on me. Close but far enough away to give me and my friend a bit of privacy.

"Only five minutes. No big deal." Her strained smile told me she had a lot on her mind, and there was no time like the present to dive right in. I missed confiding in her, and although I had so much to tell her, she looked like she needed to bend my ear first.

Before she started, though, I had to compliment her on her new hair. "Loving the new look." She normally wore her hair past her shoulder and wavy, but the cut was an angled lob, or long bob, and styled poker straight. The style brought more attention to her pale green eyes and her pronounced cheekbones. Naomi was a beautiful woman, and unlike me, hadn't used her looks, or her money for that matter, to get ahead. She worked her ass off in college to get her MBA and was now working at the firm of her choice. Although she was only entry level, being the CEO's assistant, she said it was at least a foot in the door.

"Thanks, but apparently, it was just one more thing for him to be suspicious about." Our waitress approached before she could elaborate. We placed an order for red wine and an appetizer, glancing over the menu to decide on dinner.

"What do you mean?" I finally asked, curious about her cryptic comment.

Naomi sighed and leaned against the back of her seat, looking defeated before a single word left her mouth. Her demeanor told me everything, and one glass of wine wasn't going to cut it.

"When I cut my hair, Benji accused me of doing it for Steele."

"Who the hell is Steele?"

"My boss."

"That's his name? His real name? Please tell me he's good-lookin' because if his parents named him Steele and he's like five-foot-two and chubby, I'm gonna die."

"Let's just say his parents named him well. The image you would have of someone named Steele would fit perfectly." She took a sip of her drink. "He's handsome, but that's not the point. The point is that Benji didn't trust me."

Naomi had always been a one-man type of woman. She'd never had a one-night stand, and although she could party with the best of them, she was selective about who she chose to date. Unlike me.

"What do you mean 'didn't'? Don't you mean *doesn't*?" I looked at her hand and noticed she still wasn't wearing a ring. Benji had asked her to marry him a short time ago, and it looked like she still hadn't said yes.

"We broke up."

I reached across the table and covered her hand with mine. "I'm sorry. I know how much you cared about him." For some reason, my eyes flitted toward Ford, and of course, he was watching me. I flashed him a quick smile before turning my attention back to Naomi.

"I did. After he proposed the first time, he asked again a week later, to which I gave him the same answer. That we hadn't been together long enough to make that kind of commitment. Then when I got hired as Steele's assistant, something switched in him."

"Such as?" It was wrong to feel this way, but having someone else deal with a shitty circumstance made me... not happy, per se, but content to share the misfortune.

"He waited for me in the lobby after my first day, and I just so happened to be leaving the same time as my new boss. We stepped off the elevator together, laughing at something he said. Benji immediately walked up to me and grabbed my hand, smiling at me but tightening his grip the longer Steele stood next to us. Of course, I introduced the two of them, and right before I said that Benji was my boyfriend, he cut me off and said I was his fiancée." Naomi's anger over the situation intensified the more details she gave me.

Our waitress approached with the salmon croquettes appetizer, but I was too invested in her story to grab one right away. But she wasn't, snatching two and placing them on her plate. It was then I remembered Naomi fell into the category of a stress eater, even though I had no idea where she put it because I swore she was just as slim as she was in high school. I was close to my weight from years ago, although my ass had gotten a bit rounder since then.

Between bites, she continued her story. "When Steele finally left, Benji released my hand and stalked off, leaving me to follow him, confused as to what just happened."

"Had he ever acted like that before?"

"No. And I'd been around different guys before. It was just weird. I chalked it up to me not accepting his proposal. That maybe he was feeling insecure about our relationship. Anyway, things just got worse. He'd act pissy whenever my boss texted me, strictly about work, mind you, and he about lost his mind when I told him that I had to accompany Steele to California for business. The trip was only for two days, but Benji acted like I told him I fucked my boss, which was essentially what he accused me of anyway."

"Oh my God. I don't know what to say."

"Now you know how I feel. It was like a switch flipped inside him. Every day he accused me of something. Either I was going to the gym because I was trying to look good for my boss, or I bought a new dress to look sexy for him or," she pointed to her head, "getting a new haircut." She finished the rest of her drink and signaled to our waitress for a refill. "Do you want another one?" she asked, pointing to my glass.

"I'm still nursing this one."

"I see." She pursed her lips. "What's going on?"

I quickly looked at Ford before turning my eyes back to her. "What do you mean?"

"First off, you keep looking over at him." I didn't bother to ask who she was referring to because that would have been pointless. "Secondly, you'd normally be starting your second glass by now."

"We haven't been here that long." I skipped over responding to her first observation.

"Precisely."

Trying to explain why I wasn't drinking more was an odd feat, seeing as how in the not-so-distant past, I had to justify the opposite. "I'm just not feeling it, that's all. Besides, I'm more interested in this story. So please continue."

I thought perhaps my friend would argue, but she dove back in, picking up right where she left off.

"Last week was the final straw." I leaned in so as not to miss a word. "Benji showed up at my job. I was walking back into the building after lunch, coincidently at the same time my boss returned, and there he was, giving the security guard a hard time because he wouldn't let him pass. As soon as Benji saw me and Steele, he lost his shit. He even got up in Steele's face, threatening him."

"Oh my God," I repeated, all the while shaking my head in disbelief.

"Needless to say, Steele had Benji thrown out, and I broke up with him later that same night."

"How are you handling everything? How did Benji take it? Not good, I'm sure."

"Not at all. He kept apologizing, said he would change, that he wouldn't act so jealous if I just took him back."

"And?"

"And what? I'm not going to continue to be with someone who frightens me." I opened my mouth, but she must've known what I was going to ask because her next words answered my impending question. "I'm all for second chances, for giving people the benefit of the doubt, but the look in his eyes when he went after Steele scared me. It was as if he wasn't in control of himself. I don't know what's going on with him, but I'm happy he showed his true colors now and not a year into the marriage."

"True," I agreed.

"Anyway, Steele was concerned about me, as well, so now he meets me in the parking garage in the morning and walks me to my car at the end of the night." Naomi smiled, and there was something about her grin that made me curious.

"Do you like him?"

"Who? My boss?" The inflection in her voice and the way she shifted in her seat told me everything.

"You do!"

"I don't," she argued. "Sure, he's good looking and success-ful and smart and sweet and—" Once she realized how much she was going on about her boss, she clamped her mouth shut. "I didn't do anything with him or lead him on or flirt with him while I was with Benji."

"I know. You're too good for your own good." I laughed.

Once our dinners arrived, I looked over at Ford once more, seeing if he was eating, as well. He nursed a glass of clear liquid, no doubt water or soda, and munched on a plate of salsa and chips.

"What's going on there?" Naomi asked, waving her hand between me and Ford, and not subtly, I might add.

"Nothing," I lied.

"You keep glancing over there and smiling at him. The last time I knew you hated him. Now look at you, all flirty smiles and stuff." She shoved a forkful of her pasta dish in her mouth, her attention on me the entire time.

"I'm not flirting." I took a bite of my chicken. "He's just rubbed off on me, I guess."

"Or do you mean that he's rubbed up against you?" She wig-gled her brows and chuckled.

I was mid-swallow and what she said made me choke.

And exactly like last time, Ford was behind me before I realized he'd gotten up from his seat. Only this time, I didn't mind the warmth of his hand when he patted my back.

I held up a hand when I'd caught my breath. "I'm okay. Thanks." I looked up at him and smiled. Again.

"Are you sure?" he asked.

"Yeah."

"Do you want to join us?" Naomi suddenly asked, but before I could contemplate if that was a good idea or not, leaning more toward not because there were some things I wanted to still discuss with my bestie, he answered.

"Thank you, but I am fine where I'm at." Ford curtly nodded and returned to his seat.

"I'm gonna kill you."

"Why? If I thought Steele was hot, Ford is otherworldly. How do you not jump on him every time he's near? And those eyes. Good God, I could stare into them for the rest of my life."

"Well, someone's feeling better," I pointed out, amused by her rant but also feeling somewhat possessive over Ford. I told myself not to do it, but I looked over at him.

"I knew it," Naomi blurted. "You slept with him."

"Would you lower your voice, please?" I reached over the table and smacked her hand. "No, I didn't."

"You did."

I started off shaking my head in denial, but it turned into a vigorous nod before I could stop myself. "Fuck. Fine. Yes, we slept together, but it was only the one time."

"Not good enough to go back for more? Because that would be a shame." Naomi turned to look at Ford, then back to me.

"It was good. Better than I thought it would be." Several

heartbeats passed before I confessed, "It was the best sex I'd ever had, and I can't stop thinking about it."

"Then, what's the problem?"

"Well, first off, I don't think my dad would take kindly to the fact that the guy he hired to protect me got me into bed. But then again, he didn't get me pregnant, so there's a win."

"Why would you say that of all things?" Naomi knew me better than most, so she knew when I tried to evade suspicion, as well as when I really wanted to explain, even though I'd say I didn't.

"Don't leave me hanging, woman. I told you all about my shit show of a life. The least you could do is reciprocate."

I relaxed against my seat, although I felt anything but. I was desperate for a moment to try and figure out what to tell her as well as how much.

"There's just so much going on."

"Do we need another drink for this?"

"Maybe two," I corrected.

As soon as our glasses had been refilled, I dove head first into everything I wanted to divulge to my best friend. Everything from the meeting with James Hollen, which started off things in a good way, to finding out that Emily was pregnant with Owen's baby, to my sister revealing that she was the one behind the threatening notes.

I didn't mention my biggest secret, though, because I wasn't ready to deal with the barrage of questions or the pity I'd surely see in her eyes when she looked at me from here on out. Besides, as soon as I uttered that I'd been raped all those years back, the shame, confusion, regret, and anger would resurface, as if they weren't already hiding in the shadows.

The honest truth was, it was better to live with my secret than to free it and be left more vulnerable than before.

CHAPTER
THIRTY-FOUR

Cara

The emotional strength it took to process all that I'd revealed to Naomi the night prior was enough to dredge up another headache. I had no idea where to go from here, but it wasn't completely up to me. For once, Emily would have to be the one to deal with the consequences of her actions. Her choices were the ones that brought about the shit storm that was now brewing. Not only had her decisions altered her life forever because of the pregnancy, but they'd altered mine, as well.

As I stood near the counter in Blush, waiting for Audrey to bring me a swatch of material, I couldn't help but think that the Massey men being in our lives, even while under false pretenses, hadn't been the worst thing to ever happen. I said that looking back on the situation. If the subject had been broached when they first arrived, I'd had a much different opinion.

"This is the one I wanted to show you," Audrey said, coming around the corner with a bundle in her hand, swiping a strand of her jet black hair out of her face. She'd been raving about the sample she'd received from her manufacturer and wanted to let me see it in case I chose to use it for any of my designs.

Audrey and I had started off as designer slash boutique owner and customer, but our relationship had morphed into a friendship. I viewed her as a mentor more than anything. She'd been designing for the past ten years and had a lot of knowledge and advice to offer me, and I soaked up every bit.

There was a hint of shimmer to the thick dark material, and every time she moved it, the glint would catch my eye. I could only imagine what it would look like with the sun highlighting the subtle sparkle.

"I love this." The fabric glided through my fingertips.

Her ice blue eyes shone brightly while she watched me. "Me too."

As we talked about the price and amount I may need for a few ideas I had, Ford paced near me, texting someone and looking none too happy.

"Everything okay?" I asked, catching his eye.

"No." It wasn't his one-word answer, but instead his tone when he said it. From what I knew of Ford, he wasn't the type of man to give off a questionable vibe, one who was unsure of anything. He was confident and sure of himself, so to hear the slightest tremble in his voice put me on alert. I didn't know if being around him so often had made it easier to pick up on the subtle nuances, but either way, the hairs on the back of my neck bristled.

Politely excusing myself, I walked up next to him, the crease between his eyes deepening with every second that passed.

"What's going on?" I tried to peer at his phone, but he finished his text and shut down the screen.

"We gotta go."

"Why?"

"Because your parents are at the house." He didn't wait for my reaction before he headed toward the exit. Once I was near, he grabbed my hand and led me outside, opening the door for me and waiting until I was situated inside before walking around to the other side.

Once he folded himself inside the driver seat, I asked, "Do they know?" Trapping the air in my lungs, I contemplated all the ways the remainder of the day would go. Everything rested on his answer.

Would I never see him again after today? If that was truly the case, how did I feel about that? I was no longer worried about my father putting a halt to my dating life, and I was sure if Ford and I wanted to continue our relationship, there wasn't a damn thing he could do about it. If he threatened to cut me off again, I'd call his bluff. Besides, I now had a plan for my life moving forward. One that would hopefully one day prove lucrative.

"All Owen would tell me was to get home as soon as possible."

"Shit!"

"Exactly," he mumbled before pulling out into the street and taking the exit up ahead, driving slower than normal.

I grabbed my cell and texted Emily, asking her if she'd told Mom and Dad anything yet, but she never responded. Either she ignored my messages, or she was in full-disclosure mode with our parents. Either way, my anxiety about what was to come intensified.

Ford was silent the entire ride back, and because I had no idea what to say, my thoughts sporadic and jumbled, I kept my lips sealed.

The moment we approached the driveway, my pulse raced. Did Emily ask them to come over, or did they happen to just pop in?

Was she going to confess being behind the threats?

Would they understand her reasoning for deceiving them?

Would she tell them she was pregnant, or save that revelation for another time?

If she did let that secret slip, Ford and Owen would be gone immediately.

After Ford put the vehicle in Park, he shut off the engine and reached over to grab my hand.

"No matter what happens, we'll talk."

There was no time for me to ask him to clarify just what he meant by that before the front door opened, my sister standing on the threshold and waving us inside.

As I reached for the handle, I suddenly felt hot and dizzy, my stomach churning at the thoughts of what was going to happen once we walked into the house. I wasn't in trouble, because for once, I hadn't done anything wrong or questionable, other than sleeping with Ford. But I considered that act neither wrong nor questionable. Besides, no one knew, and I planned on keeping it that way.

Ford walked a pace behind me as we approached the front porch, Emily still standing in the doorway. Still angry with what she'd done, there was a small part of me that was grateful, though, because Ford would've never come into my life otherwise. I wondered if she felt the same about Owen, now that her life had been flipped upside down.

I wanted to say something to her, but I couldn't bring myself to speak, so instead, Ford asked the question for me. "Why are your parents here?"

"I called them."

I took over, pushing any reservation I had about having a conversation with her. "Did you tell them anything yet?"

"No. I was waiting for you."

"How kind," I said, sarcasm slicing both words apart. I

brushed past her and into the foyer, turning into the living room seconds later. Both my parents were seated, but as soon as my dad saw me, he rose from the couch and walked over.

"What's going on?" he asked, looking from me to Emily, who had walked up behind me. Ford trudged across the room and stood next to Owen, near the corner. They looked like they were simply giving our family the space they needed, melding into the background, so to speak. "Your mother and I are worried something bad happened." He looked toward the brothers. "Did something bad happen?"

"Depends on what you classify as bad," Ford answered, his coded answer doing nothing to exterminate the tension, which slowly built in the room.

"What does that mean?" my dad asked. For once, I wouldn't be the one to cause him any sort of distress, and because I was in the clear this time, I sauntered past him to take a seat next to my mom.

Emily, on the other hand, headed toward Owen, stopping only when there was a mere foot of distance between them.

"I have something to tell you both." Emily's eyes were pinned to my parents. "Before I start, I know what I did was beyond the scope of rational, but I felt like I didn't have another choice." She glanced at me before looking back to them. "Because I was worried...." Her voice quivered, and for a split second, I thought she was going to make something up, anything but the truth. But she found her voice again and parted her lips. "There's no easy way to say this so..." My pulse drummed in my ear, the hands of the grandfather clock against the wall sounding louder than ever before. "I was the one who sent the notes," she finally blurted.

"What notes?" my mother asked, never suspecting her own daughter could be behind the threats, the mere mention of notes had to be something else entirely. I was sure that was what she was thinking because it was what I thought when she first told me.

"The threats." She blinked several times, watching my parents' expression switch three times in the span of seconds. My dad was more expressive, the crease between his brows disappearing before he widened his eyes. Then his expression blanked.

"I don't understand." His head flinched back slightly. "Emily, what the hell are you talking about?" The moment my sister's words clicked, he lowered himself to the couch to sit next to my mom. He leaned forward and dropped his head before looking back up at Emily. "Sit," he demanded, his voice eerily calm.

He was angry, there was no question, but the fact he learned his near-perfect daughter could do something like this had to tug at his confusion. Surely, he had to be baffled beyond reason. If I'd been the one to reveal such a thing, I had no doubt he would've started yelling minutes earlier, but instead, he waited for Emily to reveal the details.

She looked at me from the corner of her eye before diving right in. I remembered the excuse she gave me, and while I'd been too angered to stand there and listen to whatever else she wanted to say, I was curious how in-depth she'd go with my parents.

Emily concocted this absurd plan because she said she was worried about me and what I'd been doing with my life. How I'd chosen to conduct myself. So, to have to sit there and listen to her divulge her worry to my parents about me, in front of me, was certainly an odd situation.

My sister opened her mouth to speak, closing her eyes for a moment before starting. "Like I said, I did it because I was worried about Cara. I thought that if you thought she was in some sort of danger," she said, looking directly at my father, "you'd do something about it. I'm not going to get into specifics, but every time she left the house, I feared she'd end up doing something that would seriously hurt her."

"Don't you think you're being a bit dramatic?" I asked, my anger quickly resurfacing. I hated being judged and felt that everyone there was doing just that.

"I'm really not." Emily's attention was solely on me now. "Every time we went out, you got blasted, mixing in who only knows what because you wanted to have fun. I can't tell you how many times I had to drag you out of places because you could barely stand, let alone defend yourself if some rando decided he wanted to get with you. And don't even get me started on the number of guys you took off with, leaving me alone to fend for myself on how to get home."

Her mention of other men prickled my fury, mixing in a bit of shame for good measure. I briefly made eye contact with Ford, but instead of seeing disgust on his face, I saw a flicker of understanding. He gave me a tight grin before looking away.

"I never asked you to help me," I barked, feeling attacked. "You should've left me alone and got a life of your own."

She flinched, but continued. "How could I have a life of my own when I was constantly worried you would end up getting attacked, or worse… killed?" Now, I was the one who flinched because she had no idea her fear for me had come true when we were still kids. "I couldn't. You're my sister and I love you. I'm going to try and help you even when you don't want it or think that you need it. And I'm sorry," she said, turning her focus back onto our parents, "about the way I chose to handle things, but I didn't know what else to do."

"Why didn't you come to us and tell us all this?" my mom

asked, shaking her head because she was probably still trying to wrap her head around everything.

"Because I wasn't going to rat on Cara."

"But you'd send fake and threatening notes, worry us half to death in the process, and be saddled with security watching your every move? Knowing the whole time that their presence was unnecessary?" Our dad stood and walked behind the sofa and started to pace, his head down the entire time he strode back and forth.

Emily didn't have an answer for him, glancing back at Owen repeatedly.

"I don't even know what to say," our mom whispered.

"Me either," our dad agreed.

As I did my best to take everything in, struggling with trying to understand how worried she must've been to go to such lengths, I couldn't help but be thankful that she hadn't ended up going to my parents about me. She handled it in her own way. A weird, fucked-up way, but hers, nonetheless.

"Let me ask you this," I said, leaning against the couch and crossing my legs. "How the hell did you ever expect for this whole charade to end since you were the one behind it? Did you think Dad would just forget about it after you stopped sending the notes? Or were you going to continue to send them until he got so freaking paranoid that he locked us both away from society altogether." My words were laden with sarcasm, but I couldn't hold my tongue, not that anyone had ever accused me of doing so.

She looked down at her hands clasped in front of her and said something, but her voice was entirely too low for any of us to hear.

"Speak up, sis, because we'd all love to know." This little sit down had gone from Emily telling my parents she was behind the notes, to a recap of my bad behavior, and if there was the slightest chance for me to bring it back around, I had to ask her the obvious question and take the focus back off me.

She shrugged. "I didn't think that far ahead." At least she had the decency to appear embarrassed.

"And *you're* the smart and responsible one," I chastised.

"No one said you weren't smart, Cara," she corrected. "But you were definitely acting irresponsibly. You constantly threw caution to the wind, acting like nothing bad could ever happen to you."

The words bubbled up in my throat and tears welled in my eyes, the need to shout something back at her too great to hold back.

"Something bad did happen!" I yelled but composed myself enough that I didn't blurt out that I'd been raped. My brain furiously worked to form some sort of retort that wouldn't make any of them suspicious. I looked to Ford and drew strength from him, wanting nothing more than to run to him and drag him from the room before I said anymore. "This entire fiasco happened."

"Jesus Christ," I heard my dad mutter. I had no idea how this conversation was going to end, but what I did know was that it wasn't quite over yet. If she wanted to confess, then I'd make sure she told our parents all *her* secrets, whether she was ready to or not.

I felt attacked and vulnerable, and whenever I found myself in that sort of predicament, I lashed out. "Isn't there something else you have to tell them?" I asked, smirking more than I should. "Something they need to know before you can't hide it anymore?"

Emily gasped while Owen's eyes widened. I dared not look at Ford for fear he'd stare at me with disapproval. I realized why I pushed her to reveal her pregnancy well before she appeared ready to do so, but seconds after I asked her my question, I regretted doing so. The sooner my parents found out that Owen was the one responsible, the quicker both men would be relieved from their duty. Although, to be fair, my dad would no longer require their services going forward anyway, seeing as how there was no real threat. Other than me... to myself, apparently.

My sister shook her head, looking to our parents, then back to me. She cleared her throat but refused to speak. I didn't have to prompt her to answer my question because our dad spoke up.

"What's going on?" he asked, stepping forward until he stood a few feet from Emily. Owen shifted from foot to foot, and I actually felt bad for him, even though I'd been the one to open up this proverbial can of worms. "What else do you have to tell your mother and me?"

"Why don't you sit down, sir," Owen suggested, clearing his throat after he spoke.

"I think I'll stay right here."

Ford stepped away from his brother and approached me, extending his hand for me to take. "I think we need to give them some privacy." I wasn't sure whether I wanted to leave before she told them about the baby, but I wasn't sure if I wanted to stay either. And because I couldn't land one way or the other, I stayed seated. Ford dropped his hand to his side and moved to stand by the edge of the couch.

"You're starting to worry us, honey." Our mom rose from the sofa and flanked her husband on his left side. "Did something happen? Are you in trouble?"

"You can say that," I blurted, snapping my lips shut when

Ford tapped my shoulder. My parents' attention remained on Emily, and the longer she took to tell them what was going on, I feared the worse their response would be, as if their reaction wasn't going to be explosive to begin with. Well, our dad's, at least.

Emily's lips parted while her hand rested over her belly. "I'm pregnant," she finally confessed, taking a single step backward, closer to Owen. They looked to be a united front of sorts.

"But that's impossible. You're not allowed to date anyone while..." He waved his hand in the air as if to dismiss the rest of what he was going to say. "And I know you wouldn't go against my wishes. So... how are you—"

I counted the seconds until he realized that the man standing behind his daughter was the father of her baby.

Ford was next to Owen a second later. "I know this is a shock to you both. The news threw us, too," Owen said.

"Us?" My mother reached for my sister's hand, but my father stopped her, his posture straightening and coiled with tension.

"How far along are you?" he asked, clenching his right hand into a fist.

Now it was Emily who cleared her throat. "Uh... five weeks," she answered, stumbling over her words.

My mother placed her hand on my dad's arm right before he tried to move toward the man who'd been hired to protect his daughter.

"Did you do this?" He pointed at Owen, and I wished I could take back my words and allow her to tell them in her own time. But there was nothing I could do now except watch the explosion and try and dodge the aftermath.

"Sir, if we could just sit down and talk about—"

"Oh, now you want to show me some sort of respect?" He moved a step closer, encroaching on Emily and Owen's personal space. "I hired you to watch out for her, trusted you with her well-being, and you go and do this? Take advantage of her and get her pregnant?"

"He didn't take advantage of me," Emily cried. "We have feelings for each other."

"He played you, sweetheart. The only thing he wanted to do was get in your pants. And you let him." His tone was laced with disappointment, and right then I knew how Emily felt because I'd been on the receiving end of his displeasure more times than I cared to count.

"It wasn't like that, sir," Owen tried to interject, but before any of us knew what was happening, my dad reached around Emily and snatched Owen's shirt, pulling him to the side and dragging him out of the room. I had no doubt that if Owen wanted to break free, he could've, but he never attempted to try.

The rest of us followed them in half surprise and half expectancy while Owen was dragged into the foyer and pushed against the front door.

"If you ever come near my daughter again, you'll regret it," he spat, turning around and pinning Ford with his glare. "That goes for you, too." He released his grip on Owen and backed away. "Get out of my house! Both of you."

"Dad," Emily cried, coming up behind him. "Please don't do this."

"It's done." He refused to look back at her, keeping his glare on Owen and Ford. While I thought that maybe one of the guys would hesitate and try and reason with him, attempt

S. NELSON

to explain their situation, although Ford didn't have anything to do with Owen and Emily's predicament, Owen opened the door and both Massey men walked out of our house right after they placed our key fobs on the foyer table.

As they pulled away, Owen's car being housed in the last stall after they'd first arrived, warring emotions assaulted me. I bounced between sympathy for Emily's situation, even though I was still upset with her, and thinking that I'd inadvertently stunted whatever relationship Ford and I could've had.

CHAPTER
THIRTY-FIVE

Ford

"Well, that went better than I thought," I acknowledged, surprised as all hell that Walter hadn't tried to attack my brother. I could only imagine the thoughts that ran through that man's mind. I didn't have children of my own, but I'd had a younger sister, so I could attest to the sort of protectiveness that was involved when trying to watch out for her best interest.

Not only had Owen overstepped and slept with Walter's daughter, but he got her pregnant, changing both of their lives forever. Even if she didn't end up keeping the baby, there would always be that link between them.

I had no idea what the two of them planned to do from here on out. They had to have known her father would react like he did, although, he was much tamer than I could've predicted.

"When Emily told them she was behind the threats, or the fact he didn't attack me when your woman made her tell them she's pregnant?" Owen pressed harder on the accelerator.

"Cara is not my woman," I corrected, but even as the words left my mouth, I wasn't entirely sure I'd been speaking the truth. I did have feelings for the woman, but was still confused about how deep they ran.

She'd shared a part of herself she kept hidden from everyone else in her life, and if nothing else, that bond strengthened whatever was developing between us. Again, I'd fail miserably if I tried to put anything into words because I continued to try and figure it out myself.

"All I know is that everything is fucked now and it's all her fault." He babbled on a bit more, but I finally had to shut him down.

"First off, Emily made the decision to send the notes, knowing Walter would do something about it, like any good father would. He proved her right. And she's pregnant because of what you two did together, which has absolutely nothing to do with Cara. So, if you're going to try and blame anyone, blame yourself. Blame Emily. But not Cara."

"Whatever."

"Be mad, Owen. Own it. But just figure it out before it's too late."

I assumed we were headed back to Connecticut where we lived, but when he turned off the interstate a half hour later, I was confused.

"Where are you going?"

"I need to stay close in case she needs me."

"So, what? You're holding me prisoner until you two hatch a plan?" I looked out the window to see if I recognized where we were. Of course, I didn't have a clue because we weren't from around here.

"I don't know what we're gonna do, but I need some time to think. Can you give me that?" His tone was harsh, but his pleading question convinced me not to debate him. This time, at least.

Several miles down the road, we came across what looked like a college, but the sign out front read Miller Manor.

"What is this?" I asked, shifting in my seat.

"A place we can stay for now." He pulled into a spot, turned off the engine, and hopped out of the car before I could ask him for any more details.

"Just give me a few days to work through what I need to, then we can go home." Owen handed me my room key, staring at me much like he did when we were kids and he wanted my approval. And because he was dealing with a heavy load, I agreed with a nod.

"You know where to find me." He disappeared into the room next to mine, the click of his door echoing in the hallway.

Once inside, I stripped off everything but my boxer briefs and headed straight for the bed, dog tired and needing to rest my eyes. It was still early in the day, but it had been a rather long one, and all I wanted to do was forget about everything until I was forced to think about it again.

As I lay there, my mind wouldn't shut off like I hoped it would. So many variables were intricately woven into the near future. My younger brother was going to become a father, if Emily chose to continue the pregnancy. If that was the case, then I'd be an uncle. But how would that work, seeing as how Walter never wanted to see either of us again? And what about Cara and me? Was there an *us* in this equation? Did I want there to be? Even as my brain formed that last question, I knew the answer was yes. Then I had to acknowledge that we lived hours apart from each other, and I had to consider the role my job would play, as well. My next assignment could be clear across the country, the duration unknown. And now that her dream of designing her own line was within reach, she'd be busy, too.

Like I said, too many variables plagued me, fighting the edges of sleep from stealing me under.

But in the end, my body gave up the struggle and I passed out. I wasn't out long, however, before someone woke me by banging on my door.

"Go away," I shouted as best I could, still tired, my voice not as loud as it normally was. More banging. "Fuck." I looked over at the bedside clock and saw I'd only been asleep for two hours. More banging. I eventually marched toward the door, hell-bent on giving whoever was on the other side of it a piece of my mind.

I grabbed hold of the handle and pulled, snapping my mouth closed when I saw Cara standing in the hallway, her eyes red and puffy.

Without hesitation, I pulled her into the room, then into my arms as the door shut behind her.

"Did something else happen?" I asked, doing my best to comfort her as she unleashed fresh tears. Normally, I didn't do well with a crying woman, but there was a vulnerability surrounding Cara that called to my protective nature. All I wanted to do was shield her from whatever caused her any sort of distress. Maybe it was because she'd shown such a tough exterior to the world, and realizing she was comfortable with me enough to lower her guard had me bonding with her on a level I never thought would exist between us.

"Every... everything," she mumbled a moment later, clutching tighter to me while slowly regaining her composure. When her breathing regulated back to semi-normal, she withdrew and stepped around me. She headed toward the bed and took a seat on the edge, her head hung low, avoiding eye contact.

I slowly approached and sat next to her. "Wanna talk about it?"

She leaned into me and rested her head against my arm. "Not really."

"Okay, we can just sit here." I placed my hand on her knee and squeezed. And there we sat, in silence for the next ten minutes.

"Ford?"

"Yeah?"

"Why are you in your underwear?" she finally asked.

"Because I was sleeping. Normally I sleep in the nude, but never in strange beds."

A small laugh escaped her perfect lips.

"Do you want to get naked now?" Cara looked up at me and smirked, and for as much as I thought we should talk about what happened, she needed a distraction. And I supposed I did, as well. I'd previously refused to use sex as a diversion from the real issue, but I didn't have it in me to be that resolute this time.

As I removed her clothes and buried myself inside her, I pushed all thoughts of never seeing her after today aside and reveled in the feel of her body and the taste of her lips. My feelings toward Cara were stronger than I realized, and while they scared me, I was coming around to the idea that a twist of fate had brought us together for a reason. What that was, I hoped to find out together.

CHAPTER
THIRTY-SIX

Cara

Falling asleep with my head on Ford's chest quickly became my new favorite thing to do. The steady thrum of his heartbeat lulled me into a peace I hadn't known in over a decade.

Whenever I thought about not seeing him every day, I ached, and I didn't know if my reaction was because I'd simply become used to his presence or because he was the only person who knew my secret, that unfortunate instance attaching me to him in some sort of warped way. Maybe a mixture of both was the cause. Either way, I would miss him if he wasn't around.

A bang on the door woke us, and right then, being roused from sleep, I understood why Ford had the scowl on his face when I'd first arrived.

Another pound, then a jingling of the handle.

"Cara," my sister shouted from the hallway, knocking once more. Groaning, I moved to hop out of bed but was pulled back before my feet touched the ground. Ford knelt behind me, his warm breath hitting my ear when he spoke.

"Um… don't you think your sister is gonna wonder why we're both naked? I'm assuming you didn't get around to telling her about us." The way he said *us* made my heart flutter.

"Hell, I wasn't thinking."

"Besides, the last thing I need to deal with is Owen's mouth, especially after the hard time I kept giving him about his inappropriate relationship with Emily. Then I go and do the same thing."

"Cara, are you in there?" Emily yelled again. "I know she went in there." Another voice spoke but was low and muffled. I had no doubt Owen was out there with her.

"Hurry up and get dressed," I instructed, finally jumping off the bed and pulling on my clothes faster than I thought possible. When I turned to look at Ford, he had a goofy smile on his face, but he still hadn't made a move to get dressed.

"What?"

"Nothing. I just like watching you."

I leaned over and kissed him. "I know you do, perv." He swatted my ass before gathering his clothes, and in record time, he was decent.

When Ford opened the door, he narrowly missed Owen's fist because he had it raised to knock again.

He looked past his older brother and locked eyes with me. "What were you two doing?"

"Nothing," we both answered simultaneously, no doubt raising more suspicion.

"We were just talking," I added.

Emily pushed her way inside. "Then why are the sheets all messed."

"Because I was sleeping," Ford answered. "In fact, I don't appreciate everyone barging in here. First Cara shows up out of the blue, rambling on about this and that, then you two bang on the door like you're the goddamn police. What the hell do I have to do to get some peace around here?"

A little over the top but a satisfactory performance.

229

"Calm down." Owen glared at his brother before entering the room, all four of us seemingly annoyed. "We have enough to deal with, I don't need your shit on top of it." After Owen and Emily walked farther into the room, Ford turned to me and shrugged. I shook my head and joined the other two.

"What are we going to do?" Emily asked. "Dad is so angry." Owen pulled her in for a hug and kissed the top of her head.

Even though I felt betrayed by my sister, we talked on the way over here, and while I couldn't forgive her just yet, she was my sister and I loved her.

"He'll come around. Besides, Mom won't let him do anything too rash. You just have to let him calm down."

"I never wanted any of this to happen," she cried, her shoulders shaking when a fresh wave of sorrow washed over her.

"But it did and now you have to deal with the consequences." I had nothing other than the truth to say. But it did feel odd not to be on the receiving end of such talk.

"I need a fucking drink," Owen admitted, heading back toward the door to leave, his arm slung around Emily's shoulders to keep her close.

"So do I." I looked at Ford after he said that and smirked. "What? Now I'm no longer on duty, I can have one."

"I didn't say a word."

How we were going to pretend nothing was going on between the two of us, especially with a few drinks in us, was something I wondered as the elevator descended to the lobby where the bar was located.

Stumbling back toward Ford's room, he'd convinced us to stay the night because we'd all had too much to drink, except Emily, of course. He suggested that he and his brother share a room and that Emily and I take the other, but Owen shut down that suggestion right away, insisting he and Emily needed time alone to continue to try and figure things out. I acted like spending more time with Ford annoyed me, but in truth, I was happy we'd be alone.

After he hooked the latch on the door, he turned around and stared at me, a devilish grin plastered across his gorgeous face. He'd drank quite a bit but didn't seem fazed, the only indication he was drunk was the slight slur of his words and the way his eyes glassed over.

"Do you wanna get naked again?" He leaned against the door and shoved his hands in his pockets, watching me, studying me.

"Nah, I'm good." I disappeared into the bathroom, laughing, but before I could close the door, he grabbed my waist and turned me so that I faced the mirror.

"I don't believe you." He leaned in close and caught my eyes in the reflection. "I think you want me to fuck you again." His breath hit my ear, and I swore an electric current bolted through my body, my knees buckling beneath me and hitting the front of the vanity. His grip around my waist held me in place so I didn't fall. With his eyes glued to mine, he unbuttoned my jeans and yanked them down my legs. When he rose back to his full height, the irises of his eyes darkened.

"What makes you say that?" I asked, both wanting to engage and throw caution to the wind and give in to our need for each other.

He reached around me and pulled my panties to the side. "This." My excitement glistened on his fingers right before he thrust them inside me. "Tell me you like it."

I moaned and my head fell forward. The man zapped all my strength with his touch. But my eyes hadn't broken away from his for long when he bunched my hair in his hand and pulled my head back.

"I know what you want," he growled right before he removed his fingers. Before I could pull enough air into my lungs to say anything, he ripped away the flimsy material covering me, kicked my legs apart, placed a hand between my shoulder blades and bent me over. "Brace yourself."

Ford's warning thrilled me, my pussy throbbing in anticipation of him succumbing to the basest of his needs. The other times we'd had sex were amazing, but there was something in his stare this time that suggested more.

The clink of his belt buckle hitting the floor startled me, but when I heard the grind of his zipper, I knew what was coming next. Not that him bending me over and telling me to brace myself wasn't a sure indicator. Seconds later, his cock pressed against my opening, but before he slammed inside me, he teased me by rubbing himself through my folds, tapping the head of his dick against my clit several times.

A jolt of pleasure stole my breath.

I moaned and wiggled my ass against him.

Needing everything he wanted to unleash on me.

"Stop making me wait," I finally cried, moving back against him in hopes he'd decide that he'd wasted enough time and fuck me hard.

Instead of giving me what I wanted, however, he pulled back and smacked my ass. Hard. The bite of pain centered my focus, but before I recovered from the slap, his palm connected with my cheek once more.

"Fuck!" The pain radiated across my backside in waves as

he hit me again, and then a fourth time. I loved it, my mewls encouraging him to continue. But he didn't, and I was under no delusion I'd be able to change his mind. Ford was going to fuck me when and how he wanted, and I'd never been so excited to relinquish control.

"Look at me," he demanded, gripping my blonde strands in his fist once more, our eyes connecting in the mirror. "Do you want me?"

I read into his question, wondering if he was asking about more than just sex. When his hold on my hair tightened, I finally gave him what he asked for.

Me.

"Yes," I whispered, wishing that time would stop, and we could stay locked in this moment forever, for as clichéd as that sounded.

"Grip the edge of the counter," he grunted right before he pushed every thick inch inside me. I tensed up but quickly relaxed. Ford wasn't a small man, and I needed a moment to allow my body to stretch around him. "Are you okay?" Because he still held me firmly in place, I nodded as best I could.

A split moment of pleading, patience, and understanding passed between us. A squint of the eyes. A curl of the lip. Parting mouths and a shaky breath. We communicated without a single word, something I'd never had with anyone before him. The pumping of his hips tossed all sentiment aside, and my body was racked with the sweetest torment.

At first, his movements were slow and controlled. The muscles in his neck strained, and he looked like he barely held on to whatever restraint he had left. I loved that I was the one who drove him crazy, in all ways possible. I'd gotten under his skin in the past, as he had done to me, but when our bodies connected, everything else seemed to fade away.

He released my hair and rested his right hand on my waist, digging his fingers in to hold me steady. His left skated around my front, then disappeared between my legs. Without warning, he pinched my clit, the feeling similar to when he gently bit the sensitive bundle of nerves. My head would've hit the mirror from the jolt had he not held me in place.

I attempted to stand but failed, the pressure he inflicted on me borderline too much. His hand moved from my hip to my throat, his fingers applying pressure, not enough to scare, but enough to excite me, to give the promise of what I liked.

"You'll take everything from me," he confessed, and I didn't have time to dissect his words before he pulled back, then slammed into me with as much force as he could muster. My mouth fell open as I sucked in air, but one look in the mirror and I saw the question in his eyes. When I closed mine, I'd given him my answer. He assaulted my body with his, every thrust and prick of pain the sweetest torture.

I crested the wave of explosion when Ford suddenly removed his hand from my pussy and pulled me back toward him.

"Why did you stop?" I groaned, frustrated that my impending orgasm had withered away.

"Take off the rest of your clothes. I want to see all of you while I fuck you." I found his bluntness sexy, so I complied immediately, pulling my shirt over my head right before I removed my bra. I stood before him completely naked, but there was one problem. He remained fully dressed, which seemed unfair. Even though from the position I was in I couldn't see him, I wanted to at least feel his skin against mine. I wanted his heat to scorch me.

"You need to do the same." The last word barely left my mouth before he quickly unbuttoned his shirt and tossed it over his shoulder. I regretted my request, however, when he pulled out of me to take off the rest of his clothes.

"Give me a second and I'll turn that frown upside down," he teased, winking at me. He kicked his pants and boxer briefs to the side before he positioned himself behind me again.

"You're a goof."

"But a goof whose gonna make you scream." He sheathed himself inside me in the next breath, pushing me forward with the force of his lust.

Every nerve inside me ached from the potency of him, but I wanted more.

"Harder," I cried. "More."

He grabbed my waist and anchored me to him, fucking me so fast and hard I barely had time to enjoy the electricity spiraling through me. The buildup to my orgasm was almost as satisfying as the explosion itself. But the way Ford drove into me triggered my body to rush through the sweet anticipation, the sound of my ass slapping against his skin more erotic than I thought possible.

"Are you close?" he asked, reaching around to pinch my nipple, the erect bud's sensitivity sending a jolt right to my pussy. I couldn't speak. Hell, I could barely nod my response before my body locked up. "I can feel your pussy tightening," he rasped, leaning over me and resting his forehead on my back. "Take everything from me, Cara," he barked, sinking his teeth into my shoulder. Again with his coded words, but I ignored it all, focusing on the sweet release my body offered.

His grunts stole my thoughts.

His body gave mine pleasure.

His words offered me everything I didn't know I needed.

After he finally released himself inside me, and our breathing started to slow, only then did Ford withdraw and turn me around to face him. He said nothing as his lips descended over mine, the tip of his tongue begging for entrance. His kiss captivated me, promised me a future I wasn't sure I was entitled to.

The rest of the evening was spent in bed, drifting in and out of sleep. Whatever alcohol we'd drank earlier had dissipated and was replaced with a renewed energy to consume the other.

Whenever I shifted in my sleep, backing up against him while he cradled me from behind, I'd awake when he would pull my leg back and throw it over his hip, entering me lazily until all I could focus on was the feel of him. Slow and steady, drawing out my pleasure for as long as possible. By the time we fell asleep for good, I ached all over, my pussy swollen and sore. But I'd never been more satisfied in my life.

CHAPTER
THIRTY-SEVEN

Ford

"Ugh... who keeps calling you?" Cara asked, throwing a pillow over her head.

"I don't know."

"You really need to set specific ringtones for your contacts. That way, you'll know who's blowing up your phone without even looking." Her words were muffled beneath the goose down, but I heard everything she said.

My cell went quiet, only to ring again seconds later. "Where the hell is it?" I asked, sitting up to look around.

"It's on the floor. On my side." She threw her pillow at me and leaned over the side of the bed, the covers shifting to reveal her plump, bare ass. I reached out to playfully spank her, but stopped when she suddenly twisted back around right before she tossed my phone at me. "It-It's... him," she stuttered.

"Who?" I glanced down at the phone and saw Cal's name on the screen, one of the guys whom I'd convinced to fake kidnap her, and knew immediately why her complexion had paled. "Fuck, sorry about that." I lay back down and swiped the screen, already pissed off his call disrupted our morning. "What?" My greeting was none too friendly and certainly abrupt.

"Hey, sorry to keep calling, but Owen told me what happened. Are you guys okay?"

Because I wanted to end this conversation as soon as possible, I didn't hesitate when I answered, "Yeah. Fine."

"Good." He sighed into the phone but stopped speaking. Cal was a great guy. He served with Owen and me, and we'd been close for years, and while he looked scary, the exact reason why I picked him to help me teach Cara a lesson, he was a big softie at heart, if he was on your side. If not, watch out.

"Was that it?"

"No. Uh… coincidentally, we have two new clients. So, now that you guys are freed up, when can we expect you back here?"

"Soon."

"How soon, because one of them keeps calling and I—"

"Cal, I'll have to call ya back." I hung up before he could say anything else and tossed my phone on the table next to the bed.

Cara had drawn the covers up to her chin and closed her eyes. I could only imagine what she was thinking, and now was the perfect time to get something off my chest.

"Sorry about that," I repeated. She kept her eyes closed and her lips shut. "Listen, about what happened. Knowing now that you were never in any real danger, I feel awful about what I put you through. I'm really torn up about it."

"Yeah, well, it's over with. No sense in dwelling on it now because I'm not. But I don't ever want to see that guy in person again because I might just punch him in the balls." Her lip twitched but never morphed into a smile.

"I'll keep you two apart, for his safety." She finally opened her eyes and turned to face me. "Come here." She moved closer until she snuggled into my side, even though we should've been getting up because checkout was in a half hour.

"What do you think they're gonna do?" she asked, tracing her finger up and down my chest, making me squirm when she hit my sensitive spot.

"Who?"

"Our siblings."

"I have no idea. I'm just thankful we don't have to deal with anything like that." I kissed her temple before rolling her onto her back. Spreading her thighs with my knee, I lay on top of her, careful to keep my weight from crushing her.

As I leaned down to kiss her, she said, "Well..." The tone of her voice flattened my expression, and I hopped off the bed so goddamn fast I startled her.

"What does that mean?" I asked, raking my hand through my hair, glancing over at her every few seconds.

"Oh my God, Ford. Calm down." Her hand rested over her belly, but the smile on her face told me she was just kidding. At least, that's what I thought. "Everything will be fine."

"Are you pregnant?"

"How would you feel if I was?" She sat up and leaned against the headboard, the sheet that had been covering her fell to her waist. Her nakedness should've distracted me, but her words took precedence over ogling her tits.

"Don't answer my question with another question. Are. You. Pregnant?"

She leaned forward and squinted her eyes at me, the faintest of smirks hidden on her lips. "It's way too early to tell." A tense moment passed before she added, "No. I'm just messing with you."

"Christ! Don't do that." Anger rolled through me but quickly dissipated when she stood up. Cara wrapped her arms around me and flicked her tongue over my nipple. "No way, woman. Not after that." She bared her teeth and clamped down. "Ow." I tried to push her away, but she wouldn't budge. The bite of pain she'd inflicted on me was a turn-on more than anything, although I continued to play it off as if I was annoyed.

She finally released me. "That's for getting so mad."

"Can you blame me? We don't even know what's going to happen between us. The last thing we need to do is bring a kid into this." I hadn't meant to speak the truth right then, but that's exactly what it was... the truth. Our relationship was complicated, and I didn't have an answer as to where we would go from here.

Cara's smile disappeared as soon as I started on my tirade, and within seconds she walked past me into the bathroom.

"Cara," I called after her, following her, but she slammed the door in my face before I reached her. I turned the handle, but she'd locked herself inside. Leaning close, I spoke. "I'm sorry if I upset you."

"You didn't."

"Then why did you walk away?"

"Because it's almost time for check-out and I need to leave." She turned on the faucet, and as I pressed my ear to the door, I swore I heard her cry, but I could be mistaken. I knocked. Silence. I knocked again. Nothing.

Five minutes later the door flung open and she stood in front of me, fully dressed. She tried to push past me, but I blocked her way.

"I need to go." Her head was down, and she did everything she could not to look at me, which wasn't too hard to do since I towered over her and she'd have to look up to do so.

"Look at me."

She ignored me.

"Sweetheart, look at me." That got her attention because all of a sudden, she whipped her head up and glared at me, placing her hands on my chest and attempting to shove me out of her way.

"You don't get to call me that, Ford."

Baffled, I asked, "What's wrong with *sweetheart*?"

"That term indicates you care about someone, which you clearly don't... for me. You're looking for a way to end things between us. Well, here you go. I'm leaving."

I'd be lying if I said I didn't know why she was saying all this, but that didn't mean I wasn't somewhat surprised. We hadn't discussed how we would move forward after our employment ended, figuring we still had some time to figure it out. But Emily's confession sped up the timeline, and the future was staring us in the face.

She pushed me once more but was unsuccessful in moving me. And when she knew I wasn't going to budge, she sidestepped me, but I grabbed her wrist before she could get very far.

"What do you want from me?" I asked.

"Nothing." Her back was to me, and I doubted she was going to turn to look at me anytime soon.

"I'm sorry." I paused to collect my thoughts. "I like you, Cara. A lot. And I wish things were different. I really do. But I just don't see how this is going to work between us."

"Let go of me."

"Can you please look at me?"

"No!" she shouted. "Now let go!" I released her and she dashed around the room collecting her purse and keys right before she hurried to leave.

I called after her as she dashed into the hallway, and since I was still naked, I couldn't very well chase after her.

As the door closed behind her, my eyes connected with Owen's, who stood just outside my room with Emily at his side. He looked me up and down right before his mouth fell open.

"Muthafu—" The door clicked shut before he finished cursing me out.

CHAPTER
THIRTY-EIGHT

Cara

I didn't know what I expected to happen, but hearing Ford tell me all that, even if it was the truth, was hard to swallow. Shoving past Emily and Owen, who no doubt now knew something had happened between us, I ran toward the elevator. My sister had driven us there, so I couldn't go anywhere without her, but in the meantime, I needed to be alone. Which probably wasn't the best thing to do since my thoughts were pinging all over the place.

He told me he liked me. A lot. His words. But he wasn't willing to even try to make things work between us. I was, though. Or had been, to be more accurate. I would've taken turns and traveled back and forth to see him. And even though I envisioned I'd be busy with following my passion, I would've carved out time to see Ford, to be with him. Because I liked him. God help me, I liked him, and I think it was more than just a lot.

But here I found myself. Sitting in the lobby and wondering why in the hell I opened myself up to him in the first place. I wasn't necessarily upset about sleeping with him, I was more pissed he'd forced me to tell him about my past. Okay, maybe forced was the wrong word to use, but it was the only one that gave me comfort, believing I'd been tricked into revealing my secret.

"Cara," Emily shouted as soon as she stepped off the elevator, looking around the lobby until she saw me sitting on one of the sofas. Thankfully, she was alone because the last thing I needed was to be bombarded with a million questions from her and Owen about me and Ford. I was even more thankful Ford wasn't there because I didn't have the emotional energy to figure out the crap rumbling around inside my head, yet alone get into it again with him.

My sister took a seat next to me and nudged my shoulder with hers. The betrayal I felt withered away, and even though it would take me a bit more time to fully forgive her, I loved her dearly for putting her own problems aside to try and help me, even if it was only by listening. The thing was, though, I didn't know what to say. I was done hiding mine and Ford's relationship, or whatever the hell I wanted to call what we had, but I couldn't pick a point to start from.

"Was that the first time?" she asked, jumping right in.

I knew what she was referring to, so I didn't ask her to clarify, or attempt to deny anything. "No."

She nodded. "Do you love him?"

"No," I rushed to say, although, I wasn't sure if I had just lied or not.

Emily flung her arm over my shoulder and pulled me close. "If it makes you feel any better, Owen is up there right now reading him the riot act."

"About what?"

"Ford constantly gave Owen shit for things being inappropriate between the two of us. It turned out he was right all along, but he still had no right. He's a hypocrite because, well, you know... he was sleeping with you."

"Not the entire time, like you two were. Which, by the

way, I'm pissed off about. You told me you were only friends. I can understand Owen lying to his brother because Ford is rather intense, and I wouldn't want to deal with his mouth either, but why did you lie to me?"

She released a long sigh. "Owen made me promise not to tell you. He thought that maybe if you knew you'd somehow let it slip to his brother, whether intentional or not, and he didn't want to take that risk until we knew if it was just a fling or not."

"Fair enough." There was no point in arguing because I completely understood Owen's logic. There was a good chance I would've said something to Ford, to get under his skin in some way, to piss him off. I could've done such a thing before.

Before the fake kidnapping.

Before I contemplated living for something more than just partying.

Before I decided to pursue my goal of making clothes.

Before I realized that the life I led up until recently wasn't the life I wanted any longer.

"Can I ask you another question?"

"Why not." I may as well tell her what she wanted to know. I'd learned that keeping secrets was exhausting.

"What happened upstairs?" I had a hunch she was going to ask me that, and while I didn't want to tell her that Ford basically kicked me to the proverbial curb, I wasn't going to skirt around and bullshit her either.

"He said that he likes me a lot but doesn't see how it's gonna work out between us." I moved to the side and Emily removed her arm from around my shoulder. "Whatever. On to the next one, right?" I laughed, but the sound came out pained. "Are we going home now?" We both stood at the same time.

"Are you sure you don't want to go back up there and talk to him?"

"Why would I want to do that?" My brows cinched so tightly if I didn't relax my face, I'd bring on one helluva headache.

"Because maybe you didn't give him time to fully explain himself. Maybe he does want to work it out with you but needs your help in trying to figure it out."

I appreciated what Emily was trying to do, but it was pointless.

Ford and I were done, and because he'd been fired, I never had to lay eyes on him again. As I followed my sister to the car, I allowed the last tears I'd ever cry over Ford Massey to trail down my cheeks. The memory of him would fade over time. But I wasn't so sure about the ache in my heart.

On the drive home, I thought about what was going to happen with Emily and our parents. For once, I wasn't mixed up in the middle of a scandal or trying to talk my way out of a situation where I'd made a bad decision. Odd didn't begin to describe what it felt like to be on the other side of things, but I had to admit that I preferred it to the other.

After Ford and Owen had left our house the day prior, our parents, mainly our dad, was beyond furious. He rambled on about how he was the one to bring them into our lives and how deceptive they were the entire time and how he would go out of his way to ruin their business. But after he'd finally calmed enough to listen to reason, Emily stepped up and took responsibility for putting things in motion when she sent the first note. Then, the second. Then, the third. She could've confessed at any time, but she didn't.

Emily also reminded our parents that she had feelings for Owen, and that looking back, realizing the impact of what she'd done, while wrong, wasn't a regret for her. She spoke those words with her hand resting over her belly.

They left the house shortly afterward, and while our mother gave us each a hug, my father walked right past us and waited for his wife in the car. It would take him some time to come to grips with everything, and I had no doubt he would do what was right in the end, which was to forgive and move on. Walter Dessoye was a stubborn man when he wanted to be, but he was kind and loving, and his family meant the world to him. Emily just had to wait for him to come around.

CHAPTER
THIRTY-NINE

Ford

The last two weeks had been challenging. Both Owen and Cal argued with me about not wanting to accept Heather Dumont as a client. They wanted her business, but because she insisted I be the one assigned to her, she refused anyone else's services in the firm. They assured me it was only for a month, that she needed security while she did a press junket overseas, but one day in her presence was one day too long. I knew damn well that she only called for me because she wanted to get under Cara's skin. Besides, the second I laid eyes on the woman, I knew she'd be a pain in the ass, more so than Cara in the beginning, and that was saying a lot. Furthermore, if I took the job, I'd feel as if I was betraying Cara, and the last thing I wanted to do was put myself in a predicament that made me uneasy all around.

The guys had finally let it go when I refused to take their calls for four days. I came to find out shortly afterward that Owen told the persistent woman that I'd never be available for her. She stopped all communication after that.

"Don't you think it's been long enough, man? When are you gonna stop being such a stubborn sonofabitch and call the

248

woman?" Owen kicked my boot when I refused to look at him, my interest in what he rambled on about at an all-time low. At least, that was the impression I wanted to give him. In reality, I couldn't stop thinking about Cara and what an ass I'd been the last time I saw her. I'd hurt her. I'd seen it in her eyes when she fled from my room. The incident had also revealed almost everything to my brother and Emily because they'd seen my naked ass standing there as she ran past them. I had no more lies to tell when Owen confronted me, demanding I tell him the truth. And I did. Every word about the relationship between Cara and me flowed easier than I ever thought it could. Much like the woman who occupied my brain 24-7, I was stubborn, but I was tired, and my brother forcing me to talk about her was a relief of sorts.

While I confessed that we'd slept together, the first time being after her date with Caverly, I justified my actions as rash and out of character. I'd been jealous and reacted. He, on the other hand, pursued Emily right from the start. And even though we both crossed the line, his was deliberate, whereas my actions were...

Oh, fuck it! We were both wrong. No use trying to justify otherwise.

My attention remained on the television and away from Owen, but when I raised my bottle of beer to my lips, he smacked my arm and the alcohol spilled down the front of me. I hopped off the couch and stepped into his personal space, hell-bent on making him back off.

"Let it go," I demanded, snarling for good measure.

"I'll let it go when you stop being an asshole and admit that you love her."

I turned away from him and walked into the kitchen to grab a towel to wipe off my shirt. "I don't love her," I shouted over my shoulder, not quite sure whether I told the truth, to him or myself, for that matter. I had feelings for Cara, sure. I'd go so far as to say those feelings were deep, but love?

"You can tell yourself whatever you want, but we both know you're a miserable prick right now."

"I'm always a miserable prick," I agreed, plopping back down on the sofa before swallowing half my drink. Kicking my feet up on the coffee table, I knocked over two of the many empties sitting on top of the glass. I'd reverted to drinking, although not to oblivion like I'd done after Julia died.

"More so these days." Owen sat in the recliner and continued annoying the shit out of me. "Why don't you just call her? Ask her how she is. Start small, then go from there?"

"What makes you the relationship expert now? Huh?"

"Well, I am in one."

"Only because you got Emily pregnant, which means you kinda don't have a choice." My brow crooked upward when Owen's expression flattened. I'd gotten to him. Serves him right, coming over to my place and trying to tell me how to live my life.

"That's not why I'm with her," he argued. "Of course, I wouldn't leave her now that she's pregnant, but that doesn't mean I don't want to be with her. Is everything happening quickly? Yeah. Am I scared out of my mind because this baby is going to be here before I know it, and I have absolutely no clue what the hell I'm doing? Sure." Owen's sudden rambling made me smile. He shook his head before exiting his chair and making a beeline for the kitchen to grab a beer. When he reentered the living room, he took the seat next to me, resting his feet on the edge of the table in front of us. "Fuck, I guess I don't have all the answers either."

"Ya think?"

We sat in silence for the next half hour. Owen stewing on his newfound revelations and me continuing to think about Cara and if there was a possibility that'd I'd acted too rashly. Said things unnecessarily without even trying to figure out a way to work through any doubts I had. I wasn't a reasonable man by nature, but I wasn't completely unreasonable either. I realized the two concepts warred with each other, but didn't they cancel each other out, then, too? My random thoughts made no sense to me, so I did what I did best. Drank another beer.

"People come into our lives for a reason," Owen said, his voice startling me because my inner ramblings had continued to steal all my focus. "Most times we don't know what that reason is, but we have to trust that our encounter with them is for the strength of our development. I truly believe Emily came into my life so that our baby could exist. And I also believe that Cara came into yours because you needed her. You just have to decide what comes next."

My brother had spewed philosophical rantings on me before, right after our sister died and he was trying to get me back into the land of the living. But this time around what he said both pissed me off and intrigued me.

Maybe he was full of it and just trying to see the silver lining of his newfound fate.

Or maybe he was on to something.

Either way, he was right. I was the one who had to choose a path and forge ahead.

The question was... which way did I want to go?

EPILOGUE

Cara
One Month Later

"**J**ust calm down," I muttered to myself, staring at my reflection in the small mirror sitting on top of one of the makeup stations. "Don't be nervous. You got this." My little pep talk wasn't doing anything to calm my nerves, and the flurry of activity behind me wasn't helping, either.

There were so many people running around backstage, shouting for shoes, clothes, and everything else imaginable. I'd never seen anything like it, other than in movies, and they clearly hadn't exaggerated the chaos that happened behind the scenes of a fashion show.

Just over a month ago, James called and asked if I was interested in showcasing a few of my pieces right before he revealed his spring collection, right there in Manhattan. I accidentally hung up on him because I'd dropped my phone right after he asked. He laughed when I called him back, telling me he had a similar reaction the first time he was asked to show his designs.

I knew he only did one show a year in the city, the rest of them were in Paris, Milan, and London, to name a few. The man traveled the world, and I would've gone anywhere he asked but was relieved the show was close by. Traveling was one less thing for me to stress out about.

I didn't have much notice, but since I was only making five pieces, I picked my favorites, buckled down and got started right away. I enlisted Audrey for advice on the designs, and Emily and Naomi to try the outfits on after they were finished. My sister wasn't showing yet, so I didn't have to worry about the clothes not fitting her.

"Hey, girl," someone shouted, and while that person could've been addressing anyone backstage, I knew her voice as soon as it cut through all the commotion and hit my eardrums.

Neely headed straight for me, her arms outstretched and pulling me into a hug before taking a step back. Her black hair was a tad longer, but otherwise, she didn't look much different than the last time I saw her, which was at mine and Emily's birthday celebration in California. I lied. One thing was distinctively different about Neely. She was sporting a baby bump.

I quickly glanced down at her belly. "How are you feeling?"

"Weird, but good."

"Did you ever tell the baby daddy you're preggers?" She disliked *preggers* almost as much as *baby daddy*.

"Ugh, please don't." She flashed me a faux-annoyed expression. "I did, and let's just say that he wasn't too receptive."

"I'm sorry that happened." I grabbed her hand as a show of support.

"I punched the bastard in the face when she told me." Calvin appeared out of nowhere. "Hello, love," he greeted, lifting me off my feet and twirling me around like he loved to do. I knocked into one of the models, but she rushed across the room before I could apologize.

"I didn't know you were coming," I squealed. "Why didn't

253

you tell me?" He finally put me down and I gave him another big hug.

"I'm not letting Neely fly by herself."

"I'm not an invalid," she argued, smacking him on his arm. "He treats me like I'm fragile. Like I'm gonna break."

"I treat my woman like gold," he corrected, flashing his killer smile right before he pressed his lips against hers. His eyes moved to me. "What?"

I waved my finger back and forth between them. "Are you two—?"

"Yeah. She finally gave in to my charm." He laughed while she shook her head and sighed. But I caught the way she looked at him. She was as enamored as he was. I'd always suspected Calvin had feelings for her, and obviously she'd felt the same.

"So, now you're the baby daddy?" I asked him, moving back a step when Neely reached out to smack me.

"We're gonna name him CJ. Calvin Jr." He wrapped his arm around her waist and pulled her close.

"You're having a boy?" I asked, fascinated with their interaction together. He kissed her temple while she leaned into him. Then, when he dropped his arm from around her waist, he linked his fingers with hers. Anyone watching would've thought they'd been together for a long time, but I knew their romance had just started not long ago. Although, as I mentioned, I was certain it started sometime back for Calvin.

"I don't know what I'm having yet."

"What we're having," Calving corrected. I loved how supportive he was about a baby that wasn't his. I only hoped when he or she arrived, he'd continue to feel as strongly about the child as he did right now.

"Enough about us, Cara. How are you doing? You look

a little nervous." Neely left Calvin's side to stand next to me, and his face fell the second she was gone, but recovered quickly when he saw I needed some support.

"I'm nervous, of course, and I'm praying everything goes well. James has given me this huge opportunity, and I just don't want to let him down. You know, make him regret that he gave me a shot."

"You'll do great," she praised. "I'm so proud of you, and to be honest, I'm a little jealous."

"Why would you be jealous of me?"

"Because your passion is coming to life." She shrugged. "I'm just hoping one of the galleries likes my paintings enough to give me a show soon."

She'd been working on her art for as long as I'd known her, but only recently had she started trying to get one of the bigger galleries to take notice. The main reason she was in New York right now was to meet with one of them.

"It will happen for you, too," I encouraged. "And sooner than you think. I have a feeling."

"I'm sorry. I didn't mean to take any of the focus off you." She gave me another hug.

"Please, take the focus off me. I'm freaking out." I smiled, but my anxiety turned down the corners of my grin before I could take another breath.

We chatted for another couple minutes before they excused themselves and left to find their seats out front. I wasn't left to my thoughts for long before James's assistant bombarded me with questions about the garments I brought and who was supposed to wear what.

Going with the suggestion to hire a few models from a local agency, I'd done a dry run a couple days ago and tagged everyone's outfit with the model's name. Apparently, the papers had fallen off during the transport to the show, so I gathered the women and together we solved the small crisis.

I had my back turned when Emily came up behind me and startled me, although because of my heightened bout of anxiety, it didn't take much to scare me.

"Look who I found," she announced, tapping me on the shoulder. For a split second, I envisioned that Ford would be standing behind me, but quickly realized I had to get rid of any hope I had that he would contact me again. The way we left things the last time we saw each other hadn't been ideal, but neither one of us made a move to correct it. The man was stubborn, but if he really wanted to see me or talk to me, he would. His lack of communication told me everything.

I twisted around to see Nick standing next to my sister.

"Are you working today?" I asked, pulling him in close.

"Yeah. How cool is this?

"I still can't believe this is all happening." I tried to stop and revel in everything that was going on around me, but it was hard to do because of all the commotion.

"Well, get used to it, baby, because this is only the beginning for you." Someone shouted Nick's name. "I have to go, but you better start making men's clothing because I want to walk for you soon." He grabbed the sides of my face and leaned in. "You deserve it all, Cara." His words brought tears to my eyes, not only because I was excited but because I needed someone else to tell me what he just did. Whenever I tried to tell myself the same, I hadn't been very convincing. I still had my doubts, but I was getting better.

A week after I ran out of Ford's room, I was lying in bed and a commercial came on. One I'd seen many times before, but for some reason that day, the way the actress looked into the camera felt like she was speaking directly to me. She said, "If you or anyone you know has been abused, don't be ashamed. Tell someone. No one should have to live with secrets."

I broke down and sobbed, and I realized it was the first time I'd allowed myself to grieve, to truly mourn the loss of my childhood.

The loss of my innocence.

The loss of faith I had in the world, the faith that I had in me.

Whenever I did allow the memory of that day to filter in, which would only last a few seconds, I blamed myself for what happened. If only I hadn't gone into his study.

If only I hadn't been wearing that bathing suit.

Then I made the decision that changed the course of the way I thought about what happened and about the way I'd been treating myself.

When I called my parents over to the house, the first thing my dad asked me was if I was pregnant. After I shook my head, I told them there was something that I needed to share with them, something I'd kept from them since I was fourteen years old.

I'd managed to hold most of my tears back while I spoke, but as soon as I saw my dad cry, I broke down. I'd never seen him so distraught, and while my mom and Emily were also shedding tears because of my revelation, my dad was the rock of the family. So, to see him crumble because of what happened to me, I oddly felt a small sense of relief.

My family shared in my pain right then, and it was the second time in my life that I hadn't felt so alone.

The first was when I told Ford.

My family and I talked for hours that day, and while I agreed to finally go to counseling to deal with the rape, I refused to go to the police or even tell Steph, for that matter. One step at a time was the way I needed to process everything. They stood behind my decision.

Two weeks later, during one of my phone calls with Steph, she told me her father had suddenly lost his job and I had no doubt my dad had something to do with that. He knew many people in high places. She also revealed that her parents had been arguing nonstop.

I almost broke down and told her what her father did to me, to give her some inclination as to what was going on with her family, but I just couldn't do it. Maybe someday when I'm further along in the healing process.

"We're going to take our seats," Emily said, giving me a good-luck kiss before she disappeared.

"And I'm sure someone is looking for me." Nick laughed, squeezing my hand before he disappeared into the crowd of models and stylists.

Moments later, I stood facing the side of the stage, doing a last-minute check of the dresses before the first of the models stepped out onto the runway. Deep breaths left my lungs, and a calmness spread through me. Ten minutes remained before my pieces would be shown, some of the most influential people in the industry sitting twenty feet away.

Amid the quieting chaos, I heard the chime of my phone. When I turned around to go back and check the notification, my eyes collided with the sight of someone I never expected to see again.

Ford stood near the doorway with flowers in his hands,

a nervous smile kicking up the corners of his mouth. He was dressed in all black, sans shades, and he sported more scruff than I'd seen him wear before. He looked virile. Rugged yet elegant. And I hated that my lust returned full force from a simple glance.

So many questions and memories bombarded me that I had no idea what to say, if anything, or what to think.

Recovering from the initial shock, my feet propelled me back toward the table where my phone was placed. As I approached, I wanted to look away from him, but I couldn't. I devoured the sight of him and all I wanted to do was crawl into his arms and stay there for the rest of my life.

I wanted to feel his embrace.

I wanted to taste his kiss.

I wanted to share my incredible moment with him, but it was too late for any of those delusions.

For as much as I hated to admit it, my heart slammed against my chest when only a few feet separated us.

"Hi, Cara." His deep voice prickled my skin, his velvet tone smoother than I remembered. "I wanted to wish you good luck and congratulate you on your show." He handed me the bouquet of red, orange, and white lilies. My favorite flowers. "Your sister told me how much you like them."

"Emily knew you were coming? She didn't tell me."

"I asked her not to because I wasn't sure I was going to go through with it or not."

"I see." I tilted my head. "Are you regretting your decision?" Hurt and doubt sliced me apart while I waited to hear his answer.

"What? No." He reached for my hand, but I retreated a step. "I meant, I wasn't sure if I should show up here and distract you or not. But believe me, I was going to see you either way."

"Cara, we're starting in five minutes," someone shouted from near the stage. I had no idea who it was because all my attention was on the man in front of me.

"Why are you here?"

"I told you why."

"No, why are you really here?" He frowned, then licked his lips, then shifted from foot to foot. "Tick-tock, Ford. I don't have much time left." Crossing my arms over my chest spurred him to part his lips and finally answer me.

"I came here to apologize for the way we left things. For the way *I* left things between us. I should've never let you leave my room that day. And I sure as hell should've chased you down the hallway, naked or not."

The more intently he stared at me, the more my heart rate spiked.

"Go on," I prompted.

"I miss you." He crept closer.

"So."

"You're not gonna make this easy on me, are you?"

"Should I?"

"No." He shook his head. "You shouldn't make this easy on me because I've been a fool to let you get away. Do you think there's a possibility that you could give me another chance?"

I'd dreamt of hearing him say something like this for the past six weeks, and here he was giving me what I wanted, but I was skeptical. I didn't trust that he meant it.

"A chance for what?"

"To make things right again. To be with you. To figure things out."

As I stared at him, the words to form my answer eluded me. Of course, I wanted to scream yes, but my pride wouldn't allow me to react that way. Instead, I squinted and pursed my lips. In the end, I knew I'd choose to be with him, but I wanted to make him work for it first.

"You said you missed me."

"Yes, I did. I me... mean, I do." To hear Ford falter, even the slightest, tickled my heart. It meant he was willing to put aside his stubbornness for something he wanted, and apparently that something was me.

"What do you miss about me?"

His eyes darkened. "Your sass. Your attitude. Your mouth." He pulled me into him before I even saw him raise his arm. "Your passion. The way your eyes light up when you talk about designing. Your vulnerability because it reminds me to embrace that part of myself from time to time."

The heat of his body warmed me in ways I couldn't describe. My heart felt lighter, my mind clearer than it had been recently. He cradled my face in his hands.

"I want to make us work. I know it will be challenging with my job and yours, but I'm willing to put in the effort. I won't take a job longer than a week at a time if it's not close by. And if the detail is local, I'll make sure it's not a live-in job. I'll make time for us because I want to be with you."

"No more female clients." He looked hesitant, so I clarified, realizing I couldn't ask him to decline business. "No more young, female clients."

He looked entirely too sexy when he arched his brow. "And why's that?"

"Because I know firsthand what happened the last time you were assigned to one."

"That I fell in love with her?" he asked without an ounce of hesitation. I swore my jaw hit the floor.

"You what?" I was barely able to get my words out I was so stunned. Never in a million years did I ever expect him to say that to me. I knew Ford had feelings for me, as I did for him, but was it truly love?

I couldn't stop thinking about him, even when I tried. The image of him alone set off butterflies in my belly and made my heart race. I smiled at the memories we shared, even though I was angry with him for tossing me aside. I hated waking up every day for the past six weeks knowing I wasn't going to see him, or to argue with him, or to share my excitement with him. I missed the strength he offered when I needed him the most.

Did I love Ford Massey?

I absolutely did.

"I'm sorry it took me so long to figure it out, Cara, but I do love you." He picked me up and placed me on top of the vanity, not a care in the world that there were people all around us. He tipped my head upward and leaned down to kiss me. As soon as his lips brushed over mine, I knew we'd be all right. We had what it took to make our relationship work, and I had to trust our feelings for each other would be enough to push us past any trials we encountered, starting with my dad. There was no other man I'd want by my side for this next chapter in my life.

Although we'd been brought together under false pretenses, as it turned out, I'd never been so grateful to Emily for doing what she did; otherwise, my life would be completely different. I'd still be lost in the shuffle of life. Lost to my past and the need to mask what happened with drugs and alcohol. And even though Ford and I clashed from the gate, I'd needed him, even though I didn't know it at the time.

I snaked my arms around his neck and drew him closer.

"I love you, too," I whispered against his lips. The smile on his face and the glint in his beautiful eyes told me that he heard me loud and clear.

The End

NOTE TO READER

If you are a new reader of my work, thank you so much for taking a chance on me. If I'm old news to you, thank you for continuing to support me. It truly means the world to me.

If you've enjoyed this book, or any of my other stories, please consider leaving a review. It doesn't have to be long at all. A sentence or two will do just fine. Of course, if you wish to elaborate, feel free to write as much as you want.

If you would like to be notified of my upcoming releases, cover reveals, giveaways, etc, be sure to sign up for my newsletter: www.subscribepage.com/snelsonnewsletter.

ACKNOWLEDGEMENTS

Thank you to my husband for allowing me to forget about everything else while I lost myself to finishing Ford and Cara's story, not coming up for air until it was finished. I love you!

A huge thank you to my family and friends for your continued love and support.

Becky, you continue to push and challenge me. The direction I thought I wanted for this book altered because of your insight. Ford and Cara's story is more polished because of it. Thank you for everything!

Clarise, CT Cover Creations, the covers for this duet are beyond amazing! You hit it out of the park again, woman. Thank you for indulging me whenever I have one of my many last minute requests. Love you!

To all of the bloggers who have shared my work, I'm forever indebted to you. You ladies are simply wonderful!

To all of you who have reached out to me to let me know how much you love my stories, I'm truly humbled.

And last but not least, I would like to thank you, the reader. Without you, I'd just be some crazy lady with a bunch of characters in my head. I hope you enjoyed the conclusion to Ford and Cara's story.

ABOUT THE AUTHOR

S. Nelson grew up with a love of reading and a very active imagination, never putting pen to paper, or fingers to keyboard until 2013.

Her passion to create was overwhelming, and within a few months she'd written her first novel. When she isn't engrossed in creating one of the many stories rattling around inside her head, she loves to read and travel as much as she can. She lives in the Northeast with her husband and two dogs, enjoying the ever changing seasons.

If you would like to follow or contact her,
please feel free to do so at the following:

Email Address: snelsonauthor8@gmail.com

Website: www.snelsonauthor.com

Facebook

Nelson's Novels (Facebook VIP group)

Goodreads

Amazon

Instagram: snelsonauthor

Twitter: authorsnelson1

Newsletter: www.subscribepage.com/snelsonnewsletter

ALSO BY
S. NELSON

Standalones
Stolen Fate
Redemption
Torn
Blind Devotion

Massey Security Duet
The Assignment

The Addicted Trilogy
Addicted
Shattered
Wanted

The Knights Corruption MC Series
Marek
Stone
Jagger
Tripp
Ryder

**Knights Corruption Complete Series (all 5 MC books in one:
Marek, Stone, Jagger, Tripp, Ryder)**

ALSO AVAILABLE

She intrigues him. She challenges him. She threatens the secret he's been hiding for years. Will a promise make long ago be the very same thing that destroys their chance for happiness?

Grab your copy of *Addicted* today

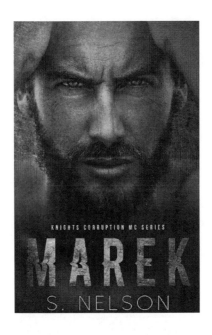

KNIGHTS CORRUPTION MC SERIES

MAREK

S. NELSON

With the weight of the club on his shoulders, Cole Marek, president of the Knights Corruption MC, had only one choice:

Turn their livelihood legit.

Everything was falling into place until one unexpected, fateful night. With an attack on his fellow brothers, Marek had no choice but to retaliate against their sworn enemy.

Swarming their compound, he comes face-to-face with the infamous daughter of his rival club, making an astonishing decision which would change his life forever.

Grab your copy of *Marek* today

Made in the USA
Middletown, DE
16 July 2019